FATED

Karma Series, Book Three

Donna Augustine

ISBN: 0692408878
ISBN-13: 978-0692408872

For my readers. When I started writing, it was for me. Then you found me. You started reaching out to me and telling me your stories. I still write for me, but now I also write for you.

CHAPTER ONE

I didn't think I could name one person who was all good or all bad. If I had to bet my life on it, I'd be as dead as the human body I'd left beside those train tracks months ago. There was no such thing, or at least, I'd yet to meet them. We're all a woven tapestry, created with threads of various shades of wrongs and rights, some brighter, some darker, but never perfectly either.

In normal times—which these certainly were not—when I'd seen a group of people, there would have been an appearance of what I'd describe as a generic average. Maybe once I started to pick these mortals from the group, one by one, and delved deeper, I'd see that this person leaned more toward evil or that one leaned more toward good. The worst of them hid their flaws, their anger and corruptness, in the dark corners of life, the times when most aren't looking.

But because most humans had the desire to fit within the norm of their culture, general civility hid the darkest traits. In better times, when people walked down the street on a sunny day, a layer of icing hid the sometimes moldy cake beneath, because most human beings had a natural compulsion to fall in line with what was considered the norm of their culture. It went all the way back to our hunter-gatherer years, when it was a necessity to be able to work as a team and being an outcast meant certain death.

But something had been unraveling, shifting in the psyche, or maybe in the very fabric that wove us all together. In the weeks since I'd met Malokin in that hotel things had changed. The threads of evil, that had been hidden from view and denied, were now being flown with banners. The few threads that had once been the shadows in the tapestry of who we were had become the dominant color of the piece.

The most worrying aspect was I wasn't clear on what was causing it. I wasn't entirely sure if this was Malokin's doing or if he was a byproduct and if it was something that could be undone. Months ago, I'd seen hints of the chaos that was beginning to unfold now, but like so many before me I had brushed off a gut instinct as paranoia.

That foresight of potential upheaval, the one my gut had foreseen and been yelling at me to pay attention to, was blooming full force. People who had inclinations towards a dark side seemed to be on a downward slide and gaining speed. Assaults and burglaries had doubled in the last month and that wasn't the worst. Murders had tripled. Rapes had gotten so bad that women were starting to fear walking the streets alone. It wasn't only here in coastal South Carolina, either, or just the United States.

Crime was on the rise everywhere, and if you paid attention to the trends, like I did, you knew it was getting worse every day. The decay of the moral fiber of the human race had hit a tipping point and the downward slant was steepening.

It wasn't all bad. There were some people who were going in the opposite direction. The good within them had blossomed. Strange how sometimes it took the worst of times to bring out the best in some. Unlikely heroes were rising all over the place, lending aid to the weak and easy prey. It gave me and everyone else around us— those who were still hanging on to who they were— hope, and we desperately needed that. Especially now, when everywhere I looked lately, things seemed to be unraveling.

Even as Smoke and I sat by the ocean, something that would have been uneventful a couple of weeks ago before the hotel and the rioting that went with it, there was a threat. A group of five boys, all in their teens, approached from a little way down the beach. They were close enough though that I could see the way they were appraising me. They were looking for trouble and considering me for some sport.

Was that what things were coming to? Would I have to fight children to survive? The idea of snuffing out a life before it even reached manhood sickened me.

It didn't matter that every one of them had karma

that was as dark and dingy as a used ashtray. Only the very best of humans, people who would've been near blindingly bright before, weren't dark at this point. A month ago, they might've been normal. Perhaps a month from now, if we could figure out what was wrong, they would be light again. They wouldn't have that chance if I killed them. And even if it were I who dealt the killing blow, in essence they'd be another victim of Malokin's. The walking and talking personification of anger on Earth would have another notch on his belt and I'd again be doing his dirty work.

Smoke, more companion than cat and one of the best judges of personality I'd ever met, hissed as they got close. The black cat who had been born grey had been doomed to a position as an underachiever by factors of birth. Sort of like a ballerina with stumpy legs, some things just couldn't be overcome.

"Keep walking," I said, doing a little hissing of my own as they came within human hearing range, which was considerably shorter than my own.

The group of five eyed me, debating on if I had the claws to match the warning. Their step slowed in unison as they came closer. Then something caught their gaze behind me. Their steps quickened and they kept moving.

I leaned my weight back on my hands and then my elbows, letting my head fall back and my dark ponytail graze the sand so I could get him in my view. The tension, which had surged a moment before in anticipation of a fight, turned into an altogether different type of awareness. As I watched him come closer, there was a hint of something that I wasn't quite ready to feel stirring in me.

"You know, I had that handled." My hair blew as the wind kicked up and I enjoyed the ocean breeze on my skin.

"I'm sure." Fate shoved his hands in his jeans' pockets as he walked forward, looking completely relaxed even as he scanned the beach for any other possible threats.

"If you have any doubts, I can go chase them down and offer a demonstration." I smiled as I said it, having no desire to do any such thing. It was a comment that simply continued on the larger unspoken discussion we'd been having. I was capable of protecting myself.

"But then you'd miss dinner," he replied, going along with the ruse he'd been carrying out—that he felt completely comfortable letting me go off and handle things alone.

Fate and I had a strange way of communicating, or lack of it. I wasn't sure how it had started or when, but we rarely discussed the important matters. We'd talk circles around them. Maybe we'd fallen into the habit back when I'd killed Suit, and we both decided to let the why of the situation drop.

It might have gone back even farther, to the very first time I met him. I still didn't understand why, when he hadn't wanted me there, he'd agreed to stay with me all those long days I'd been teetering on the edge, after my human form had died.

At this point, the habit of not actually saying what

we meant was becoming pretty ingrained, for better or worse. We didn't discuss any of the real issues between us. If it hit too close to the raw emotions that made us tick, they weren't spoken of or asked about.

"If you chased after them, you might have to do that weird glow thing with your eyes. We wouldn't want that to happen," Fate said.

He dropped down to sit on his haunches by my side, and Smoke immediately went in for the petting. His faded denim looked nearly bare in places as Smoke rubbed her cheek against his knee, claiming him. His hands rubbed over her as she purred on full blast, eating up the attention. Hooker.

It was ridiculous that I was jealous of a cat but I'd felt those hands on me. They were masculine perfection and always knew just the right way to touch. A small thrill shot through my system at the memory of exactly that. It wasn't often that I saw him and didn't think of those times or breathe deeply when I was next to him, loving the masculine scent that reminded me of sandalwood and cedar.

"We don't need to have dinner together every night." The words came out and I immediately regretted them, as I often did, not understanding fully why I felt compelled to pull away when what I wanted was the exact opposite. I stared off at the horizon, watching the waves break, and tried to keep my demeanor relaxed while I awaited his response, like a sword held poised above my head.

We'd been dining together every night since things

had started to get crazy. It had been another unspoken compromise. He'd shown up with boxes at my condo one night, telling me how perhaps I should store some things at his place, just in case. I'd agreed but then kept everything I actually used at my condo. It made sense with everything going on and also because of the vision of my fate he had, the one we didn't speak of, where I was lying dead in a pool of my own blood.

I'd had dinner with him that night but then went home afterward. We'd fallen into a routine, one night turning into a standing dinner date. Sometimes I'd cook, sometimes he would, and occasionally we would have take-out. We'd strategize about work, Malokin, and what was happening then have a coffee afterward on the deck or maybe a drink. At some point I'd force myself, against my baser instincts, to leave. There'd be a moment before our goodbye when the invitation would be crystal clear in his eyes; a glance down the hall to where his bedroom was or a lingering hand at my waist as I moved to get up from the couch.

The thing was, I wanted to be with him. I wanted to live there and go skipping down the beach, watch the sunrise hand in hand and every other goofy cliché I'd never thought I'd need or experience since I'd started this new life. But that wasn't what was being offered.

Protection? Check. Sex? He'd been dropping plenty of hints he was ready and waiting.

But love? Now that didn't seem to be on the menu, or not on his, at least. No mention of deeper feelings or even a carrot, far off in the future to chase, a dangling promise that would allow me to rationalize that maybe he did have deeper feelings for me. Something that would let me think this was the real thing for him and that he just needed time. But he wasn't giving me anything to hang my hat on and reality, a pesky nuisance I'd never been able to ignore very well, would hit me upside the head.

Fate had lived for a minimum of centuries. That I was fairly certain of. And in all the details I'd gleaned from him, over the time I'd known him, not once had there been any mention of a long-term relationship. If, in all these years, he'd never once had a commitment that lasted longer than a week, what made me think I'd be different?

It wasn't like that for me. I was going down and hard. There are a few things in life that suck really badly. Loving someone who doesn't love you back is one of them. I'd thought I'd learned my lesson with Charlie, my ex fiancé. I'd thought losing him, and then having to watch him build the life I thought we'd share from the outside, had been bad.

When I looked at Fate—when he gave me that flirty smirk he sometimes did or a part of him brushed against a part of me—I glimpsed what true heartache looked like. What I'd felt for Charlie had been love; I was certain of it. Or a type of love, anyway, the kind that was comforting and calm, soft and let you sleep easy at night.

"You're not bailing on dinner."

Hearing those words, I could breathe again, and he turned and gave me that smirk.

8

I wondered if he knew what he was doing? If he had any idea how some of the things he did affected me? The sizzle I felt being near him was so intense but I couldn't figure out if they were fireworks or warning flares.

As far as my gut instinct was concerned, the only thing it was telling me as far as Fate went was, there was no soft fall. I'd go down hard, with no chance of bouncing back. He'd be it. If it was just a fling to him? There would be no rebound after he broke my heart, just a hard crash that I'd never recover from. And as much as I thought to myself that I needed to *not* walk down that path, because I might be going alone, I nodded, taking another step, again, like an addict saying I'd quit tomorrow, just one more time.

I'd once heard a Chinese proverb that said, "*You'll end up where you're heading.*" All those little steps would still take me to the same destination, just a bit slower, and it scared the hell out of me.

"It's getting worse and the decline seems to be increasing," he said, his eyes scanning the horizon and his voice edgier than before, when he'd been teasing.

Work. That was safe ground. I wasn't sure what that said about me, that I'd prefer a discussion about the coming apocalypse over my feelings for a confirmed bachelor. Still, I'd grab the lifeline with both hands if it got me out of my own head for a little while.

I nodded. He *was* right. You could taste it in the air every time you stepped out of your door. The feeling of violence, which had been just a taste weeks ago, had been growing steadily into a full on all-you-can-eat buffet.

"I don't think anyone should be staying alone at this point. It's not safe." His eyes, appearing so dark sometimes, practically glowed with green emerald flecks as they stared at me.

"I know," I replied, agreeing with the sentiment but not offering any solution, wondering if I'd be better off fending for myself against the angry mob than sleeping feet from him. How long would my willpower hold up? Death by fire or a beating from an angry mob? I'd have to think on that a bit more.

"But you're not going to listen." He didn't need to elaborate on how he felt about that. It was clear in his voice.

"I'm listening. I just haven't made a decision." I let my head drop back to stare at the clouds. Why couldn't he say *I'm falling for you and can't spend another night without you in my arms?* It was so much more romantic than *I think you're going to be raped and murdered so let's shack up together and probably have sex because, hey, you're right there and isn't this convenient.* At least if he'd said he was falling for me, I'd have an excuse. When it eventually went bad, I could fall back on the position that he had lied and how could he have done that to me. It would have been a lot easier to go down with delusions and a scapegoat neatly lined up.

"Not sure how long you're going to have an option."

My head popped back up as I looked at him, trying

to gauge where he was going with that last statement. Did he mean the situation was going to force my hand or him? Neither would surprise me, but I couldn't read his expression.

Now that would give me plausible deniability. See, it wasn't my fault. We had been thrown together. The whole thing was becoming ridiculous. I was preparing an excuse for when I was heartbroken and looking to place blame, and it wouldn't matter. I'd still be heartbroken.

A flurry of action caught my eye as I saw the group that had eyed me up as a potential target before. They'd stopped underneath a pier about a mile down. Another group was heading toward them from the opposite direction. I knew the fight was coming before the first fist swung. Then it was an all-out brawl between the two groups.

Fate turned to watch as well, neither of us making any move to stop it. It would be as pointless as blowing in the wind.

He sighed then stood up. He stepped in front of me, faded jeans and white t-shirt hinting at the tanned perfection I knew lay beneath. His palm reached out to give me a helping hand up, and I let him pull me to my feet.

He tugged me up hard enough that I was propelled into his arms, which he then wrapped around me, to keep me from falling I'm sure.

"Sorry." His mouth was alarmingly close to mine. "I really don't know my strength sometimes."

Another smirk. Another hint. And my pulse was off to the races.

"No problem." I shrugged it off as I stepped out of his embrace and started walking back to his house. The guy was completely screwing with me.

CHAPTER TWO

I groaned as I opened my eyes and looked at the clock beside me. It was four in the morning and the third time in the last two weeks that a throbbing pain near the region of my tattoo had woken me from a dead sleep.

I closed my eyes, telling myself it wasn't a big deal and that nothing was wrong. It was a strain or something. I sighed deeply. That excuse had worked so much better the first few times I'd used it.

Something had felt off with me pretty soon after Paddy had taken a piece of him and somehow forced it into me. It was supposed to keep me connected, let me move on from this place someday and reconnect the link Malokin had broken. That little bit of Paddy, which was inside me, was the equivalent of my retirement plan. Without it I'd be stuck here, on Earth, forever.

I guessed there was an argument to be made for remaining on Earth, never aging, eternally young when you didn't know what your retirement home might look like. Fate's guys had chosen it. Lars, Bic, Angus and Cutty—none of them would move on from this world. This was it for them, and that was exactly how they wanted it. Plenty of people would want it.

But I didn't. I'd made the choice. I wanted to know what lay beyond this realm, even if only for a short while before I was doomed to forget it all and walk the Earth again as a mortal. As much as I'd been mocked for once being human, there was a value to it that someone who isn't a transfer couldn't possibly understand.

Maybe the day-to-day minutiae of being human didn't seem appealing to my current co-workers but they couldn't possibly understand how much joy the simple things can bring. What it felt like to win my first case or go to the movies with a boy for the first time. The human experience was loaded with things that made your endorphins sing. I wanted to experience this place as a human again one day with all that it entailed.

But it looked like there was going to be a price to pay. This part of Paddy in me, the part that gave me the chance to go on and live another life, it was doing more than just keeping me in touch. I could easily have rationalized the pain away as my body adjusting to a foreign part if I hadn't felt other things happening. Lying still on the bed, I could feel it spreading through me. It was too crazy to say aloud but I couldn't shake the feeling.

Dr. Hamil had been my family's doctor since I'd been a toddler. I still knew his number. Too bad I couldn't call it, shoot in for a quick X-ray, get a script and be good to go in a week.

I closed my eyes, trying to go back to sleep, but I just lay there, trying to think about anything other than what might be going on within me.

I went into the bathroom, downed what pain medications I had left in the medicine cabinet, and made a mental note to stop at the drug store tomorrow.

***

I rapped my knuckles on the open office door even though I knew Harold was aware of me standing there. He didn't look up so I kept knocking and knocking. I could've walked in and sat in front of him, but somehow, forcing him to acknowledge me and utter an invitation was far more entertaining. My current frustrations needed some sort of outlet.

After a solid minute of knocking, he finally looked up. "Come. In." His lips barely moved as he spoke, and I realized perhaps he'd missed his true calling as a ventriloquist. Hell, even his hair—as bright red and bushy as it was—would look perfect on a dummy. I'd never seen such a color occur naturally. There had to be some better career for him other than running this place.

I bit my tongue, holding back the lyrics from *The Heat Miser*, but failed somewhat as the melody slipped out in a hum. I smiled in greeting and walked in gingerly, taking the seat in front of his desk. His forehead had become one continuous wave of wrinkles. I should've known instinctively he'd recognize that song.

They'd probably modeled the character after him.

Still, somewhere deep down, so far down I wasn't sure I could find it anymore, I was still a southern girl. There were manners in here somewhere. I really needed to try and shake the dust off them and let them see daylight once in a while. "I think it would be nice if we had a little chat." *Smile, don't forget the big smile.* I put so much umph into it my cheeks hurt.

"Can I avoid it?" His droll monotone had my face muscles burning in rebellion. Harold was about as far from my side of the Mason-Dixon Line as he could get.

I'm sorry, Mama, wherever you are right now, but good manners are a total waste on him. I sucked air in through my teeth, most likely ruining the smiling effect but making a dramatic show of considering his question. Hanging on by a single raised pinky, I shrugged and said, "No."

The sound of skateboards skidding across linoleum stopped me from continuing. The Jinxes were here and I was probably one of the only people happy about it. But when the shit had hit the fan, they'd been there for me. Were they rude, obnoxious and all sorts of undesirable? Yes. Downright repulsive? On occasion. They were the pariahs of the office and they embraced the position, but they'd become *my* little pariahs.

They entered the office seconds later. I held my fist up, knowing them well at this point, and they each cruised by in a line and fist bumped me as they found their places.

"Why are you three here?" Harold's voice, always

nasal, seemed to be hitting a new whine with the question. "Did she request your presence? Because I didn't."

"We don't need a request. We're her posse, douchebag." The Jinxes were the antithesis of southern but as welcome as sweet tea on a hot summer day.

Bobby pulled up the chair that had been tucked in the corner, sat down and then kicked his sneakers up onto Harold's desk. It was reminiscent of a move I myself had made not long ago, except my shoes hadn't been caked with dirt in the treads, which now fell like sprinkles of love onto Harold's never-ending paperwork. Oh, the charm of the Jinxes. Three pre-pubescent looking packages with more swagger than James Dean in his prime and more experience on the job than I could claim. I wasn't sure how old they really were, but looks were deceiving and never more so than with them.

I tilted my head toward the door and, right on cue, Billy went over and slammed it shut. Buddy remained behind me, his small arms crossed over his chest as if he were my personal bodyguard.

Harold stared at the dirt on his desk and then me, his eyelids drooping ever so slightly more than usual. "What do you want? Let's get this shit over with."

I crossed my legs, repositioning my summer dress in supremely ladylike fashion. "I informed you not long ago, as have others, that we've got a problem."

"And what do you want from me?"

"Something. Anything. The world out there is on the brink of falling apart and you sit here and do

17

nothing." I folded my hands on my lap, trying to remain composed. I didn't want to encourage the Jinxes by turning into a raging lunatic. Their social graces were hanging on by the barest thread. One bad example could propel them into a black hole of social uncouthness they might never recover from.

"You're being dramatic." He lowered his head and returned to scribbling away at whatever useless notes he made.

This had been my last ditch effort to try and recruit Harold to my way of thinking. Hell, the whole office's way of thinking. It would've been nice to have him on board for once but it wasn't a necessity.

I stood, applauding myself for not contributing to the further demise of the Jinxes' downfall in social skills, and walked out of there with the three of them trailing me.

"Why are we leaving? He ain't doing nothin' still," Bobby complained as we left.

"It's called rising above." Memories of my mother's voice, telling me a lady rose above the fracas, whispered in my ear like a bittersweet memory. I'd always thought that one day I'd be teaching my own children lessons like that.

Bobby elbowed Billy with a saucy grin on his face. "I want to rise above *some* people, just not that dweeb. I think we should sink real low, where it's nice and comfy, and kick him in the teeth, if you ask me. This manners crap is bullshit. We look like a bunch of pansies letting him disrespect us like that."

I looked at the three of them tagging behind me and wondered how many people had decided not to have children after meeting them. "Don't worry, boys, you haven't risen very far. I'd say you're knee level at best."

This seemed to uplift their spirits somewhat as they fist pumped each other encouragingly.

The main office door creaked open, and the room seemed to shrink to half its size as Fate entered. His head turned to me for an infinitesimal moment before he took in the rest of the room. For a while I'd thought I was imaging that he did that, sought me out first, until it happened over and over and over again.

I kept walking toward my table where he seemed prepared to intersect with me. I'd told him of my plans to approach Harold again, for one last ditch attempt, over dinner last night. He hadn't said anything; he had simply raised his eyebrows at the mention and taken another bite of his steak.

I leaned a hip on the table as he came over and he did the same beside me. He didn't say a word but *I told you so* was written clearly in the shrug of his shoulder and one raised eyebrow.

"I felt like it was the right thing to do."

He didn't say anything about it and I didn't continue with the subject.

Of course, the Jinxes were there so it wasn't case closed until they got their say in. "The guy's a total douche. Not sure what you expected," Bobby said, his blond locks shimmying with the shaking of his head. The Jinxes were always useful for saying the things most people were thinking but tried to hold back.

Murphy walked over to where we were gathered and Buddy was all over him as soon as he approached. "Hey, Sloppy Jo, you trip me this morning?"

Murphy rolled his eyes. "How many times do I have to tell you, you're a klutz. I don't get the urge with any of our kind." Murphy took a chair nearby and crossed his legs, looking like someone had plucked him right out of a detective show from the fifties. Trench coat and hat, I could imagine him pulling out a badge at any moment. This morning, he looked like an episode where he'd been on surveillance all night.

Death, who was only now entering the office, looked closer to a rerun of Mr. Rogers, complete with sweater, and was probably finishing up a grief counseling session. I'd recently learned he charged over three hundred an hour. I guess knowing the deceased personally gave him a certain edge in effectiveness.

Death saw the group of us and came over. It didn't take long before almost everyone in the building had made their way to that portion of the office. Of course Lady Luck was there, looking as tousled as ever. Her dry spell, which had coincided with Kitty's disappearance, had ended the night she found out Kitty was okay. She'd been going strong ever since, trying to make up for lost time and missed pillow talk.

The Tooth Fairy and his assistants had come by, Santa appeared with some of his elves in tow, Mother brought her gardeners and Jockey popped in; in essence, the whole awkward gang was there.

The Jinxes were still carrying on with their tirade over Harold's less than desirable traits. They had got the group so rattled that by time Cupid showed up that no one even made a run for Harold's office.

The truth was, Harold was merely a scapegoat for the real problem. We were all alarmed at the turn of events lately and the state of the humans. There wasn't a day that went by when someone wasn't walking in and saying, "You're not going to believe what they did now," and it took a lot to surprise this group.

So when Cupid walked in slowly, palms raised, and said, "I won't do anything, I swear. I just want to know what's going. Those mortals are getting weirder by the minute," no one ran. We put aside the past.

He was nervous, like the rest of us, and no one had the heart to exclude him. Plus, right now we needed the numbers. I turned to Fate. "We've got to let him stay."

"Agreed."

Luck came and stood beside me. "Cupid's right. It's getting real strange. I've never seen anything like this in all my years on the job." There was a lot of grunting and agreeing noises after her statement.

Santa stepped forward and addressed the group. "I just stopped by to let you all know that Mrs. Claus and I have decided to head up to the North Pole for an extended leave. Things are getting too rough around here, and I'm worried for the safety of Mrs. Claus and the elves. We'll seal up the entrance until things calm down."

Santa was leaving? It felt like first grade all over

again when I found out from my classmate, Susie Wilkins, that he was made up. All the grief that girl had caused me. I should track her down right now and give her a piece of my mind for spreading such lies.

It wouldn't change anything though, as Santa made his goodbyes and his elves handed out candy canes as they left. As I watched his departure, the only thing that repeated over and over in my head was, what if things never did calm down? Screw everything else, what if Santa never came back?

"How am I getting good cookies now?" Luck asked. "I can't go back to store-bought. All of this because of that angry guy?"

Everyone in the office knew Malokin, or Angry Guy, as Luck called him. After Kitty and the hotel incident, Harold's determined lack of cooperation, and things getting strange and violent, everyone in the know had sat down and decided there was no more hiding. Malokin was a threat to all of us. Everyone deserved to know what was out there.

Luck took a seat on my table beside us, a pout in full bloom. "I don't like that angry man."

"None of us—" A loud crashing sound, coming from behind Harold's closed door, interrupted me. The high-pitched sound of his screaming came next. He was plenty loud but I still couldn't make out what he was saying. There were no other voices. I'd left him in his office alone not more than fifteen minutes ago.

Maybe he was on the phone? Or—the more interesting possibility—maybe someone had come through the retirement door, the one that had an inch gap underneath that glowed funny light. I'd never seen or heard of anyone using it.

My eyes scanned the rest of the group, and they, like me, couldn't stop staring. The only one not paying attention was Fate. He was looking at his phone.

"What are you doing?" I tried to look over and see what was on the screen.

"Nothing," he said as he tilted his phone away from me.

"Are you playing a game?"

"Maybe."

"Aren't you concerned?"

"No."

He certainly didn't seem it.

The sound of a door slamming echoed through the office, but Harold's door hadn't budged, nor any other in view.

Instead of moving closer, I perched on the table, nudging Luck over slightly. "Maybe we should go in?" I asked but no one was moving forward or doing anything other than making themselves comfortable as they watched Harold's office for signs of life.

"It's fine," Fate said, distracted, as he sat on the table next to me, squeezing us both over a bit.

"What if something really bad is happening in there?" I turned around and looked for the chips I'd been snacking on earlier. Luck had already snagged the bag and was sharing them with Murphy, who stood next to her. I reached out a hand and he tilted the bag in my direction.

"Ugh." Fate grumbled from beside me and pocketed his phone.

"Lost?"

"Don't worry, I always win in the end," he answered as he grabbed my wrist and directed the chip in my hand to his mouth, grazing my finger with a nip of his teeth.

A sensation I'd become all too familiar with churned inside me. What the hell was going on with him these days? His sexual overtures were becoming a daily occurrence and picking up steam.

Harold might be getting bludgeoned to death as we sat here. Had he no shame? I tried to muster a look of moral disgust but couldn't. I didn't know if I cared that much either.

But still, as dilapidated as the office might be and as dysfunctional as the staff definitely was, we were at work. "Harold could be getting murdered in there," I said, trying to sound as disapproving as possible and failing pathetically. It didn't matter at the moment. This had nothing to do with Harold and everything to do with Fate screwing with my head.

"I can't help if I'm hungry." It was the "*so sue me*" tone he used so often.

I narrowed my eyes.

"Why are you so opposed to sharing a couple of chips?" He shrugged, as if he hadn't just asked me in a roundabout way why I wouldn't sleep with him.

"Maybe I don't feel like sharing my chips. A girl

24

doesn't have to share." I crossed my arms, jostling Luck in the process.

"It's not like you've never shared before. Why so stingy now?" He reached in front of me and grabbed a chip from the bag Luck held and made a show of eating one.

"Maybe I'm just not in the mood to share my chips. I don't have to share my chips simply because I've shared my chips in the past." I grabbed the bag of chips from Luck and rolled the top closed. "See? Nobody is getting chips."

He stared at my hand, bag clinched tightly in my fist and then he gave me that smirk. I had a love/hate relationship with that smirk.

"I think deep down," he leaned in slightly closer before he continued, "you *want* to share your chips."

I inhaled sharply. "Are you insinuating I share my chips freely?"

He squinted. "What I'm saying is, someone might get the foolish notion that once you've shared some chips with them, you'd be likely to share chips on a regular basis."

"You didn't even like the chips! Why do you have to have my chips now?"

"That's completely misrepresenting how I feel about chips. I wasn't looking to expand my diet at that moment. It has nothing to do with whether I liked the chips or not. Or whether once I had some chips, I wouldn't want them in the future."

One of the Jinxes groaned loudly where he stood in

front of us. "I think I'd rather be in the office with Douchebag, getting beat up."

"Why is she getting so crazy about her potato chips? Am I in trouble for eating some?" Murphy whispered to Luck, underestimating my hearing.

Luck leaned closer to him. "It's one of those weird talks I was telling you about. They never mean what they mean. It's not chips, it's—"

I kicked her before she could finish.

"What? What is it?" Murphy pressed.

Luck paused before blurting out, "Lipstick."

"He wants to share her lipstick?" Murphy asked and I saw him peeking over at Fate and me.

"Um, sort of," Luck responded.

Fate leaned over towards them, pressing against me as he did, and said, "I like her to apply it personally though."

Murphy made a questioning face before I saw it finally click and he made a loud "ohhh" sound.

I'm not sure where our conversation would've led because we all fell silent when Harold's door started swinging open.

A man, who definitely was not Harold, stepped out. Close to Fate's height and build, but light where Fate was dark, his thick hair couldn't seem to decide what color it wanted to be—blond or brown. He looked to be in his late twenties, although that meant absolutely nothing where any of us were concerned. He wore a black suit with a white shirt, which was unbuttoned at the neck, softening the appearance.

He must have come through *the* door. It was the only logical explanation. He was handsome, but his mode of arrival alone would've been enough to garner my interest. I tried peeking around him and got enough of a glimpse into the office to see that the door was closed and it didn't look like Harold was in there any longer.

The new guy cleared his throat as he looked over the group of us. His eyes scanned every person in our group but when they landed on me, they paused.

My spine straightened a little, and I wondered what he found so interesting about me. I wasn't dealing with any more transfer bullshit.

Fate rose beside me and straightened to his full height, suddenly taking some interest in the situation. He took a step slightly in front of me and I had to shove Luck farther down the table so I could see around his broad back. It was nice that he thought he could protect me from possible danger but all he was doing currently was blocking my view.

"Harold has retired," the man said, his voice sounding as refined as his appearance, and he turned his gaze on the whole of the group again.

Bernie the leprechaun, all three and a half feet of him, walked over and stood in front of the newcomer. "Who the fuck are you?"

Bernie was especially cranky today because some woman had found three four-leaf clovers in the period of one week.

The man looked down, unfazed, and then looked

back up as if Bernie were of no consequence. Hands
resting loosely on his hips, he said to the group, "Harold
retired. I'm Knox, his replacement."

No one spoke.

Just like that, Harold was gone. And who had given
him his pink slip? Was it Paddy or the others? And was
Knox going to be useful or was he just for show, like
Harold had been?

Knox's chin edged up slightly. "Do you have any
questions?" he asked.

Fate inched closer, drawing Knox's gaze.

"I do," Fate said.

Knox made a single nod, acknowledging Fate
before he spoke. "I'll be in my office." He turned around
and walked back into what used to be Harold's office
and left the door open. I watched as he settled in behind
the cluttered desk and started to sort through papers.

Fate stepped forward, heading toward the office,
and I followed. There was no way I wasn't going to be a
part of this conversation. I was hoping Knox wasn't
going to be another paper pusher. We needed help.
Hands on, feet grounded, walking beside us help.

I bumped into Fate's back as he stopped short of
what was now Knox's office.

Knox raised his gaze and gestured Fate in. Fate
didn't move.

"You know where to find me," Fate said.

"Yes," Knox replied.

"Twenty minutes."

Knox nodded.

I stepped outside the opening of the door and made mad gesturing motions towards the inside.

Fate shook his head.

I moved forward.

Fate blocked.

What are you doing? I mouthed, having no idea what kind of hearing the new kid had.

Our terms, not his, he replied silently.

I threw my hands up. Seriously? *We can't just go talk to the guy?*

He didn't have to shake his head or nod. The resounding no was written all over him, punctuated by his arms crossing and his feet braced apart.

I shook my head and waved for him to lead the way to wherever this meeting was to take place, rethinking my choice of partners the entire time. Maybe I would've been better off with Luck. Oh wait, that's right, Fate had chosen me.

CHAPTER THREE

"Why couldn't we just chit chat with him right then and there?" I asked as I followed Fate down the hall towards the stairs. Why was I following him? And where? I hoped it wasn't because he smelled particularly good today and his jeans fit oh-so perfectly. Nothing else made sense, because I really couldn't figure out why it would be a bad idea to talk to Knox in what was now his office.

Fate stopped and held the stairwell door open for me. "Because we talk on our terms, not his."

Our terms? I didn't remember him asking me for *my* terms, and yet it felt kind of nice to have standards, even if I'd only found out about them afterward. Maybe this was something I could get behind after all. "Where are we going to achieve these terms we require?"

He followed me into the stairwell and then passed me on the stairs. "My office," he said as if it were no big deal that he had an office and I was just finding out about this now.

The balm of "our terms" went out the window with those two words. "Your office?" It wasn't *our* office. First the car, then the pay, and now he had an office? Who could blame me if my voice had come out like a shrieking witch? "Excuse me, but when did you get an office and why am I only finding out about this now?"

He looked back at me briefly. "I've always had one. All that time you spent laying out the building, one had to assume you knew."

"That's bullshit. You knew I didn't know."

He didn't have to drag me with him this time. He'd have to block my path. There was no way I wasn't seeing *this* office. I was hoping it would be a dump, like the rest of the place, but knowing Fate he'd have the one nice chunk of real estate in this crumbling 80s carpet and Formica dive.

"This is why you don't have a desk in the pit of hell." In the entire time I'd been here, Fate had flitted in and out of the main office, and I'd never realized he did this because he had his own space. I'd assumed he went somewhere—anywhere—that wasn't here. I'd thought I'd known every nook and cranny of this building. He himself had seen me pouring over it, and his comment now added to the insult of not knowing.

We didn't stop climbing until we made it to the top floor. No surprise there. If he was going to have an office here, I couldn't imagine any other place. I wracked my brain, trying to think of any unchecked door up here, and I couldn't.

He took a left and I followed him to the very end of the hall. He stopped in front of what I'd thought was a maintenance closet. It wasn't labeled and it was always locked. He turned the knob. There was no way whatever lay behind that door would be nice. There wasn't enough space. I'd figured the interior of this building out. It was four-by-four at best. He'd converted a closet. It was probably just big enough to squeeze in another Formica desk. There was no reason to get irritated.

The door swung open to a twenty-by-twenty room. It shouldn't have fit, but it was here, gleaming hardwood floors and all. An expensive looking wool area rug sat under the wooden desk centered against the back wall, the antique detail contrasted by the largest flat screen TV I'd even seen. It was the latest model and took up almost the entire west wall.

"In case you don't know," I made a grand gesture of pointing toward the screen, "*that* is an absurd size for a TV. And, it doesn't go with the decor." Uh huh, take that Mr. I'm So Cool I've Got a Corner Office. I flopped down on the impossibly soft couch that sat opposite the TV. You fell into it like a leather hug that whispered of sweet siestas as it nestled your head. All those mysterious disappearances made a lot more sense now.

"Do you have cable?" I asked in a threatening tone, ready to kill him if he said yes.

"No. I've got *cables*. What do you want to watch?"

"Show off."

Fate walked around and sat on the arm of the couch and his eyes roamed slowly up my legs, exposed by the shorts I'd worn today. When his eyes eventually met mine, an image of him completely naked, my hands gliding up the skin of his abdomen before they wrapped around his neck popped into mind. The vision excited my cells like I'd been popped in a microwave.

Get a grip. It was just some flesh lying over some toned muscles. Big whoop. I could go to the gym down the street and find all the muscles I wanted. Yeah, they wouldn't be Fate but so what? A girl could only handle so much sexy. He had too much. It was a big flaw.

That wasn't helping at all.

Staring at him from a reclined position was also another very bad idea.

"How do you want to handle the new guy?" Getting up, I tried to make my way to the chair behind the desk several feet away as casually as possible. "And what was the big deal about talking there?"

He sank down onto the couch, taking my position with a look that begged me to join him. He folded his arms behind his head and got settled before he spoke. "I'm not sitting on the interviewee's side of the desk in a folding chair. As far as what I want? Him to stay out of our way." His lips turned up. "There's room for two over here if that chair is uncomfortable."

I immediately forced myself to stop squirming about. "I don't think we should be hasty. He might be able to help us."

I kicked my feet up onto the surface. The movement disturbed the air and caused a slip of paper to gently drift to the ground.

I reached down and grabbed it to set it on the desk. I shouldn't have looked but I couldn't stop myself. What did Fate have receipts lying about for? What was he out buying himself that his shopper couldn't get?

Perfume? He'd been trying to get me into bed nonstop, maybe not saying the words but laying it all out there nonetheless, and he'd been buying perfume for someone else.

Returning my feet back to their previous position on the desk, I tried to act normal even though I was furious. I couldn't say a word. I didn't have a leg to stand on. Trying to get me in bed wasn't saying he was committed to me. It was just sleazy to be that big of a pig.

"Did you see something that made you upset?" Fate said from the couch.

It pissed me off how well he read me. It made me even angrier that he obviously knew what I'd read and didn't even care.

"Nope. Nothing important."

"Anyone ever tell you that you have a lousy poker face?"

"Not until I landed in this dump."

He got off the couch and headed over toward the desk while I used my feet to kick off and wheel myself to a more comfortable distance. He looked down at the desk as if he found something incredibly amusing. "So, nothing is bothering you? Nothing you want to ask me about?"

"Like I just said, there's nothing that concerns me here." I kicked my feet back up onto the desk from my new location on the other side of it and leaned back, turning my head away from him and toward the window I wanted to slam a fist into.

I couldn't believe the jerk thought it was funny that I found his receipt for a gift for another woman. The world was falling apart at our feet but that didn't slow him down any. Good to know. I might have started to think I was something special.

Fate perched himself on the desk near my feet. "Can we talk business or are you too upset?"

I didn't need to look at his face. I could hear the smirk and this time I didn't have torn feelings about it. There was no love of the smirk, only hate. Why he thought it was so funny that I'd find a receipt that confirmed exactly what I feared was beyond me. "I'm not upset. Go ahead. Talk away."

He sighed, the amusement fading fairly quickly. "As much as I'm enjoying this, it wasn't what you think."

I sniffed the air. "You don't smell particularly feminine today. You wear perfume?"

"No."

"You have a sister who does?"

"You know I don't but I do have a Mother who does."

Mother. Her name sounded like a curse when I heard it. "If you have a thing for Mother, that's fine. It's none of my business."

He stiffened. "It was a work thing. Why would you think there's something between me and Mother?"

Why? Was he kidding? She was utterly enamored with him and he certainly hadn't been pushing her away when I'd seen them together. "Like I said, it's none of my business."

"I've known her a long time, and when she's upset, I'm the only one she'll listen to. From time to time, I give her little gifts. It makes her happy and makes the situation easier."

"Easier for you?"

"You don't get it."

"I completely understand." I just didn't like it. Although, I did like it better than the alternative.

He stood and took a couple of steps away from me, shaking his head, and then turned back. Good.

"It's—"

There was a rapping at the door a second before Knox walked in, cutting off Fate's sentence.

He stepped a few feet into Fate's office and stopped. The guy looked like he'd come ready for battle.

"Have a seat," Fate said as he himself stood and made no move to relax.

"I'm fine," Knox replied, not bothering to look for a seat, even with the invitation.

They stood staring at each other for approximately three and a half seconds before Fate leaned against the desk, looking completely relaxed.

I wasn't sure if Knox understood what had just happened, but I did. Fate had sized him up and found him to be of little consequence.

"Paddy sent you?" Fate asked casually.

"Yes."

Fate nodded.

Knox's eyes darted to mine and the lines of his mouth softened. He gave me a nod of acknowledgement, which I returned. His attention went back to Fate. I wasn't insulted. I wasn't the one who'd called him out and made beef with him.

"You wanted to talk?"

"Shit is about to hit the fan. You plan on helping out or getting in our way?" Fate crossed his arms in front of him, ankles doing the same. Yeah, he really wasn't worried about this Knox guy at all.

"I think there's a bit more to discuss. Don't you?"

I leaned my head back on the chair as I eyed Knox and answered the question for Fate. "It's the only question that matters."

Fate's gaze met mine and something flickered.

I looked back at him. *Yeah, I get it now*, my look said. After months of Harold, I'd better. After the last few weeks, I knew. None of us had a cheat sheet or syllabus that laid out what was coming but you didn't need a textbook to tell you that when the winds started picking up, a storm was on its way. This one was promising to be a real doozy.

We needed to know what type of person Knox was before it hit full force. There were three categories of people—and I used that term loosely—two types were okay. One type had to go. He would either help and fight with us, not help but stay out of the way, or be a hindrance.

Knox's eyes went from Fate to me, and I could see the opinions forming there, wondering just how deep our relationship ran. He'd eventually hear the tales and I didn't care. I guess that was one good thing this office and my coworkers had done for me. I'd lost almost all my ability to feel embarrassment. The only thing that mattered was which type of person would he turn out to be.

He rocked back on his heels. "From what I know, I'm prepared to help at this time."

That hit about a seven on the lame answer scoreboard. Maybe it was a little cheesy but I'd hoped for something a little closer to "*I know what's going on and I've got your backs,*" instilled with even the tiniest amount of passion, maybe?

Fate was staring at me with the same expression he'd had downstairs after my Harold meeting. I rolled my eyes. I was quickly realizing that silent *I told you so*s were just as annoying as the out loud varieties.

Hell, at least Knox had ended the unwanted conversation I was having with Fate. And, I could ride this lame horse right out of here and avoid the tail end of discussing the finer points of perfume.

"Knox, let me show you around," I said, getting up heading toward the door before he could think of declining.

"Thanks." I could see him visibly rethinking his opinion about Fate and I.

I wanted to pat him on the back and say, "Good luck figuring us out, because I certainly can't."

Fate's eyes narrowed with annoyance and a promise of tracking me down later. I silently replied with a, *so sue me.* It was an expression that he liked to pull out often and it hadn't gotten any less irritating with use.

His eyes narrowed even further.

I smirked, pulling out another weapon from his arsenal.

He shook his head and grunted.

I tallied a win for my column.

Knox scooted in front of me to open the door and then his hand reached out in my direction, like it wanted to land on my back. It dropped before I could make out its true destination. I nodded at him to go into the hall first, since I didn't like being corralled. For all I knew he thought because I was a transfer I needed help walking or something crazy.

I shot a final look back at Fate as Knox exited first to see Fate's eyes on the guy's back. Wow, he really didn't like this guy.

I closed the door on Fate and Knox and I walked down the hallway. Then I started counting down the seconds, thirty, twenty-nine, twenty…

"You two a thing?" he asked ahead of schedule.

It wasn't a question I was prepared to answer, even for someone naturally good on her feet. The fact that I knew it was coming didn't seem to help much. Awkward didn't become less so because you got prior warning.

"What kind of thing would that be?" I said, shooting for ignorance.

"Enough said."

Maybe Knox wasn't so bad. He'd agreed to help and now here he was, taking the hint. Have to love a person who knows when to shut up. It was almost like he was human.

It made giving him the most rudimentary tour of the building I could get away with not entirely horrible. I was positive he didn't need it though. He'd known where Fate's office was before I'd known he had one. He should've given me the tour.

But that wasn't why I was doing it and not why he was going along with it. We both sized up each other's measure as he was pretending to size up the halls.

With that in mind, I felt very little guilt when I gave him the bum's rush at the lobby door. I shook his hand and went my own way.

CHAPTER FOUR

"There are some people who would like an official introduction."

The apples fell out of my hands as Paddy's voice came from beside me when there'd only been a pile of pears a split second before. I turned to look at the old man. His fedora hat sat low on his brow and the cane he carried was looped around his arm, useless as ever.

I was grateful he'd decided to appear. Hearing bodiless voices, even if I was certain they existed, was still disconcerting. You never knew when that one last push of crazy, which was flying my way almost daily, might thrust your brain into a spiral of mental illness.

As far as falling apart, I was hanging in there mentally but the body wasn't holding up quite as well as it used to. I had a part of Paddy in me, whatever he was; it would sure be nice to know. The fact that if I didn't gauze and tape up the tattoo on my hip every day, I'd glow like a bug zapper on a starless night, left some glaring questions. The pain that woke me in the middle of the night was a little easier to ignore, at least during the day.

I sometimes wondered if going along with Paddy's plan had been akin to eating a *special* brownie and not knowing it wasn't made by Betty Crocker until after it was digested.

"Who would these people be?" It would be nice to place blind trust in Paddy but there was no one I trusted that much, not anymore, and especially not the brownie baker.

Well, maybe there was one.

"You know who. My people." He reached into my cart, grabbed a Granny Smith and crunched down on it.

"People?" I raised a single dark eyebrow and nailed him with my, *and now let's hear the truth* stare I'd perfected during my days as an attorney.

"Let's not split hairs." He patted my hand, the one that was closest to him.

The look had worked wonders on clients. Not so effective on beings of the Universe.

I grabbed a bunch of bananas and placed them in my cart and then skirted around some women arguing in the aisle, who looked like they were going to break out into a brawl at any moment. It sounded like someone had taken the tomatoes the other considered theirs. It wasn't just the teens; people from every age group, every socioeconomic level—basically everyone—was acting strangely.

"Why do I want to meet these people? I'm not

looking to expand my current circle of acquaintances at the moment, considering the limited pool I've been delegated to choose from. I'm sure they'll understand." I'd met enough nonhumans for an eternity, and if the world didn't go to shit soon, that's how long I might live.

Eternity. That was a really long time. How many birthdays could you have before they didn't matter anymore? After a couple hundred, would I even keep count? Was there even a point to counting if it wasn't to calculate the years to old age? A futile exercise to help guess how many years were left using an equation that proved wrong so often.

Paddy grabbed a chocolate bar as we turned down the baking and candy aisle. How good would chocolate taste after I ate it a thousand more times?

The wrapping on the candy bar crinkled as Paddy opened it. "Consider it a favor to me?" he asked before he took a bite.

I watched the joy of a sugar rush spread across his features. Okay, I'd still have chocolate. Coffee never seemed to lose its appeal. How bad could it be?

"No." I used to have a problem rejecting favors outright, always squirming to find a plausible excuse. But that was before I'd stomped my manners into the ground and kicked some dirt over them. I only dug them up and rinsed them off for special occasions now.

"No," a deep male voice seconded.

Paddy disappeared the second Fate's voice hit the airwaves. Well, that was rude. Even my buried and dirtied manners were rolling over in their grave, aghast.

I turned at the sound of Fate's voice right behind me. "What are you doing here?" I asked even though I knew he'd been keeping tabs on me lately, or worse, sticking the Jinxes on me. He was definitely the lesser of the two evils. The Jinxes tended to get bored with guard duty, even if it was supposed to be covert. At least they flattened the car's tires beside where the Honda was parked, or turned on their lights. Unfortunately, I tended to feel responsible. After the third time, I put jumper cables and a pump in my trunk.

"I had some shopping to do." He shrugged as if it were a perfectly good excuse as he stood there without a single item and his hands in his pockets.

"You don't do your own shopping, or not most of it," I said, still thinking of the perfume. I believed that he didn't have something going on with Mother but not from lack of interest on her part.

But as far as shopping went, it was probably a good thing he didn't do most of his. With the level of testosterone he pumped into an area, he was going to give the ladies more than tomatoes to fight over. Even now, I could hear carts turning down our aisle. We were in the process of picking up a caravan and he hadn't even been here long.

Women were so silly, some nice built biceps and broad shoulders, face to die for and they got all... And now he was smirking, so I needed to stop looking at him.

"I do my own shopping as of today. My shopper is missing." He moved closer, his side brushing mine as we stepped forward. "Want me to push your cart?"

How had he made that sound like sex? And what had happened? When had sexual innuendos become a total free for all with us? What switch had been tripped without me knowing?

I stopped pushing the cart, blocking him when he would've taken the handles. "What are you buying?"

He looked around, grabbed a bag of marshmallows and threw them in my cart before he tugged on my ponytail. "Nice get up," he said, eyeing me.

I thought it was. My tank top, although disarmingly lacy, allowed for good mobility, and my flirty skirt hid holstered knives, strapped to my thighs, which were easily reached. The only sacrifice I'd made was the beaded flip-flops with wedged heels. The girl in me couldn't pair sneakers with this outfit, no matter how practical.

"It's highly functional."

"Just so we're clear, I don't want you disappearing anywhere with Paddy."

He had a point, but it was a point I'd seen for myself. "When did I become incapable of handling my own affairs?"

"I've got more experience than you."

"At handling my affairs? I think that might be impossible, even for you."

"At handling everything."

His tone made it clear exactly what he meant to handle and the smirk made its return. It never seemed far away anymore. It was hard to be angry, frustrated, or really anything else when he looked at me like that.

And I wasn't the only one. Some dippy lady ran her cart into an end display, too preoccupied by Fate and his smirk to pay attention to where she was going.

The pickle jars crashing to the floor broke the spell for long enough to get my senses under control. It was taking more and more these days but the overwhelming smell of vinegar helped. "I can't do dinner tonight."

"That's the deal we made." The smirk was gone.

"We didn't actually ever make a deal."

"Is this about your twisted bucket list or the perfume?"

I paused a minute. The perfume for Mother annoyed me but I wasn't going to screw up the only reliable working partner I had because of it. Besides, flirting aside, we had a working relationship. I didn't have any claim on him and I had to keep that straight in my head. Maybe the perfume was a good thing. It clarified things. He'd flirt and use all sorts of tactics to his advantage but it didn't mean anything.

I hoped the perfume was something sickly sweet as I tried to keep my voice from coming out as nauseating as I found his gifts to her to be. "Bucket list. I have to get them off the street."

I'd been trying to track down every person I'd saved for Malokin and had made a bucket list of sorts. Some people had a list of things they needed to do before they died. I had a list of people who needed to be killed before Malokin used them.

"What time did you plan on having your killing

spree?" He asked the question the way someone would inquire about when a tee time was.

"Not a spree." My shoulders drooped a bit. "It's not that easy to get them all in one place. More along the lines of serial killings."

"I'm sorry. That's tough."

"Are you mocking me?"

"No. That really is a pain in the ass. I had to make sure a war started once. It was an ordeal getting everyone together long enough for things to click into place."

"Which war?"

"I'd prefer not to say. I don't like to brag."

"Did you feel bad about it?"

"No. The guy was a total ass and I knew he was going to lose."

"But what about all the deaths?"

"You're letting your human show again. Death isn't final, not for humans. It's just a layover before you get back on the train. Why would I be upset about that?"

"What about the people left behind and grieving?"

"It's not like they aren't going to see them again."

"But they're distraught for a while, sometimes for years and years."

"Years are nothing. You really need to get those human thoughts under control. It's why you can't lose the transfer nickname." He reached over and grabbed an unbroken jar of pickles left on the display and placed them in the cart. "What time do you have slotted for your murder tonight?"

"Why?"

"Because I'm going with you."

I pushed the cart down the meat aisle, swerving to avoid two men about to fist fight over a shank of beef. "Is it that you like to be involved in everything or do you just think that I'll end up dead if you don't get involved?" And as I said it, I realized that question was my biggest problem with his attentiveness lately. What if he had some sort of savior hang up and that was all this was? He felt good about saving the helpless girl who couldn't save herself.

"Why are the two exclusive?"

"Be at my house at seven thirty." Sometimes I wondered why I gave him a hard time. In all honesty, I wanted the help and I didn't particularly care for having my entire existence wiped as if I'd never existed.

It also wasn't going to be a lot of fun trying to kill the people who should have died, but it needed to be done. I'd already chickened out on a previous attempt. I'd had the guy in my aim but I hadn't been able to go through with it. Maybe if Fate were there with me, having a witness would literally force me to pull the trigger.

Fate tossed a bag of salt and vinegar chips into my cart, highly unusual for his diet but not such a shock to see in my cart. Fate actually preferred healthier food. He had to, since it didn't matter that much what we ate.

"Comfort food? Afraid Mother didn't like her gift?" I hope that didn't sound as bitter as it had tasted crossing my lips.

He smiled. "They're not for me."

"For who then?" It didn't matter. They'd be eaten, and most likely by me, but I liked to downplay my junk food tendencies around him, shamed into silence by his salads and tuna tartar. I wasn't even human, the world was falling apart and a maniacal lunatic wanted to kill me, but I was still closet-eating bags of chips?

He looked at me like I had a screw loose. "For you. You might need them after you shoot someone tonight. If you shoot someone, that is."

I pushed the cart forward, having no idea why him thinking I might need comfort food after my possible kill tonight made me soften toward him. And wasn't there something integrally wrong to that entire train of thought?

"I have killed someone before." And not just one, but he knew that. He'd been there each time. "I had no problem then."

He didn't know about me chickening out a couple nights ago. I'd bribed the Jinxes with more booze to keep their mouths shut after they'd stopped laughing long enough to hear me speak. I was going to have to buy them an entire distillery soon. Those three knew how to negotiate.

An image of the wad of cash they'd had on them when they were buying their smokes came to mind. "They told you."

"What did you expect? I pay better. Plus, I'm me. It's natural. The problem is that cold blood is a whole different game. You had strong motivations with all the others. You were protecting either yourself or someone else."

He was right. It was why I froze last time as well. I hadn't been able to do it but I had to. The idea of those people walking around and becoming Malokin recruits drove me on, whether I wanted to turn down that road or not. There was no choice. Savior had become assassin.

I turned down the shampoo aisle, already feeling the need to cleanse myself of the blood soon to come. This aisle also had the added benefit of being devoid of any comfort food he might feel the need to get me.

I looked at the bottles, wanting to change everything in my life right now but only having the ability to change my soap. Fate was popping caps and bringing them to his nose making it obvious which ones he preferred.

"You know, I can finish shopping on my own," I told him. He was getting as distrustful of the crowds as I was but the people today seemed to be a relatively harmless bunch. It was still manageable at this point.

"I've got nowhere to be." His face froze as I grabbed shampoo and conditioner off the shelf and threw them in the cart. I decided peaches and apricot would be my new signature scent for my hair; it reminded me of the peach pies my mother made.

"What are you doing?"

"Uh, buying items to cleanse myself so that I don't become offensive?" It had seemed like a pretty obvious action in my opinion. Was I missing something here? I looked down at the cart, his tone making me wonder if

I'd grabbed Rogaine, or men's shaving cream, by accident.

He roughly grabbed both the shampoo and conditioner bottles hastily, and shoved them on the first open shelf spot, as if he disliked having to touch them too long. He turned and scanned the other bottles, dismissing my choices as he said. "Wrong ones. I don't like those."

I wasn't sure what he was looking for until he grabbed my old brand.

"What was wrong with the ones I just had? It was new. I want new."

I reached down to grab the shampoo he'd replaced it with but before I could, he started dragging the cart forward, effectively cart-jacking my groceries.

"Hey!" I said, having no choice but to move into something close to a jog to follow him if I ever wanted to see my cart again. "You can't cart-jack me."

He ignored me as he built up more distance between him and the shampoos.

"You don't wash your hair with it," I shouted after him.

He didn't stop, just yelled back, "I'm with you all the time. I'm the one who smells you more than anyone. I should have a say. Plus, you've been using this one for years. Why do you want to change now?" He took a sharp corner down the frozen food's aisle.

It took about three seconds, or the length of time for me to catch up to him in the ice cream section, for what he said to hit home. "I think we should stock up on some cookie dough too, just to be safe," he said, reaching in and grabbing a gallon of my favorite brand.

"The shampoo you put in the cart, I haven't bought *that* brand since I died." I'd stopped using it a week after my death, from the first time I'd gone shopping for myself. I took a quick look around, belatedly realizing what I'd said in the middle of the supermarket and making sure no one was too close before I continued. "How did you know what I used before I joined you guys?" I asked in a much more subdued tone. The humans might be getting riled up lately but that didn't mean they'd become deaf and stupid.

I'd guessed he had some knowledge of my previous lives; he'd alluded to it with a couple of comments but my shampoo? How could he have known such an intimate detail such as that?

"I don't. I meant months."

I looked at him and part of me didn't know if I believed him. I just had the strangest feeling he was lying. But why? Because that meant he'd known me? Had he watched me, and if so, how closely?

I remembered seeing my brand stocked in the condo when I'd taken my very first shower there. I'd thought it had been a coincidence. It was a popular brand. Now I wasn't so sure anymore. And if he had known me that well, how come he never really talked about it?

"Did you ever come around me when I was human? Did you know what my fate was then? Was I meant to end up here?" The implications of it all started churning in my mind, and I was sure I'd end with a bellyache once it was done. "Did you?"

"Do you really think I had nothing else to do but follow you around all day? Nothing personal, but there were much more interesting lives to watch than yours."

He wasn't looking at me but walking away, and I grabbed my now discarded cart and followed after him.

"For your information, I hadn't been going for burn down the walls, non-stop adventure. I was building a career and looking to start a family with Charlie—"

"I have to meet the guys. I'll pick you up at seven."

Looking as cold as ever, flirty smirk long gone, he moved past me and started heading out of the store.

"If I ever live again, I'll try to live life more recklessly for your amusement! Maybe I'll even be a crack whore if that would be more entertaining for you," I screamed after him, not caring how crazy I sounded.

He walked out, leaving me with my memories of the past. I couldn't take a step forward without them dragging like a weight around my ankles. I guess that's what pasts do, weigh you down, anchor you in another time and place. Sometimes it's a beautiful bay, with sail boats and warm breezes that uplift you, and other times you're holding onto your last breath in the cold waters of Antarctica and hoping to crawl your way back out alive. Good or bad, we all had them, and they didn't sit idly by, forgotten in the rearview. They walked beside you, tainting everything you saw.

CHAPTER FIVE

In two minutes, my neighbors—also known as the condo next door's current weekly rental—would be pounding down my door. Or worse, it might be the cops banging their sticks, trying to gain entrance.

Or maybe not.

We hadn't exactly become a close-knit unit in the two days that they'd lived in the building. They might not have even heard the high-pitched scream when I walked into my living room, not prepared for company.

After all, Fate was early, and although I was used to him strolling in without an invite, I thought he'd be preoccupied with his boys until later. He must not have liked that plan, and instead of telling me he did what he felt like doing, in typical Fate fashion.

So there he sat, fully reclined with an arm running along the back of the couch like he owned it, hogging up all the space in my small condo with his larger than life presence. He was dressed in black from head to toe, ready for our covert mission, and looking as tempting as the devil handing up my heart's desire, trying to lure me in for one small taste.

His head didn't move but I saw his eyes flicker, taking in the still damp exposed flesh.

I gripped the towel around me closer, not from fear of him ripping it off but to keep from dropping it myself and letting the devil take me. When I saw him look at me, like the way he was now, I could almost feel his hands gliding over my skin. Memories kicked in to full gear. They always started an avalanche of heightened senses.

I liked to pretend sex with him hadn't been that good. Problem was, it had been. Of course, Cupid had been involved. Logic dictated that he must have added some extra bonus points on because I'd only had sex with Fate twice. We should've still been in the awkward getting to know you phase. I tightened my grip. Yeah, it had been Cupid for sure.

"I thought you weren't coming for another hour?" I licked my lips after I said the words and then had to stop my hand mid-motion as it sneakily approached my hair. I might not have been sleeping with him but my body kept sending the signals that I was interested. Every time I let my guard down, a little sneaky telltale sign would slip out. From the look on his face, he was reading me like a scholar well-briefed in the ancient language of desire. It was probably where that smirk had crept up from.

This was all Cupid's fault. Maybe I should sleep

with him just to prove it wouldn't be that good again. Yeah, that was a plausible excuse to do what I wanted, a solid reason for walking straight into my emotional demise with eyes wide open. That would surely make me feel better when I was picking up the tattered pieces after he dumped me. I mentally snorted at my own twisted thinking.

"I was running early."

That was a lie. Some people thought Fate ran late, later and sometimes early. I knew him well enough at this point to know he just didn't give a shit about time. He came and went whenever he felt like it and that was when he meant to get there.

He stood and my lips parted. I shut them quickly before my tongue had the chance to moisten them again. Goddamn it, they weren't even dry. I'd just put on lip balm.

"You didn't forget that there is a psychopathic non-human creature running around this town wanting us both dead? Maybe a little heads up, next time, so you don't scare the hell out of me?" I leaned my shoulders against the wall and realized my back was arching. Why was I not sleeping with him? Sometimes I couldn't keep the reasons straight. Oh yeah, this week it was the perfume. I wasn't sleeping with him because he was a flirt and he bought Mother perfume.

No, that wasn't it. It would be a disappointment. That was the most current excuse. Or was that why I should sleep with him?

Nope, that wasn't it, either. Now, I remembered.

56

He'd crush my heart like a meat pulverizer.

While I was flipping back and forth between do or don't quicker than they were serving up flapjacks down at the diner, he was getting closer to me, close enough that I could smell him, feel the heat he threw off and that other certain energy that was pouring off of him right now at levels not seen since Chernobyl.

If I didn't move soon, I'd be in trouble…or ecstasy. He was close enough that he had to tilt his head downward to look me in the eyes. "Malokin won't."

"Won't what?" My brain was getting fogged with Fate pheromones. He should bottle this stuff up and sell it. He could make a fortune, not that he needed it.

"He won't give you a warning."

My chest rose and fell with his words; they seemed to take on a different meaning. His eyes darted to the tops of my breasts above the towel and watched a drop of moisture drop from my hair to travel their surface. I had an image of his tongue licking it off. He moved another inch closer and I was torn between running or staying right there and dropping my towel.

Another inch. I should move. I should go into the other room and stop this; I should be running from him. I stood there as he moved yet another inch closer.

And another.

A palm landed on the wall on either side of my shoulders. He was everywhere but not touching me at all. I felt overwhelmed and longing at the same time. My back arched further, my body seeking the contact that my heart feared.

"How long are we going to play this game?" he asked, his eyes moving from my mouth and back again.

"What game?" Was he changing the rules on me? Did he want to *talk?* Warning bells were flaring as loud as a car alarm outside my door. Sleeping with him was one thing. In no way was I ready to talk about it, too. Oh no, that would be way too intimate. If I slept with him, I might still be able to pretend I wasn't attached. If we talked, it would be *out there* and somehow real.

"We both want this." A jolt shot through me as we made contact. His hips pressed against mine, letting me know exactly how much. His head tilted down to mine, closing the gap and I couldn't or didn't want to stop him. I couldn't decide which and my brain wasn't functioning on full steam. My libido had kicked it out of the wheelhouse.

His tongue brushed across my closed mouth as I tried to keep myself in check. His teeth nipped at my lower lip, pulling on it, teasing me, tempting me to play.

My lips parted on a moan, not able to reject the invitation and his tongue dipped inside and tangled with mine; trying to draw me into a kiss I was still attempting to fight. But I knew I'd lose. I didn't have the will to resist completely.

His hand came up, cupped my cheek, his thumb under my chin. Tilting my head back slightly, his lips followed the line of my jaw working his way toward where it met my neck, only breaking to whisper, "Come on, I know you want it too. Why not have a little fun?"

I'd had fun with him before. Then watched his back

as he walked away taking all the fun with him. Fun. That was all this was to him.

I stiffened.

So did he.

His head pulled back. "I don't understand what the problem is." His eyes were intent on mine. He really didn't get it, and I wasn't going to explain. It was bad enough without the words.

I would've stepped away but his arms were there again, on either side, blocking me. "What is the problem?" he asked, repeating himself. "Those other times, they weren't only Cupid. We both want this."

"It might not be a good idea is all. We work together." I turned my head because if I kept looking at him, I was going to go down again, hard and quick.

"Why? It's not like it would be the first time for us." He took the opportunity of my exposed neck, kissing his way upward toward my ear where the tingle of his breath made it hard to remember what was stopping me. "I can see the way you look at me," he whispered in my ear.

His hands went to my waist and lifted me to my toes for better access as his chest brushed against mine. We were flush from the shoulders down.

He stopped talking and so did I, as I let the sensation of being so close absorb into my senses fully. God, I missed this but it was dangerous.

How did you tell someone that you cared more? It didn't change anything. It wouldn't make the other person magically love you equally. Why did I just use the word love? Why did that word even pop into my head? No, I didn't love him. The word made me go stiffer than rigor mortis.

Sensing my hesitance again, he took a step back.

"Go." The word was a pardon and a sentence from his lips.

"What?" I asked, partly sad he was letting me off the hook and not understanding why. The logically side of me was screaming *run* but still had a death grip on the steering wheel.

"Go. Now."

Logic won and I hurried into my bedroom, taking the coward's way out. I shut the door, my whole body alive and tingling, my hands shaking. I got dressed quickly, feeling much safer fully dressed when Fate was so close by. I tugged on a pair of dark jeans that would fade into the night and the first dark tank top my fingers touched on in the drawer.

Fate was standing a few feet from the door when I came back out. "Do you have something with long sleeves?" he asked. The mood of a few minutes ago still hovered in the air between us, also evidenced by the slightly deeper sound of his voice, which was not quite back to normal yet.

I grabbed a dark sweatshirt I'd left on the dinette chair and tried to avoid his eyes. He was like some sex Medusa; if I didn't look in his eyes it would all be okay.

"Let's get going," I said, looking to break the tension that was still there.

"Sure." My words seemed to jolt him from

whatever sexy trance he was in.

I followed him out of the condo and settling into our purpose for the evening somehow took the edge off of the mood, enough to make it bearable anyway.

"I'll drive," I said as we made our way to the parking lot.

His step faltered for a minute and I paused to look at him. "What?"

"You need a new car."

I stared at my Honda. All the sheen was gone from her paint and there was rust eating away at her wheel wells. "I like my car."

It was true that I hadn't at first. I'd resented everyone else having a better car but now I was sort of used to her. We'd been through a lot, my Honda and me, and she'd always pulled through. She'd never once stalled at an inappropriate time. Not that she didn't stall, but she seemed to know when she could slack off.

"We can't go after people in this thing. It sticks out too much." He had a look on his face like a kid with a plate of lima beans in front of him.

"And you think your car is more low key and appropriate?" I asked, pointing toward the flashy Porsche. "Trust me on this, no one's looking at my old Honda."

"That's part of the problem, I don't want to look at it either. I propose we get another car for the bucket list."

I scrunched up my face, feeling bad at casting aside my old car. "I don't know. It feels wrong somehow."

"You don't have AC. I can't drive around like that."

"I do have AC," I said. "You just have to turn it off when you drive over thirty. Why? You think your fancy sports car makes you better?"

"What makes me better has nothing to do with my car. I just like to actually move forward when I hit the gas as opposed to how you occasionally slide backward."

"That only happened once and we were on a hill!"

"Look, I'm not forcing you to ride in mine. I'm compromising. Me. Compromising. For you." He raised his eyebrows, stressing with his expression how difficult this was for him.

"You do have a problem compromising." I nodded in agreement.

"That wasn't what you were supposed to say. I am not the only one with this problem. And if we are going to make it as a…team, you need to as well."

I was fairly certain team was his second choice of words. Was he going to say friends? Coworkers? He was trying. I had to take what I could get.

But I wasn't very fond of compromising either. I crossed my arms, sighed and I knew I must have had a puss on my face but I finally forced out the word, "Fine."

"Was it really that bad?" he said, laughter in his tone.

"Yes."

"There's a used car lot around the corner. You can pick. Tonight we take the Honda. Tomorrow, we get a real car."

He wasn't exactly asking but I answered anyway. "Okay."

CHAPTER SIX

A lifetime ago—or more accurately, last month—I'd saved a man on a yacht. Thinking back on it now, it felt like a different person had done that. It had been my first "save" job, robbing someone from death's hands—and by death's hands, I mean the process of the body dying, not my buddy back at the office—so that I could deliver them into Malokin's. He wanted them for his own nefarious needs, the exact details of which I had blissful ignorance of.

I'd never been a willing participant but Kitty's life had been hanging over my head as Malokin's noose had tightened around my neck. I hadn't known until then how much I would hate being under someone's thumb. How could I have? I'd never been a puppet before. If it hadn't been for Kitty, I would've taken my chances and told Malokin to do his worst, even if that meant being strangled by the threads that held me.

And here I was now: new marina and agenda, same

yacht and target. It wasn't surprising that they had decided to move the yacht to a new location after what had happened.

I hesitated only a second before I turned off the engine, parked in a spot between a Mercedes and a Lamborghini.

Fate threw me a look that said, *yeah, we blend*, before climbing out of the car. The Honda was making some especially foul smells today so I followed quickly. He might have a point.

We walked through the parking lot and then toward the slips filled with boats.

One of the things I hated about remaining here, so close to where I'd been born and raised as a human, was it was filled with memories that flooded back when I least expected them. The last time I'd been at this marina was when my number could still be counted among the homo sapiens.

I'd gone on sailing trips from this place, back in better days when the only worries we'd had were if we'd brought enough booze and sandwiches. I wished those were the only things that came to mind now. I'd even settle for those memories to be the second or third of what came to mind, instead of being buried under a whole lot of ugly crap.

"This guy, this was the first time I did something for Malokin." I walked down the dock, staring up at the changing sky and wondering about all of the things I still didn't know. "It keeps me up at night wondering how my saves contributed to what's happening now." It might have been the most honest thing I'd ever uttered to Fate.

He looked at me as if he understood, right down to the sleepless nights. "Something was going on way before that. Maybe it helped him, maybe it didn't, but this was coming either way."

He sounded so sure of it that it was easy to cling to the belief he was correct. I remembered the day I went to Montreal on one of my first jobs. Things had seemed off then, even to my novice transfer sensibilities. "Maybe you're right."

"You know I'm right. I was searching for the cause way before you got involved."

He had been. I'd thought at the time it was a fool's errand. Now look at me; if he'd been a fool I was now a court jester dancing to the same tune.

"Even still, I didn't help things."

Fate stopped in the middle of the walk and grabbed my hand to stop me as well. "Kitty would be dead if you hadn't done what you did. He would've killed her."

"Would you have done it? Helped Malokin to save Kitty?" I asked.

He didn't answer, and that was all I needed. I'd known anyway. As playful and flirty as this newer version of Fate could be, it hadn't been that long ago for me to have forgotten what he'd been like when I'd arrived and what I knew he was deep down—black and white, all steel and sharp edges. He would've let Kitty die.

"You think I'm soft?" I didn't know if it was a

question or an accusation.

"No. Everyone has to follow their gut. You did the only thing you could live with."

He looked at me like he believed in what he was saying, even if it was the exact opposite of how he would've dealt with it. I nodded and started walking again. So did he.

"Don't judge your actions against mine. We're different."

Don't judge. That was a joke. How could I not? Everyone judged whether we admitted to it or not, usually saving the harshest criticisms for ourselves.

"What about Murphy or Luck? What do you think they would've done?" I asked, fearing the worst. Was I the only one that didn't have the heart to let her die? Or was what I called heart actually just human weakness? Maybe they were right; transfers were inferior.

"It doesn't matter. It was your choice to make." His eyes, that sometimes burned so hot, were cold as he said it.

"But it's not what you think I should've done. Admit it." I could see it there in his face, and I needed to hear it. "I can handle the truth but respect me enough to say it to me. I don't need to be handled with kid gloves."

"I would've let her die."

That hadn't taken much prodding. "Why?"

"Does it matter?"

"To me it does."

He didn't speak and I thought he wasn't going to explain. We paused within view of the boat, he finally said, "Because I couldn't let anyone have that much control over me."

I'd expected something along the lines of sacrificing one for the greater good.

"You would've let her die because of your control hang up?"

"No. Not because of my hang up, because of what could happen if they did ever have control over me. It could've been much worse than arming him with a few more people. Like so many other things, it's all in the numbers. Kitty's life wasn't worth the possible damage. No one's life is worth that many, no matter who."

It had been what I'd thought after all. I got it. In the larger scheme of things—as a whole—it made sense. But standing there, being the one that had to walk away and let the single one die, I wasn't built that way and probably never would be.

The fact that he would make the same choice if I were the single life … . That was why I needed to keep my distance. Because if it had been him, I wouldn't have ever given up.

"And what exactly are you that would be so lethal? I highly doubt you were ever supposed to be human. You finally going to tell me?"

"Depends. What are you willing to pay for the information?" He smiled.

I faked a smile in return, trying to forget what his earlier words had meant, that he would sacrifice anyone including myself if that was what it took to save the whole. I wouldn't. Justified or not, it caused a hurt somewhere deep within. Seemed even if I didn't acknowledge how I felt about him, it didn't stop the feeling of it.

"There it is," I said, motioning towards the large yacht I remembered. The door I'd crashed through had new glass and lights were shining inside.

"Do you want me to do it?" Fate asked as we got to the ladder that would lead us up to my target.

"No. I saved him; I should kill him."

He paused with hand on a rung. "It'll be easier for me."

He had no nerves. He was calmer than the water in this inlet, gently swaying the boats to and fro as if they were rocking a baby to sleep.

"I know. But it still has to be me."

He wasn't human; he never had been, and I doubted he ever would be. The idea that he would be capable of having a relationship with me was ludicrous.

Even watching him now, I could feel something potent growing. Preparing for obstacles, it replaced the flirting Fate, who had just resided in his place, with a more ruthless creature.

We were so different on the most fundamental level. It was pointless to pine for something that could never be. I'd fallen into this position by some crazy twist of luck. I'd do my time, see if I could get Paddy to spring me early for good behavior, and go back to a normal human life. There was something animalistic in Fate that took to this life. The two of us would be like a bunny and a wolf mating. Even if I were to become the most vicious bunny in the warren, it just didn't work. We were different animals.

"You ready?" he said, but I could tell he was wondering what had made me pause.

"Yeah," I said as I nodded, trying to shake off my thoughts and get my head back in the game.

He nodded and started to climb up onto the deck. I took a deep breath and followed after him, thinking of how sturdy the ladder was this time around. The Universe really didn't like when you messed with its plans. Now that I was trying to correct them, it seemed much more magnanimous to my presence here.

We hit the deck and crossed to the door, then made our way into the lavish interior of the boat. A guy walked into the room and stopped short, clearly startled to find us standing there. I recognized him immediately. It was the man that would've shot his partner. I wished he were the one I needed to kill. Pulling the trigger would've been a lot easier.

"You!" he said, looking directly at me.

"Where's your partner?" Fate asked.

The guy threw his hands up. "I don't know what beef he had with you people but I don't want any trouble. He's gone. I know he was involved in some shady things but I just want you all to go away."

"Gone where?"

"He's dead."

I advanced on the guy, ready to bang his head into the wall until I got the truth. "Dead? Why didn't I see an obituary?" I'd done extensive research and nothing I'd found had led me to believe Malokin had got to him already.

"He disappeared a couple of weeks ago. They declared him today."

The guy was sweating bullets, and I was starting to believe his story. I'd known my target was missing but I'd thought that he was hiding on the boat. "Fate?" I asked.

"On it," he said, pulling out his phone and checking. Only a couple of seconds elapsed before he confirmed the information. "Yep, declared today."

I turned toward Fate, not caring if the guy took off anymore and knowing my reflexes were quick enough to stop an attack from a single human, back turned or not. "Let's go. Nothing left to do here."

"Would it make you feel better to kill him?" Fate asked, pointing to the guy.

I watched the potential target's back as he ran from the room. I waved my hand to let him go when Fate raised his eyebrows. "No. I wanted to kill *my* target."

He walked over and patted me on the shoulder in a slightly mocking way. "It's okay. There'll be other murders."

"I know. It's just so disappointing." I'd really thought this one would be a slam-dunk.

"Come on, I'll buy you an ice cream."

CHAPTER SEVEN

The Honda spluttered like it was on life support as we pulled out of the parking lot. The disappointment was so thick that I was having a hard time keeping it contained.

"I think we need to focus more on Malokin. These names on your bucket list mean little to nothing."

I knew what he was trying to accomplish but it didn't make me feel any better. "Maybe by themselves they don't but as a whole, they can't be helping the situation."

"It's more important to locate Malokin."

Frustration and disappointment warred within me, and I wanted to bang my forehead into the cracked vinyl of the steering wheel. It did always come down to finding him, slippery eel that he was. I'd hunted him down before. Malokin didn't get found until he wanted to.

"Turn left over here," Fate said, pointing.

"Why? What's down there?"

"You losing your memory? Ice cream."

"I thought you were kidding. I really don't want any." Ice cream would sit like cement in my stomach the way I was feeling.

"I want it."

72

I turned my head toward him. "You don't eat it."

"I do once in a while."

"What, once every century?"

"No, once a decade or so."

The sound of my phone vibrating in the middle console filled the car. We both looked down. It was ringing but no number came up on the caller ID. That could only mean one thing. Maybe he was coming to us.

I hit speaker on the phone. "Malokin."

His voice was as smooth and genteel as ever as he spoke. "I'd like to offer you a proposition."

Propositions from Malokin never leaned in my favor. "Which is?"

"I'd like to discuss it in person tomorrow night."

"She won't be coming alone," Fate added making his presence known.

"Didn't expect her to." And from the sound of his voice, he really hadn't.

Malokin rattled off a time and place before hanging up abruptly.

I let the shock of what had just happened filter slowly into my system for a minute before I spoke. "I'm not sure how I feel about that. Why would he agree to meet us when I'm sure he knows we want to kill him?"

Fate threw his hands up as I passed the ice cream stand. "Where are you going?"

"My condo."

"I still want ice cream."

"You *still* want ice cream?"

"Yes."

Those calm waters must be a really nice place to dock your psyche, I thought to myself as I whipped a U-turn.

I parked in the crowded lot and we got in line, me still pondering the situation and waiting for Fate to voice an opinion about something other than ice cream.

"Order me a hot fudge sundae, extra whip and cherries," Paddy said. "Tell them double fudge, too."

"I hate when you do that," I said, as I turned to see him standing beside me when no one had been there a second before. I looked around, wondering why no one else noticed him just appear.

"And sprinkles. I want a lot of sprinkles. The rainbow kind. Open table! I'll go grab it before someone gets it."

His cane barely touched the ground as he ran toward the four top, nearly knocking a couple of kids who were eyeing up the same space out of the way.

Crazy, rude misfits, the whole lot of them, even the ones at the top. Of course things were falling apart. How could they do anything but if we were the ones in charge?

Fate handed me a bowl of cookie dough ice cream I hadn't ordered as we made it over to the table that Paddy was actively protecting, waiving his cane around like a senior samurai. He plopped down a bowl in front of Paddy as we both took a seat.

"Are you two aware that the chaos breaking out around here isn't a limited occurrence?" Paddy asked right before a shovel-sized spoonful hit his mouth.

"Obviously." Fate took a spoonful of his ice cream then made a face. He turned and dipped his spoon in mine. He raised his eyebrows and nodded his approval.

"Do you have anything to add that we don't know?" Fate went to reach over and eat more of mine. I slid the cup towards him, not caring if he took the whole thing.

"Not exactly, but I think we should be cautious about trying to completely do away with Malokin."

Fate shoved his spoon in my ice cream and left it there. Finally, there was something that dimmed his appetite.

"What do you mean, we can't kill him?" he asked. "If this is happening because of him we have to. If we don't, what then? You know he's at the heart of this somehow. We can't let this keep building and have everyone going crazy."

While Fate had been speaking, two ten-year-old boys had started going at it. That wouldn't have been anything surprising except both fathers, who I'd thought were heading over to break it up, were now punching each other as well.

"Why can't we get rid of him?" I asked, glad that the brawl was a good fifteen feet away but keeping my purse in hand in case we needed to dart out of the way.

"Everything is connected. Every leaf, bug, speck of dust, it's all part of the same whole. I've been searching around through the most basic make-up of the Universe, looking for where Malokin originated and, well, when he formed, something pretty severe must have happened. He seems to be integrated into the fabric of things more than he should be. If you kill him, I'm not sure what will happen. Killing him could be like a mortal taking a gut shot. You wouldn't just take out the small intestines, the poison would spread and kill all the other tissue. It might make things worse."

"How sure are you?" I asked.

"I can't be a hundred percent sure unless you kill him, but I'm not eager to be proven correct in that manner. I need to keep digging. Until we do know for sure, don't do anything irreversible."

"So we're stuck with him?" I asked, as he continued to stuff his face with ice cream.

"Sort of." Paddy pointed an arthritic finger toward both discarded ice creams. "Are you going to eat that?"

I shoved both bowls his way and Paddy dug in. With a mouthful of ice cream, he said, "I've got some people you—"

"She isn't going," Fate answered.

Before I could say anything, Paddy gave Fate a sour face and disappeared with his ice cream.

***

After almost twenty-four hours of debate, Fate and I finally agreed that we couldn't take the risk of killing Malokin as we pulled up at the designated restaurant. The place was known to have the best steaks in all of South Carolina. Malokin was seated in the corner but his elegant looks, set off by his expensive suit, commanded as much attention in the room as if he were on a stage.

An open bottle of wine sat on the white clothed table in front of him, a glass already half full of red that probably cost more than I made in a month.

We all nodded in greeting, none of us speaking yet as we sat. The tuxedoed waiter came over within seconds of us settling in. Neither Malokin nor Fate ordered anything and then the waiter turned toward me.

"Miss?"

I was sick of having Malokin ruin my appetite. I was going to eat a meal, even if I had to chug a gallon of water to get it down. I suspected Malokin had been behind the train accident that had killed me and he had been responsible for both mine and Kitty's mental anguish. I'd leap over this table and kill him right in the middle of the restaurant before I let him take my dinner, too.

"I'd like a Caesar salad to start and for my main course, I'll have the filet, rare, with a side of the garlic mashed potatoes and French cut string beans."

The waiter nodded and walked away.

"Thank you for meeting me," Malokin said.

Fate leaned back in his chair but said nothing. I couldn't speak. I'd just dunked some bread in the dish of seasoned oil in front of me and was too busy chewing.

"You've changed," Malokin said to me. "You used to be so nervous when we met."

It aggravated me that I'd been so transparent and that he'd clearly enjoyed my unease. "Yeah, well, we're all young and stupid at some point." I forced a smile as I picked up my phone and sent a text. The smile came naturally after that.

"Your manners were better as well."

"I've learned to conserve my energy for those worthy of the effort," I replied, adding to the insult by not bothering to look up from my phone as I made sure my message sent.

Fate was silent but I felt his hand come to my leg under the table and give a squeeze, telling me silently to not let him goad me into anger.

Fate cleared his throat before he spoke. "Move on or this meeting is over. You were the one who wanted to talk, not the other way around. Get to your point."

Malokin nodded stiffly. "I asked you here because I know that you two are the only real threat to me. But let's be clear, if we went head to head, I'd win. I just don't see why we need to expend our energies."

I took another bite of bread, having no desire to speak to him. I might laugh if I did. He was offering us a truce when we couldn't do anything to him anyway.

"I think we can come to some sort of agreement," Fate said, stone faced.

"I propose non engagement, at least with each other." Malokin leaned back and brought his glass of red wine with him. "Before you answer, I'd think really hard on this. You don't know what I'm capable of."

"And what about everyone else? Do you plan on increasing your numbers while we do nothing?" I asked, feeling forced to speak because I wasn't sure it was very high on Fate's list of priorities.

"I'll stop actively recruiting if you stop actively

trying to reduce my numbers." He pulled a cigar out of a case and lit it up. "You mind your business, and I'll mind mine. I don't touch any of yours and the same for anyone with me."

"Agreed," Fate said. I couldn't speak as I was already mourning my bucket list.

I knew we didn't have a choice. Not much of one. If we could hold everything in check, at least for a while, until Paddy could figure out what our options were, a truce would protect our people and hopefully stop the downward slide of the human race.

I waved toward the waiter. "Pack my order to go please?" I asked as Malokin stood to leave, no one feeling comfortable enough with the other to touch hands.

As we watched him leave the restaurant, a flash of bodies zoomed by one of the windows.

Fate looked at me. "Did I just see the Jinxes skating by?"

"Yep."

CHAPTER EIGHT

"You're scuffing the dash."

I looked at my boots, where they were still sitting on the dash of the new *work* car Fate and I were sitting in. I thought they looked feminine yet assertive, with their modest heel and lace up front. They held my knives quite comfortably tucked into the side, too. When I wore leggings, sometimes a thigh holster was a little too Rambo for the look I was going for, even on an occasion such as this.

It had been a week since the truce and things hadn't gotten any better. They hadn't stayed the same either. They'd become progressively worse.

Fights were breaking out everywhere and businesses were becoming too scared to open their doors.

If one of the names from my list disappeared now, post truce, we needed to know. It would be the first signal that Malokin had broken his word and was recruiting again. They might not make it into my bucket, but they still made a list.

We'd been watching the apartment across the street for about an hour, waiting for one of the people I'd saved for Malokin to show up. This one had been a junkie who'd knocked off a jewelry store. The ones who were still human weren't hard to locate. Flipping through possible suspect photos had led me to most. Not surprising that the majority of them had a criminal history.

It made my skin crawl that I'd ever been on his recruit list. It still didn't make any sense. Had I been a saint? No. But I didn't fit in with this gang.

Fate insisted on coming, and I didn't mind having the backup even though I wasn't doing anything risky other than criminal watching. Lately, simply leaving the house could be considered endangering your life.

"Your boots?" he asked, reminding me of their unwelcome position.

"Are quite comfortable where they are. If you hadn't snuck off and picked this car without me, we wouldn't have wood trim on the dashboard we needed to worry about, now would we? It would be aged and cracking plastic, as befitting a car for this type of job. I don't believe I should have to be uncomfortable because of your poor choices." I turned the dial down on the temperature-controlled seat.

His eyes shot to the control and then me. I was complaining but the amenities were quite nice, not that I'd admit it to him.

"You don't look like you mind much. And it's a used Audi. What would you have us drive? Should I have gotten something worse than the twenty-year-old Honda? Maybe you would prefer having to stick your foot out as you drive and pushing it along?"

I leaned over, acutely aware of exactly every inch of space his frame took up, which was way too much in the front seat of this car, and painstakingly avoided even an accidental brush. I tapped the spot above the odometer.

"Used? Demo at best. A couple trips around the block is far from what I'd had in mind." I reclined back into chilled bliss.

"I know how you feel." His voice had turned husky.

I knew that tone and it immediately set off a chain reaction in me. Just like that, he'd brought the discussion back to sex. He had a crazy ability to do that. Somehow, everything turned into a sexual innuendo with Fate these days.

"This was supposed to be a compromise?" I asked, playing tug of war with the conversation until the ribbon was back in safe territory.

"It was gently used. Not like it was ridden hard for hours on end and thoroughly abused, pushed to the very edge, until it gave over every ounce of soul it possessed to the feel of the ride."

The air in my chest froze and it took a bit of conscious effort to get my diaphragm expanding again. Conversations with Fate had become like tiptoeing through a minefield and waiting to step on a trigger. It seemed like there was no subject that he couldn't turn sexual.

I stretched out as much as I could in the car, which was more than if we'd gotten an automobile of my choosing. "Seeing as murder isn't on the menu, I need to move around a bit and expend some energy." And get a couple of deep breaths of fresh air in before he says something that sounds sexual again and I decide to throw caution to the wind.

His hand wrapped around my wrist as I went to leave. It was strange how when he touched me, my entire physical awareness shrank down to that one place where we touched, as if my entire body was running on a dead battery and he was feeding the current.

It was downright embarrassing how I reacted to him. He'd probably had so many women that nothing was a big deal and here I was, jumping at his touch. Another reason it wasn't a good idea to go down...

Great, now I was turning everything into sex too. I wasn't going to have many words left in my vocabulary soon.

He let go of me and held out the same hand, motioning for my notebook.

"You're going to take notes?" My eyebrows would've touched my hairline if I raised them anymore.

"No," he replied, confirming my impression. "I just want to see what you wrote."

Yeah, now that was more like Fate, controlling to the core. I tucked the notebook in my purse, ignoring his request. And that was more like me, flaunting his demands. Plus, I didn't think he'd get much out of my house and flowers doodle with the occasional heart accent. I could already hear the mockery.

"Fine. Keep your notebook. I'll make my own."

I shook my head as I got out of the car. Never, ever, would he keep a notebook.

"Don't go far," he yelled after me.

I nodded like I resented his watchful nature. I didn't. I wasn't sure why I acted as if I did. Maybe it was because to admit that I liked him worrying about me meant that I wanted him to care. That then reminded me that he didn't care, at least not the way I wanted him to. Ta-da, it was better to not think of it at all. I was actually mad at myself for letting this train of thought take over in the first place. I was acting like a soft human again. Damn, it was hard to break that habit.

Tugging my purse higher on my shoulder, I pointed over to a convenience store that had somehow managed to stay in operation and not be looted. Only about thirty percent of businesses could boast such a thing. That percentage was dropping rapidly and on a daily basis. Soon it would be down below ten percent, the same rate as a new restaurant surviving its first year.

"You want a soda or something?" I yelled back to him, an afterthought as those southern manners I was still fighting reared their pretty little head like a game of Whack-A-Mole.

"*Something.*"

I could see his smile in the reflection of the rearview mirror.

Shaking my head, I pretended that I didn't like the overtures. I was getting really good at all this pretending crap.

I walked away and headed toward the store.

CHAPTER NINE

The place was in relatively good shape, and I relished in the fact that I could still pick something off the shelf and not have to scavenge off the floor. It was a small perk but I'd always liked to think I was a smell the roses type, or as with this case, stop and taste the Ho Hos.

The large tattooed guy behind the register, with piercings from ear to nostril, watched me hesitantly as if I'd try and kick his ass at any moment. Even though he was twice my size, and assumed I was human, so many were carrying weapons at this point that no one was totally safe. I understood.

I gave him a smile and a wave, trying to put him at ease. He nodded and went back to flipping through last month's issue of People magazine. I continued to peruse the offerings, unoffended.

I grabbed a pack of Twizzlers off the shelf and looked at the sticker. "Ten dollars? Are you people crazy?"

His left shoulder angled up toward his ear. "Supply and demand."

"Oh, well thank you so much, Mr. Harvard Economics. You ever hear of ethics or price gauging in those classes?"

"Hey, no one's forcing you to buy them." He looked back down at his magazine.

I tossed the Twizzlers back on the shelf and moved on, not sure if I was going to be purchasing anything but not ready to go back to the love bug yet.

I forced myself to move on to the next overpriced package of empty calories as the Twizzlers continued to taunt me in my peripheral vision.

The door squeaked open as my internal clock told me it was three minutes past my unspoken allowed time frame when Fate would start getting edgy. I couldn't leave though, not while I had a raging debate going on in my head over whether two Ho Hos were worth twelve dollars. Those Twizzlers were looking like a bargain but I couldn't get them now, not with Mr. Economics ringing me out and my prior statements. But I really wanted that damn twisted red licorice. Maybe I could make Fate buy them. I'd have my candy and my pride.

"Mr. Healthy, you want some brownies?" I asked when a tall body cast a shadow on my package.

I suddenly knew it wasn't Fate. It didn't smell like him and even though whoever was hulking behind me wasn't touching me, it didn't feel like him either. Fate caused a certain sizzle in my senses when he came close.

It was probably some idiotic human drinking

whatever crazy juice Malokin was handing out. I should handle him before I eat my snack. Didn't want to fight on a full stomach.

"No, that isn't what I was looking for." The voice was deep, and monotone. I couldn't explain why, but I'd guarantee the guy who owned it had less IQ points than the lump of chocolaty goodness in my hands.

I also recognized it immediately. I'd saved him— Eddie, the petty thief. I'd dragged him kicking and screaming out of an alleyway when he would've been stabbed with his own knife.

Somehow, I didn't think he came here to show his gratitude. I wasn't sure if he had found me intentionally, although I couldn't imagine how, or perhaps the lack of shopping opportunities had created this chance meeting. Either way, he was on my bucket list. And here he was, serving himself up like a chilled bottle of champagne and yet I wasn't allowed to pop his cork, so to speak.

I turned to face him and realized someone had already beaten me to the killing. He was already dead or at least not human anymore. Oddly, he didn't look that much different from when he'd been mortal. Or maybe he did and it was just me?

It was still strange how I could recognize anyone after they changed but I did. Like with this guy, I knew he looked different but it was still him somehow. And it hit me. This was the first time I realized I wasn't recognizing him as a human would recognize another human. I was recognizing him on some other deeper fundamental level that had my thoughts spinning.

All those times I'd thought I'd recognized someone in my human life but couldn't put a name to the face, this is what it had been. The thing that makes us who we are, that goes with us from life to life, it never changes. We always know the people that have surrounded us deep down, whether they are meant to be in our lives at that moment of time or not.

As much as I wanted to drift off into my memories and musings, standing before me was a problem wrapped up in a black tracksuit. He wasn't alone. He had two others with him, neither of whom I recognized, but definitely not human either, and it looked like they'd all done their shopping in the same place.

I didn't know what happened when people were recruited outside of the agency but I knew it made them stronger, quicker and, in essence, a match for me. The biggest problem was, there were three of them and, if I had to guess, everyone outweighed me by almost double.

A couple of things immediately ran through my mind. Firstly, how had I been so lax that I hadn't noticed three large men approaching me? Secondly was that Malokin must have been very busy and it better have been before the truce *he'd* called for.

The fact that there was a truce should've put me at ease but something didn't feel right about this. I saw intent in their eyes, their stances, in the forward tilt of a head and the way one was rolling up his sleeves. They wanted to inflict pain and wouldn't be happy until they did. They probably wouldn't be happy afterward either, but that was their shrinks' problem.

I belatedly scanned the store. The clerk was gone, and the back door was also wide open. I was glad for it even if I was silently calling him every name for coward that existed. This had the smell of something that was going to get ugly. The clerk hadn't needed any more help in that area. He'd had a face that perfectly matched his shitty attitude. I wouldn't want to be partially responsible for kids everywhere running away in tears.

I held up my hands, palms outward, toward the three undead amigos.

"I'm not looking for trouble." I sounded like a bad action flick. Even in those movies that line never worked. I needed something extra. "Seriously," I tacked on. *Oh, yeah, that made it so much better. Now they wouldn't screw with me, for sure.*

I could always try the honest approach and tell them I didn't want to fight because I was outnumbered. I'm sure that would get them to leave me alone.

In actuality, I wasn't adverse to a fight. My mouth drooled at the idea of taking out Eddie, just not three on one. If I could only get them to take turns, my night would be perfect.

Most likely it wouldn't matter what I did or said. I was fairly certain a fight was coming. This wasn't bluffing and showmanship.

Eddie reached out with his club-like hand and grabbed my arm, yanking me to him. Immediately I knew something was off. I felt like a rag doll. The guy was freakishly strong, even for one of us.

One hand wrapped around my back as the other

groped my breast. "Nice and full, just how I like them."

"Wow, what a charmer you are. I'm even getting foreplay and dirty talk." There went my mouth, taunting him when I should've been trying to calm him down, especially since I couldn't budge him. I was torn between pure rage and full blown "I really stepped in it this time" panic. He shouldn't have been that much stronger than me.

No, I couldn't get nervous. Panic was bad. So was rage. This wasn't anything worse than I'd already dealt with. It was certainly less intrusive than a wiretap on my entire existence, like Malokin had done. Plus there was the truce. They wouldn't kill me. They couldn't.

Remain calm and talk to him. "Listen to me. We have a deal with your boss. You can't do this. It would be very bad for your newly burgeoning career. Don't you want to be Mr. Second Bad in Charge someday?"

He smiled. His teeth were perfect but that made him as appealing as getting bitten by a viper with gleaming scales.

"You're right. I can't off you. No one said shit about having a little fun with you." His eyes looked even smaller when he smiled like he was.

I was shoved backward, the metal shelves of the rack pressing into my spine. His hand went from my breast to my hair, gripping it and pulling back on my scalp painfully as his mouth tried to close over mine. He didn't want to have sex with me. He wanted to humiliate me and it looked like he had some experience at the job.

I pushed and shoved but he still didn't budge. What

the hell was up with this guy that I couldn't move him even slightly? Eddie the pickpocket had just shown his value for recruitment. It wasn't that I'd grown weaker; he'd become much stronger.

When his tongue shoved into my mouth, I bit down hard and then gagged on the taste of blood. He yanked back quickly, yelling out in pain.

"Grab her arms," Eddie said to his two companions.

"You're not grabbing anything," I said, but Eddie still had a grip on me, and no matter how hard I punched or pulled, I couldn't break it. Without being able to get clearance, both arms were grabbed and I was soon being turned and shoved face down over the ice cream fridge.

I struggled, pulling at my arms and seeing what leverage I had. The two holding me down weren't as strong as the dick I'd saved but they had an arm each and they weren't holding back. It felt like both limbs had the entire weight of each man bearing down on them. I yanked at my arms again and again, refusing to give up easily.

And where the hell was Fate? Was he taking a nap in the car?

A thought hit me like a kick to the teeth. Maybe he would let this happen to maintain the truce and limit the damage. Maybe he was out there right now, watching everything happen but wasn't going to get involved. The idea made me sick but he'd already said as much just the other night. I was in this alone.

I never thought I'd be this vulnerable again. I was Karma, for fuck's sake. How did this stuff keep happening? But there I was, stuck like an insect in sticky tape, and I'd been just as oblivious to the trap as the damn fly. Helpless, that was me. Again.

It was strange how my mind went to the oddest thoughts as I was about to be raped, like the way I couldn't stop surveying the ice cream in the case below me. I was going to be violated as I stared down at my favorite Toll House ice cream sandwich. Even if they didn't kill me, I'd never be able to eat one again.

The fact that I was even thinking about an ice cream sandwiches probably meant I was already mentally screwed up from this. Shouldn't I be crying? Screaming? Was I really this tough or was I just in some sort of shock? I'd like to think I was strong but time would tell, if I lived past this, how many pieces of who I was would still be intact, how human I would be.

My leggings and underwear were roughly yanked down together and I heard fabric ripping. Bastard. Those were new leggings.

"I bet that made you feel really tough, ripping that flimsy fabric like that. Gotta give it to you, Eddie, you're the man."

"You'll know exactly what kind of man I am." His hand reached forward, at least I thought it was his, and slammed my head back the several inches I'd lifted it off the cooler. I was lucky I'd had it turned to the side or it would've been my nose absorbing the blow.

"Look at that ass." I felt two hands on my back before his friend chimed in, "I get her next."

"Fuck you. I do," the other said.

Donna Augustine

"You can flip for it. Now shut it, you're fucking up my hard on."

Such a diplomat. Now I knew what was causing the delay. "Poor Eddie, can't you get it up?"

My head slammed into the cooler again and my vision wobbled in and out, taking with it my bravado. This was definitely happening and nothing I said would goad him into a fight instead. I could handle a beat down. Nothing about that was new. I didn't know if I could handle the three of them taking turns on me.

Finally, the dread I'd expected—the sheer horror of the situation—was hitting home and seemingly all at once. It started an avalanche of other thoughts, all the way back to when I'd first signed that contract with Harold.

Greed. It had been my time to die and I'd refused to accept it. I should've moved on but I'd taken any opportunity I could. I'd cheated death and for what? To end up like this? What good had come from it? I'd lost everything that I'd been trying to hold on to—my family, my career.

The new situation hadn't turned out well. I was falling for someone out of reach while the world was falling apart and I couldn't do a thing about it. Every time I thought I was getting my bearings, I went spinning again. Hell, I spent more time spinning than standing still, until lately it felt like the entire world was shifting with me.

It was too late to dwell. I needed to get past this first, and then I could have the luxury of picking apart my choices. I closed my eyes, trying to put myself somewhere else mentally. This didn't matter. Nothing mattered. I'd get out of this and forget it ever happened.

Okay, forget might have been an overly optimistic prognosis. I would get over it though. And if they let me live, I'd kill them. One by one, in the most painful way I could devise.

My cheek was cool against the freezer and I imagined myself lying in a field far away. It was a pristine snowy evening, with flakes gently drifting down, coating the ground around me. And there were fireworks above.

Wait, that wasn't imaginary fireworks, that was gunfire.

"Let her go." I opened my eyes to see Fate standing in the door with a shotgun, looking like a demented demon. When his eyes glanced my way, I was glad he was on my team. The way he stood, feet braced apart with the butt of the gun against his shoulder, eyes blazing…forget a demon, he looked like the very devil waiting to escort us all to hell.

"We aren't killing her. There's nothing you can do about this." Eddie was speaking but it didn't sound like he truly believed his own words.

I felt a little slack in my arms but not enough to break free; just enough to be less bruising. I guess his friends heard the same hesitation I did.

"You really believe that?" The words were succinct, crisp and layered with something else that made the hair on my body stand up and pay attention.

If I didn't know better, it sounded like he was goading them for a fight. But I did know better. *Sacrifice one for the greater good.* We'd just talked about this the other day. Now that I was the sacrifice, I didn't expect him to think differently, protective instinct or not. He would've let Kitty die and he'd known her for centuries. Letting some girl he'd only known for months get raped wasn't going to change a philosophy that seemed pretty ingrained in his nature.

He was bluffing and I'd prefer that he just left rather than witness the act.

My current position was humiliating but I forced myself to meet his eyes anyway, and I found the strength to take control, if not of the situation, of at least myself. "It's okay," I said but broke eye contact quickly before I followed those two words with something more desperate and truer to how I was feeling.

It would have to be okay. I wouldn't grovel for help simply to be denied. I had too much pride. I wouldn't cry for these men to stop. They wouldn't. I could only control myself and that would have to be enough, because Fate wasn't going to break a truce for me—one person.

The gun rang out and the hold on my wrists released. I was frozen for less than a second before I stood and yanked my pants up quickly, covering myself. I looked around. It was a good thing I'd developed a stronger stomach because there was blood and little fleshy bits everywhere. He'd shot all three of them quicker than I thought was possible. I'd expected a mess from the warm spray that had hit my exposed skin and there it was. All three of my assailants no longer had faces.

I heard Fate approach as I was tying off the ripped corners of my pants to keep them up. I was still staring at the dead bodies around me. Who knew we'd break the truce first?

I tore my gaze away from the bodies lying there to look at Fate. He looked worse than he had a minute ago and I saw his eyes move from my torso to my wrists. I looked down at myself, not realizing that the guy had torn my shirt as well. There was blood spattered all over me and marks on my arms. "Wow. I'm a wreck." My voice was flat, in distinct contrast to the chaos I felt ricocheting within.

His hands reached behind him and pulled his shirt up and over his head. Standing there naked from the waist up and completely at ease, he held it out to me. I took it and quickly swapped out shirts with my back turned, self-conscious now.

I turned back, resting my hands on my hips to keep them from wrapping around myself. Some loser had almost gotten the best of me, raped me a foot away from my Ho Hos. I was not going to compound matters and look even weaker by having a mental breakdown over it.

"The truce is definitely broken." I took a deep breath and exhaled loudly. "Do you regr—"

"No." The single word cut me off and echoed with power and finality.

As soon as his attention was off of me and on the

bloody bodies, I searched his features for some sign of regret. I should've let it go but I couldn't, and when I couldn't find any, I tried to pull it out of him.

"I know this wasn't the outcome you were hoping for." I thanked my years in front of hostile juries for my ability to hide stress under duress and my continued blasé attitude when I felt nothing of the sort.

"It wasn't planned but I'm not unhappy with the results." His voice was stiff and I felt like I barely knew this man. Or maybe I did. I just hadn't seen him in a long while.

He walked closer to where I was and looked over his *results*.

"We should get out of here." I looked over my shoulder, toward the glass door. All I could think of was escape. They were dead and I still wanted to run. I felt like a coward of the worst kind, worse than the names I'd called the tattooed employee who had taken off. I turned to Fate again, my back to the doors, refusing to show any more weakness.

Fate looked at his watch. "Why? The police response time right now is a joke." He knelt down next to one of them, looking the bodies over.

He was right. The cops who were still showing up for work were so overtaxed it was almost as if there weren't any at all. I'd heard reports of up to a twelve-hour response time in certain areas.

"I knew that one." I rattled off the bare details as he concentrated on the other two. I knew what he wanted. He was looking for ID. If there was some way to link the bodies to their former past, we could determine if the truce had been broken before this incident. I didn't see a reason to care. The truce was broken either way. "What's the point?"

"All knowledge is good."

My arms were wet. I needed to get the blood off. I walked down an aisle and found some baby wipes and made my way back to where he was still inspecting the dead, only one question on my mind. "What about that thing you said to me the other night?" I asked as I scrubbed my forearms to baby softness, trying to concentrate on the clean smell and not the wet feeling on my leggings.

He looked up at me from where he was and cocked an eyebrow as if he had no idea what thing I was speaking of.

"You know, *the thing*?" I'd just escaped rape. Did he have to play games right now?

"What thing?" He shook his head, still proclaiming ignorance.

Was he trying to be obtuse? "*Sacrificing one for the greater good* thing."

"This was different." He went back to his inspection, dismissing the question.

I took a second, wondering if I was the one missing something. "How is this different?"

"It is. That's all."

"I don't see how."

"Did you want to get gang raped?" His voice was off, the tiniest little bit. It was so slight, I wasn't sure my human ears would've picked up on the difference of a 16th of an octave at most.

"That was uncalled for." Anger that was boiling inside of me, choking me with its fight for prominence in a myriad of unhealthy emotions, was starting to gnaw its way out, beating past the humiliation, ineptitude and self-pity.

"Then stop questioning it and be grateful."

This tone I knew well. Irritated.

"I just don't understand why you did it." I went to grab another wipe to realize the packet was empty, all the used ones in a pile by my feet. I ducked down the aisle to grab another container.

"What don't you understand? Didn't you want me to stop it?" he asked, his voice carrying over the aisle as I debated between baby wipes or going for some disinfectants. I opted for Lysol wipes and walked back.

When I returned, he looked at me as if I were the stupidest being walking the planet. He was the one contradicting himself.

"I want to know why you did that. Why you broke the truce when it's the exact opposite of what you said you'd do? And I want to know why, whenever I need you most, you act like the biggest asshole I've ever met?" I looked at the spot where the incident had almost happened as I vigorously scrubbed my skin. No. I wouldn't let that rile me. They hadn't done it, and if I acknowledged how close they'd come I might start losing it a little, and I was fairly proud of myself with how I was holding it together thus far.

His eyes narrowed on the Lysol wipes I was scrubbing my cheeks with and then rubbed against my lips. "Can you just say thank you and—for once in the last twenty lives you've lived—act like a normal girl?"

"You're a complete ass. Can't you ever have an ounce of compassion?" Wait…twenty lives? I had him! He slipped. Didn't really watch me *my ass*. "Twenty lives?"

He let out a loud sigh and ran his hands through his hair, still clean and pristine in comparison to myself.

"I might have seen you around."

"When?"

"Can't say. Against the rules." He shrugged as he stood there.

"Well that's the biggest load of bullshit I've ever heard from you. Yes, you can. And even if some stupid rule existed, you don't listen to rules." He walked out of the store but stopped just outside of the threshold holding the door open for me.

"You're right. I can. I just won't."

"You're really not going to tell me anything?"

"No."

"Why?"

"Don't feel like it."

"What do you mean, *you don't feel like it*? I was just attacked in there! You can't cut me a little slack?" I was screaming at him like a banshee in the middle of the parking lot and he seemed completely unperturbed.

Then it clicked into place. He'd *wanted* me to scream at him. I stopped, now feeling like an even bigger ass than I had a moment ago. My shoulders sagged and I let out a long sigh.

"Better?" he asked.

"Actually, yeah, a little," I admitted, embarrassed at how easily he'd manipulated me but grateful for the release. "Was that a lie? The twenty lives?"

There was a flicker of indecision before he answered, "No."

"And?"

"What?"

"You're really not going to tell me about them?"

"Nope."

"Why?"

"That wouldn't be any fun." He walked toward the car, opening the trunk and grabbing a T-shirt out and throwing it on.

"But..."

"I know, *you were almost raped*."

"I can't figure out if you're really a bastard or sometimes you just play one for kicks."

He smirked but the light in his eyes wasn't there this time and I had a feeling he was faking it.

"Just so you know, I won't ask any more questions for now, since you are obviously flustered by this situation, but this is not the end of it." I tilted my head toward the store we'd left. I didn't even want to look in that direction. "What about them? We can't just leave them there in the middle of the store."

"They won't be there long. If they do manage to get the police here, the bodies will be gone before they show, energy reabsorbed into the system. Nothing will be left but some dusty residue."

I nodded, feeling an overwhelming need to go home and scrub my skin in the shower for hours. "I need to get my car at the office. It's been a long night."

"I'll drive you. You're in shock."

I shook my head. "No. I'm not. I've been in shock enough times in the last several months to know what it feels like. I'm a little off balance but I'll be fine." The scariest part was I would be. Close call, but I'd made it out relatively unharmed, physically anyway.

His silence made me look at him and the stern set of his mouth as he stared off into the distance, surveying for anymore threats.

"I would've thought that would make you happy. I'm getting tougher, jaded if you will." I let out a long sigh before I continued. "Less human."

He shook his head, a profoundly sad look on his face. It wasn't an emotion I was used to seeing him wear. He leaned his forearms on the car hood in between us. "No. Not even a little."

"Why? It's for the best." How many times had I heard the word *transfer* like it was a disease of the worst kind since I'd come here?

"I never wanted this life for you."

Every time he said something like that, so brutally honest and from the gut, it flayed me until I was raw. Maybe that was why we didn't speak honestly with each other.

"Come on. I'll drive you." He straightened and

opened his door.

"You don't need to come. Just give me a lift back to the office where I'm parked."

"Not tonight." His voice was soft. He wasn't just asking me to let him do this, he was asking me to not fight him on it, and it revealed more than anything he'd said to me tonight. He wanted to drive me.

He wasn't going to budge and he was probably right. I might not have been in shock but I wasn't great, either. A ride wouldn't be the worst idea.

I got in the car, letting him drive me away from the place I'd been attacked. That wasn't how I'd remember it though. I had a frightening feeling that from this point on, I'd remember it as the place I'd lost yet another chunk of my humanity. I just wished I knew how many pieces you could lose before you had none left.

CHAPTER TEN

We didn't speak as we drove. I wasn't sure what kept him silent. For me, the scene kept replaying in my mind. If I kept accumulating moments like these, I'd be able to run an entire movie theatre's worth of traumatizing images soon. Murder, torture, beatings—I had a plethora of horrible memories to draw from next time I was staring down one of the numbers on my bucket list and trying to find the magnitude of strength I needed to pull that trigger. Thinking of it that way, a near rape wasn't such a big deal. I'd shown more skin on the beach, I'd just been more selective about the parts.

I redid my warrior ponytail, as I'd come to think of it, and set my mind to a more useful purpose than dwelling on what might have happened. It *hadn't* and there were plenty of things that were happening I needed to concern myself with.

But I couldn't let the scene go completely. "He was really strong."

"I'd suspected as much," Fate said, without any question.

"Why?"

"Because I didn't see any bruises on them. You were overpowered too easily, and I know you wouldn't have gone down without a fight."

"Was that…"

"What?"

"Nothing."

Fate had just paid me the first compliment I'd ever heard him utter, and it made me feel like I was glowing and not just from my tattoo. First he saved me, then he helped me vent when I would've swallowed all those horrible feelings, now a compliment? That was a big problem. I could feel myself getting dragged down further into the quicksand of emotions that were Fate.

I wanted to smack myself upside the head and might have done it if I wouldn't have had to then explain it to him.

Work—world is falling apart, need to concentrate on work.

"So Malokin is tapping into a human's natural inclinations."

He nodded.

"If you knew, you could've mentioned it to me."

"Sorry. I thought you knew that that's how it works. I forgot you were a transfer."

"Don't flatter me so." I lifted my head and took a deep breath. "Do you smell that? The air smells weird."

"I do."

I hit the down button on the window so I could get a better sense if it was coming from the car or outside and that was when I knew something was wrong. This time, it had nothing to do with gut instinct.

We were a mile or so from my condo when I saw it. Smoke was billowing up into the night sky over the area of my building like an ominous cloud of dread or, maybe more accurately, a personalized billboard from Malokin. It might as well have had the words *you fucked with me* carved into the smoke.

That there'd be retaliation wasn't surprising. There was no way Malokin would let the death of his men— and a break of the truce—go unanswered. Not for a second had I ever believed his southern charm act or doubted his ruthlessness; not even before Kitty's torture or that first offer of a drink. But I hadn't expected payback to come so swiftly. The shit was about to hit the fan in a very large way and I was pretty sure we weren't prepared.

Fate hit the gas, giving the work car as much juice as he could, which was quite substantial since it wasn't the wreck he'd promised to buy.

Traffic choked up the streets when we got a couple of blocks away. Without having to discuss it, we abandoned the car and ran the rest of the way on foot.

The fire department, or the skeleton crew who were still reporting for work, was trying to put out a raging fire that looked like it had been burning for a while from the amount of damage already done. Or more likely, had gotten some help in the way of gasoline. Half the building was blackened and half was in sticks. My condo looked like it wasn't fully gone yet, as if Malokin had orchestrated the fire to burn in just the perfect way that I'd be able to witness its destruction in person.

My condo didn't matter right now. All I could think of was Smoke, my cat. If that bastard had killed my cat…

I didn't think of the fire, or Fate, or anything but Smoke as I took off toward the building. A fireman blocked me immediately.

"Ma'am, you can't go in there," he said, but I was pushing past him before he'd finished the sentence.

He screamed something along the lines of *crazy bitch* after me, but I ignored him and ran for the stairs that led to my floor. He didn't know what crazy was if my cat wasn't okay.

I barged through my door, flames creeping closer as the fire burned through the cedar siding like it was a book of matches. "Smoke!" I screamed.

A howling preceded Smoke leaping into my arms and digging into me with a clawed death grip. I ignored the discomfort as I hugged her closer, feeling utter relief. The overhang in front of the door fell, blocking the way. The deck was in flames at the back.

I turned, with Smoke in my arms and howling up a tirade like I'd never heard before. Both doors were burning flames. And then sheet rock started crumbling from above. I thought the ceiling was collapsing until I looked up to see Fate leaning over the new hole in the ceiling. That's where he'd gone.

I reached up toward him before he had to ask and was quickly pulled up through the hole in the ceiling he'd made that went through the rafters of the attic to the roof.

There was only one clear path but it led to a deck on the side and we were able to climb down. We hit the beach where a different fireman thought we'd escaped the fire.

"You okay?" he yelled after us as we gained some distance from the burning building.

"Fine," Fate yelled back.

I wasn't sure what the guy would've done if we'd said no. There wasn't an ambulance to be seen.

Standing on the beach with Smoke safe in my arms, as a crowd gathered to watch my home burn to the ground, the impact of what happened hit. "My stuff."

"Is all replaceable. Nothing in there would be salvageable anyway."

He was right. Even if something did survive, which was becoming more and more doubtful, it would all be smoke damaged.

For the second time in less than six months, I'd lost all my possessions, and it felt every bit as bad as the first, maybe even worse. Smoke let out a howl and I loosened my grip.

It hadn't taken long for the truce to fall apart and the gloves to come off.

***

Morning light had just started to disrupt the dark sky as we met in the office for an impromptu meeting to discuss the latest development. My fingers pushed the hair from my face and a fluttering of ashes floated to the floor. Then there was the smell of eau d' ashtray that permeated the air in a ten foot radius around where I sat in the middle of the office, Smoke on my lap, even stinker than I was.

Fate was leaning on the desk in front of me, Murphy standing to his right and Luck to his left. The Jinxes were doing laps around the room on their skateboards, each go around punctuated at the sharp turns with skidding sounds.

Knox—who was looking pretty good in another high end suit of navy blue, bought with an obviously much higher salary than I received—followed them with his eyes in a way that confirmed they'd managed to irritate the new guy.

"Don't tell me the agency doesn't have another condo," I said to Knox. I wasn't sure how he'd found out about this little get together, since I was certain it wasn't from Fate. Still, maybe I could make use of him.

"No, nothing," he replied, still not turning away from the Jinxes like a housecat staring at an annoying fly it couldn't reach. Wow, they'd really gotten under his skin.

"You aren't staying alone." Fate crossed his arms in front of his chest and the muscles in his forearms looked like they were geared up for a fistfight. His eyes stared hard and his mouth was tense. It was what I thought of as his emotional lockdown face. It was the look he gave when he was unmovable; I'd come to know it well.

Luck edged back to sit on the desk, crossed her shapely legs and trim ankles, all the more attractive for being donned with five inch red stilettos. "It's not like you have much of a choice anyway. Duh, your condo looks like the remnants of last night's bonfire, and an extremely festive one at that," Luck added, stating the obvious.

"Thanks, Luck. What a wonderful visual that is." I could imagine all the psychos toasting marshmallows as the fires died down. I hadn't stuck around that long myself, having seen all I'd needed in the fifteen minutes I'd been there.

"You should stay with me," she added, undaunted by my sarcasm. The only sign of nervousness from her was the continual digging out of her red lipstick as she reapplied it to already pouty fresh red lips. It was the fifth time she'd done it since she'd heard what happened, beginning with the convenience store attack and followed by my condo building being burnt to a crisp.

Being overly groomed in response to Malokin declaring war wasn't a sign of weakness to me. In my book, it meant you had some balls if that's the most you were slipping. And if he won, at least she'd go out looking her best.

"No," Fate said, countering Luck's offer. His body was so tense I could actually trace the line of his veins visually all the way from his elbow to his hands. This was going to be a tough battle, and I wasn't sure I had the gas left in the tank to take it on. The only thing that gave me any fuel was wanting to curl up in a ball in a dark room and be able to process this all in solitude. And if I couldn't be left alone completely, Luck won hands down. She was far easier to ignore.

"I'm tired. I've had a very rough day and I'm not arguing. I'm going home with Luck for tonight, and before you start asking who's covering my back, I've got Luck. Who's covering yours? Do you think you're untouchable?"

"Yes. I do," he said.

"Really?" I leaned back in my seat, feeling much more bravado than I thought I'd be able to muster. He'd walked right into my hands with that last statement, and I could never walk away from a challenge. "And why is that?" I said, backing him into a corner. Fate had secrets and I was fairly certain I wasn't the only one he kept them from. If he wanted me to stay with him badly enough, he could come clean.

"Because I'm me." He smirked.

I'd thought I'd laid a trap. Traps didn't work on Fate. He didn't feel the compulsion that normal people did to defend themselves or explain. I should've known better.

"You're in that house *alone* so you don't have a leg to stand on. At least Luck and I will have each other. "

I leaned back and let my eyelids droop closed over gritty eyeballs, thinking I should have splashed some water on my face. I couldn't wait until the day was over. Once I went to sleep, it wouldn't be the day my home burned down or the day I was almost raped while I stared down at my favorite ice cream. It would be a fresh new day where all sorts of wonderful things could happen.

Or maybe it would just be the shitty day after everything went to hell. Still, probably an improvement.

"She's got a point," Murphy said from his position next to Fate, his trench coat rustling with his finger pointing.

My eyes widened and fixated on my unexpected ally. I hadn't thought I'd get any support from his corner, not when it went against something Fate wanted. He wasn't as bad as the Jinxes but he had a slight Fate crush. Embarrassingly enough, there seemed to be a long list of us on it.

"Thank you, Murphy." The count had just hit three against his one opposing vote.

Fate threw him a look that I thought would send him scrambling, but Murphy looked back at him and kept talking. "I'm on your side. I don't think anyone should be alone," Murphy added.

Now I was the one shooting dirty looks in Murphy's direction. *This* was more along the lines of what I'd expected from him.

Fate raised his eyebrows and turned his gloat glare all the way to maximum output for my benefit.

"Oh, so now *Murphy* is the be-all and end-all on tactical matters?" I didn't care if it was a valid point. I didn't like getting ganged up on. I'd had enough of gangs for a while.

Murphy, who'd been in a slouch, straightened his shoulders. "I'll have you know, I'm very good tactically. I'm an excellent chess player."

Knox, forcing his eyes away from the long skid marks on the floor left by the Jinxes' last lap, dragged his attention back to the group.

He did that weird sleeve jerk, which men who wore suits a lot often did, to look at his watch. "He's right. No one should be staying alone."

"Are you kidding?" I nailed Knox with a stare that said *I'd thought maybe we could be friends but not anymore*. Of all the people I'd expected to back Fate up, Knox was the last. He and Fate hardly had a bromance brewing.

Didn't anyone get it? I wasn't looking for attention or someone to take care of me. All I wanted was to crawl into a bed, be left alone to digest the shitty day I'd had and go to sleep. Why was this turning into such a fiasco? This day just kept getting longer. It felt as if the last twenty-four hours had magically stretched into forty-eight.

Knox's eyes softened when they landed on mine. He shot me a look back that silently asked me for patience. "He's right. The entire office should condense. After what happened with you, it's for the best." He looked at the occupants again and then his eyes came right back to me. "I've also received orders," he added.

I knew it was Knox's way of apologizing, and he didn't need to tell me who issued them. *Paddy.* There was no way Knox would go against him, not in all eternity. The chips were piling up against me, and I was getting too tired to argue. A quiet corner was starting to outweigh who was there.

"How many people do you think you can fit at your place?" Knox questioned Fate. "The larger the group the better."

"I'll take whoever wants to come," Fate said. "We'll make it work."

"I want to come! I love a good slumber party!" Luck said.

Murphy jumped on the bandwagon and I saw the Jinxes' ears perk up as if they'd heard something of interest.

Would these people ever not seem weird? I didn't think so.

I forced my legs to straighten underneath me and set off another dusting of ash. "Smoke and I are going to Luck's tonight. That's final. Tomorrow is soon enough for everyone to have to climb all over each other."

Luck started rubbing a hand across her brow like someone would rub their cheek if you had a dirt spot on your face.

"What?" I asked, having a hard time thinking what could be seen on my face past all the dirt.

"Your eyes are glowing," Fate offered.

Shit. I'd thought I'd gotten that under control. They were all looking at me like I was finally starting to crack.

"Now can I go to Luck's in peace?"

"I'll pick you up tomorrow," Fate said. I think he was taking pity on me.

Luck stepped forward. "Come on, I've got an outfit you can borrow for now. Let's go to the bathroom and clean you up a bit."

I didn't argue with that. I was leaving a trail of dirt as I walked away.

"Looks like we have a base," I heard Knox say as we left.

Huh? Did that mean he was coming too?

CHAPTER ELEVEN

Everyone was treating me with kid gloves since fiasco one, the near gang rape, and fiasco two, the condo burning down that almost took my cat with it. Fate had picked me up from Luck's house the next evening. But he'd backed off only to sic his boys on me. I'd seen both Cutty and Lars in Luck's backyard throughout the evening.

Luck was planning on staying with him too so I wasn't sure why I needed a personal escort. She'd promised to drive Smoke over with her since Fate had wanted to make a stop. I'd burnt out my arguing skills over the past day—something I never thought would happen—and I was slightly more agreeable while I waited for my words to replenish.

Fate pulled the car up behind a closed strip mall about halfway between Luck's place and his house. Every store in the row had been boarded up in the past week. I knew because I'd slowly watched it happen. I passed by here every day on my way to the office and I'd kept count. The last store in this strip mall had closed as of a few days ago.

"What are we doing here?" I asked.

"You're going to need clothes." He got out of the car and waited until I followed. He pulled out a set of keys and opened the backdoor to a place called Sandy's Boutique. I'd shopped here when I was human and made better money. I hadn't stepped foot into the place since I'd begun my new job.

"You own this place?" Fate and a women's boutique went together about as well as a wolf in a hen house.

"I own the building, not the store." He held the rear entrance door open for me and flipped on the lights. "Pick out whatever you need. I'll cover it with the owner."

Who would cover it with him? I walked around the store, knowing I couldn't afford anything here without even having to look at a tag. Wow, this was awkward. Maybe I should just get one outfit to hold me over.

No, this was ridiculous. I was going to pick up two items that would cost me my whole pay for a month? "I can't afford this place. There's a clothing store down the street that's still open. I'll go there tomorrow."

"I told you not to worry about it." He shrugged, as if he didn't understand my problem. Dismissing the issue, he looked back down at his phone as he leaned against the counter.

"But I can't not worry about it."

"You can pay me back if it makes you feel better."
He was still looking down at his phone as if he didn't
understand the concept of worrying about money.

"On my pay, it'll take me fifty years with the price
of things in here."

"You've got the time." His voice faltered on the last
word and I looked away.

I knew what he was thinking because I was as well.
I might *not* have the time; not if the vision he'd seen of
me being killed was accurate. Neither of us brought it up
often but it wasn't something easily forgotten, not when
you were the walking dead.

I grabbed a shopping bag from the counter beside
him, figuring debt was the least of my issues right now
and tried to forget the reminder from a moment ago.

I walked around the store debating on which was
more depressing, ceasing to exist or minimum wage for
an eternity. My intention had been to grab the basic
essentials but the reminder of my throat getting slit
added an additional level of stress that drove my need
for shopping therapy way past the point of subduing.

Twenty minutes later, Fate looked up from his
phone to the bags and heaps of shoeboxes I was trying to
juggle. He reached into his pocket to add another wad of
cash to the pile he'd already left near the register. He
scribbled a note and placed that and the cash in the
drawer before we left.

We got to his place less than five minutes later and
he helped me carry in all my new belongings. I'd
thought he was being a gentleman when he'd grabbed

them for me.

He walked past the kitchen and living room. Things didn't go bad until, instead of taking the stairs to the bedrooms above, he headed straight towards the master suite—his suite—the lair of the… That was the scariest part about it. I didn't even know what the hell he really was.

My body, which had been simply watching, finally sprang into action and chased him down as my bags disappeared inside with him.

He was placing them on the bed when I walked into the room.

"Why are you putting my things in here? I know you have guest rooms. I've seen them."

"We need the space. You heard them back at the office. We're going to have half the place staying here. No one can afford to have their own room. Going to have to double up at minimum."

"Double. Up." I said the words as if I'd never heard them before. How could I have not thought of this scenario? That's right, I'd been worried about everything falling apart while he'd been worried about falling into bed.

He said it as if he had no control of the situation. No—worse—like he was as stuck as I was. Fate didn't do anything he didn't want.

It all made sense. It was why he didn't mind the entire office cramming into his house.

"You did this to…" My words faltered. I couldn't say he did it to win. Oh no, that might lead to an outright discussion about what he wanted to win. Next thing, we'd be talking about sex. Then what if it led to a discussion about why I wouldn't? The warning bells were starting to chime. I needed to abort this conversation immediately. I could picture it now, me in a pile on the floor crying *why don't you love me?* Because that was the only thing left that could make this week complete.

And it could happen. I never would've imagined I'd be *that* girl, the kind who would grovel and beg. Now it hung over me like a looming threat. If I veered too close to the edge, I'd fall over, broken, desperate and clinging to whatever flimsy root I could.

"I don't need to double with you. I think it would be better if I doubled with another female. Luck is coming tonight."

He shook his head. "She's rooming with Mother."

"What about—"

"The Jinxes are in with Knox."

He hadn't merely been texting or surfing the web on his phone while I'd been shopping; he'd been tightening the noose. I guess that was what I got for being lured in by pretty linen sundresses. Oh the shame of it! He'd used the lure of frilly things in my time of need to distract me. A row of pretty colors and strappy sandals and I'd been a lamb to the slaughter.

"You've got other rooms."

Legs wide, hands in his pockets, he said, "Taken." The low husky way he pronounced that word gave me an altogether different idea of what he meant.

I watched him walk past me and shut the door while I was still looking at my new things on his bed, like a piece of meat sitting in the center of metal claws ready to snap its teeth into me. What would I do? Would I go quietly or would I chew off my paw?

So stunned at how neatly his trap had been set, I didn't realize he was still there until he was standing before me, smelling all sorts of good and looking all manners of broad and handsome. How was a girl supposed to fight against this caliber of ammunition?

"I like when Luck dresses you," he said, as his hand lifted to run over the swell of my hip. Luck had lent me the dress this morning. Her washing machine had mysteriously not been working. I knew I should have put my smoky, stinky clothes back on.

"Thanks." I wasn't surprised he liked it. Luck's wardrobe had one goal in mind, make as many men drool as possible. She was extremely good at it. She never gave it all away, just hinted enough here and there to keep their eyes glued to her, waiting to catch another glimpse, a little more cleavage when she bent over or a bit more thigh when her step went a little wider at just the right moment. She was like a sex appeal ninja and she'd armed me with one of her secret weapons.

"I'm sorry about this," he said, not demonstrating an ounce of remorse. His fingers tested the span of my waist where the dress showed it off to its best, before returning down to the swell of my hip again, fingers splaying

"Sorry about sharing the room?" I needed to break

off contact because I was going down hard and soon. Maybe I wanted to. No, I *knew* I wanted to, and I couldn't remember why I was fighting it. Maybe the ride was worth the crash.

"No. Not that." His right arm wrapped around my waist as his left hand bunched in my hair, angling my head back, the better to access it. I was too shocked to think or doing anything before his lips were on mine. The only thing that came to mind briefly was what had happened to covert tactics, subtle attacks that came from the side and nipped away slowly at my reserve? This was nothing like the kisses he'd been stealing over the last few weeks. This was a full siege.

I quickly realized that he'd been going soft on me but he wasn't anymore. The other thing I was sure of was that it hadn't been all Cupid those other times. In fact, I might have highly overestimated his contribution. He might have pushed us both into the same boat but he wasn't the one who'd raised the sail to full mast.

He walked me backward and I was too overwhelmed to even think of stopping him. The bed hit the back of my calves as he bent forward, and I fell back upon it, him following me down. He pulled me with him further onto the center of the bed. His legs wedged in between mine as he settled his weight against me, full erection pressing exactly where it would do the most damage and feeling absolutely exquisite against me. The only thing I was thinking then was I wanted him in me.

My arms were holding him close and I would've crawled inside him if I could've, just to get closer. I loved the weight of him pressing me into the mattress, being surrounded by him on all sides as his arms cradled my head, as if I'd pull away. That wasn't an option.

"Whoa, sorry!"

Murphy's voice and then the sound of the door closing broke my lust-induced state enough to pull back just slightly.

He rested above me, his face inches from mine and the look on his face was about to make me melt right back in oblivion.

His eyes shot to my lips again before he rolled onto his side. He had me, bed to rights—no, that was supposed to be dead to rights—and he was pulling back? He was stopping?

I quickly scooted off the bed while I could still think straight and he changed his mind.

"What the hell was that?" I asked once I had a good distance between us and my brain was functioning on all cylinders.

"You should know. It's nothing we haven't done before."

Leaning on his side, completely at ease, just waiting on the bed for me, a slight smile touching his lips. It would be so easy to walk back over and let all my worries fall to the wayside. Except for the prospect of an eternity of pining for him. "Why did you do that?"

"I want you in my bed, and I'm tired of waiting."

He did not just say that. Knowing a man like Fate wants you can have some serious potency. Delivered from his lips, it was devastating.

"And that's what you apologized for?"

"I was apologizing because I've reached the point that I've decided to stoop to unfair tactics if that's what it takes." He shrugged.

I should've been more alarmed than anything else. Instead I was intrigued. This was a very bad reaction. The normal car alarm that went off was blasting like a five-alarm fire was burning. I needed to evacuate the area immediately.

I practically ran to the door and just as I had my hand on the knob, he said, "You know it's going to happen."

I slammed the door shut, not looking back.

CHAPTER TWELVE

"Sorry about the intrusion." Murphy was standing in front of the TV looking at the remote with a confused expression when I entered the living room. I hoped he'd keep looking down at it or that my face wasn't as flushed as it felt.

"Don't worry about it," I said, trying to brush off what he'd seen a few minutes ago. "That wasn't what you thought," I added. That sentence made it sound like it had been *exactly* what he'd thought. When had I become so bad at this?

Now he did look at me. His mouth twisted and his eyebrows rose, confirming my suspicion, but he didn't say anything more about it.

"When did you get here?" I asked.

"A couple minutes ago. Same time as Luck and Mother. You didn't hear us come in?"

"No." He didn't comment on the fact that I'd been otherwise occupied, while I was trying not to roll my eyes. Of course Mother was here already. I was surprised she hadn't come over last night.

Luck broke the awkward tension with her heels clacking down the hardwood stairs, armed with lip-gloss in her hand and Smoke following her.

"I'm not staying in a room with her!" she hissed under her breath the second she got within ten feet of the two of us. Smoke started howling, as if backing her up.

"Mother?" Murphy confirmed. "She's not that bad."

"She's horrible!" Luck blinked her eyes as if she could barely hold back the tears. "I was supposed to be with you," she said, pointing her lip-gloss at Murphy.

"We had to make room for the Jinxes," Murphy explained.

All of our eyes shot to the bar at the mention of their name. They did have a propensity towards being on the wet side more often than not. Perhaps an unguarded liquor supply wasn't a good idea. But they'd probably had more booze in bribes from me than Fate had stocked, so who was I to talk?

Luck walked over to the bar in question and poured herself a shot of peach Schnapps.

"She can't be that bad," I said, thinking of my own arrangement and how much easier it would be to room with anyone but Fate.

"She *is*." She threw back her shot and shivered like she'd just put down 180 proof moonshine.

I heard a door shut from somewhere behind me and then Luck called out Fate's name, rushing across the room to him.

For the most part, Luck didn't have the same effect on the guys in the office that she had with human males. I'd never confirmed it with her but my hunch was she dulled the sex ninja down on purpose.

Fate came into the living room just as we heard Mother's annoyingly high voice singing *We are the World* upstairs. She was very loud and extremely off tune. I had to concede Luck's point. I didn't think I'd make it long with her either.

Luck grabbed on to one of Fate's arms. "I need a different room. I can't stay with *her*."

"She's not that bad," he said.

A screeching ripped across the house before we all realized Mother had brought a karaoke machine with her.

"Really?" Luck asked. She threw her hands up in the air and broke into full dramatics.

Another screech of an amplifier had Fate relenting a little. "I'll talk to her."

I'd been avoiding eye contact with him until I heard that. There it was—again. Fate having to swoop in with his soft touch and handle Mother. Maybe he'd buy her some lingerie to go with the perfume.

All the jealousy I'd never wanted to feel came bursting out of calm surface waters like a dolphin doing a flip to amuse the spectators. "Of course you will. Why don't you have her room with you? I'll room with Luck?" The evil words spewed from my mouth before I even knew what I was saying. I wanted to reach out and yank them back. The green demon would eat me alive if what I'd just suggested came to pass.

Why did I keep doing this? Saying the stupidest things I didn't want to happen? And now I was doing it with an audience?

Luck froze, her hysterics ceasing almost immediately when she realized there was a better show available. Murphy's eyes grew large. This was one of those times that it was painfully clear they weren't human. Polite humans would've been surprised by my words and would've made their excuses to leave the room and give us some privacy. With these two, I was waiting for them to decide who was going to make the popcorn.

Fate, never human either, didn't seem to care that we had company. "Is that what you would prefer?" I'd lobbed the ball to him and he lobbed it right back at me.

We stood about eight feet away from each other but it could have been a chasm for the connection I felt. There wasn't so much as a muscle twitch to tell me what he was thinking. Stone. Because he didn't care? Maybe I was simply a game to him.

"Well?" he prodded, nailing me with an intense stare when there was no forthcoming reply.

He wasn't going to accept my silence and let me off the hook by not answering. He'd wanted me there, in his room, but I couldn't decide if I wanted to be there or not. What I did know, without the tiniest little sliver of a doubt, was I didn't want anyone else there.

But he'd let the whole situation go up in flames just to force me to admit it.

I was damned either way. I couldn't insist on staying with him and then *pretend* I had no feelings. And that left me the option of letting Mother move into my place. I tried not to curse, even mentally, because the more foul words I spewed in my head, the more likely the words would eventually slip from my tongue. But *fuck* that! I wasn't handing him over on a platter.

I stared right back at him. "And if I did?" It was an evasive stall tactic wrapped up in a bluff.

His mouth firmed. It was the only movement he made before he finally spoke. "Do you?"

He'd called the bluff and I couldn't bring myself to answer. The word yes was stricken from my dictionary. I didn't care if it was immature or petty. He was mine, even if he technically wasn't. And if he wanted her, fine. There wasn't much I could do to stop it but he'd have to make the call himself. I wasn't going to be the catalyst.

"Do whatever you want. That's what you always do anyway." I turned and started walking toward the kitchen, toward anywhere that wasn't there, in front of him and his questions.

I heard Fate's rich deep laughter at my back before it receded down the hall. That bastard. He called my bluff and I realized that no answer was an answer. I'd just admitted I wanted him.

***

We were all there, everyone that was staying in the house, piled into Fate's living room. Knox, who'd shown up this afternoon, had even lost his suit jacket and was down to the shirt. The Jinxes, banned from skateboarding in the house, were sulking where they sat at the dining room table.

Mother was there, sulking as well but for another reason. Her karaoke machine had magically stopped working a few minutes after the Jinxes had arrived, right in the middle of her rendition of *Girls Just Want to Have Fun*.

Even the people who weren't staying were there, like Death, Bernie, and Crow, who'd moved into Kitty's. She was still under the weather so it made sense to have someone stay with her.

Even Fate's guys were there and current Death meeting Lars—retired Death—was a very awkward moment. Lars didn't look like he approved of new Death's sweater vest, while new Death's eyes kept staring at the snake tattoo wrapping up Lars's neck.

Disapproval aside, everyone kept the peace. Everything was on the table, every resource in use no matter what people's hesitations might be. We all knew what the meeting was about. The very short-lived truce with Malokin had come to an end. The tipping point had arrived.

Fate stepped into the center of the room, casual as always and the focal point without trying. He didn't need a suit to imply authority or status. He had more presence in his jeans and t-shirt than anyone I'd ever met.

I relaxed slightly as I saw him lean against the table behind him. If he was leaning, maybe things weren't too bad, not yet. Or not worse than I thought, anyway. Then I looked closer at the lines of his form, and not for the appreciation of the fine figure he made, but to the telltale signs it revealed. His hands were resting at his sides, fingers curved a bit too firmly around the edge of the table. No, not so relaxed after all.

Fate pushed off the table before he spoke. "I killed three of Malokin's people and broke the truce. Anyone have a problem with that?"

Not the intro I would've used but I guess it got to the point quick enough. I looked around the room.

Exactly as suspected, no one said a word.

"Now that things are about to get ugly, we need to establish a watch," he said to the packed living room.

It was greeted by several yeses and many nods.

"Maybe we should find another location. This place with all the doors and glass is going to be really hard to protect," Knox said.

"Maybe for you."

I cringed inwardly. Talk about a warning shot across the bow. But why? The tension I'd sensed between these two from the very start seemed to be trying to bubble up. This wasn't the time for it. They needed to bury whatever their issues were, although I couldn't imagine what they could be if they'd just met.

But for now, I needed to diffuse. Nervous energy drove me to my feet. "I agree with a watch but it won't be necessary to move. The only people that will bother us here are humans and they're running around in a disorganized and chaotic mess. They won't come at us in substantial enough numbers to be any kind of threat. Malokin won't come here either. It's in his best interest to stay in his own corner."

"He went to your condo," Knox argued.

"When no one was there to stop him. A hit and run. As of right now, he's winning. Why risk a confrontation that he might *not* win? The watch is more of a show of force, because we know he's going to be watching. It's best not to look too lax and invite a problem, even if it's from one of his lackeys trying to climb the ranks."

Knox was staring at me from one side of the room with a strange look I couldn't place. Fate was looking at him with an expression like he'd been forged in steel. What was I missing here?

"What about retaliation? We just gonna let this dick burn our shit down and do nothin'?" Bobby asked from the side.

"We can't retaliate against someone we can't find. And we can't find him, can we, Knox?" I asked.

"No. We can't. He blends into the surroundings. He's completely off our grid." Knox looked ill at ease admitting this shortcoming.

Fate stood and walked over to the Jinxes. "He's got a very good ability to hide. We've known this from the start. I want you three out scouting for any scent of him or his men tomorrow."

"You got it, boss man," Billy said, the other two nodding their agreement.

"Same for everyone. Keep your ears and eyes open but make sure to stay in pairs. Don't get into anything on your own." His voice carried over the room as he spoke to everyone.

"I'll tag along with you, guys," I said to the Jinxes.

Fate was shaking his head as he came and stood beside me. "I need you for something else tomorrow."

"What?"

"We need to pay Jockey a visit." His voice was low and he said it in a way that bordered on a question.

I nodded although I was cringing at the idea. I didn't like my own nightmares. Running around in Malokin's head was worse.

CHAPTER THIRTEEN

The steps in the hallway heading toward the bedroom were my first signal. The door opened moments later and my eyes popped open in the dark. A silhouette I knew as well as my own stood in the doorway, pausing briefly as his eyes moved over me.

Fate walked in, shutting the door behind him. He pulled his shirt off, revealing the male perfection that had left a permanent image in my mind. His hands went to his pants and started to unbutton. He wasn't going to strip in front of me, was he? His eyes never moved from me and I realized that was exactly what he was going to do. I snapped my eyes shut again.

"You could've switched rooms with Mother," he said, teasingly reminding me of my loss by default.

I *should've* told him to room with Mother.

I flipped on to my other side, facing away from him. "I'm martyring myself for the greater good of the housemates."

The bed shifted with his weight. My eyes were wide open again as I sprang up into a seated position. "You're really going to sleep in here? On this bed? What about that air mattress I saw you bring in from the garage?"

He settled onto his side, still shirtless with a good expanse of skin showing above the blanket that only came to his waist. I hadn't watched him strip off his pants but I was certain he had only underwear left on, at best.

"That was for someone else. I don't need an air mattress. I've got a nice comfortable bed." He fluffed the pillow before he positioned it behind his head, looking a little too good for comfort. How was I supposed to sleep next to him?

"This isn't a good idea."

He wasn't even looking at me anymore but lying there with his eyes closed as if on the brink of drifting off. "Where did you think I was going to sleep? You knew we were roomies," he said.

"The floor."

His eyes popped back open. It was better when he hadn't been looking at me. "I didn't sleep on the floor during the stone age. I'm not planning on starting now." He turned on his side, his arm grazing my hip. "We're both adults. There's no reason we can't share a bed." His fingers grazed the side of my thigh through the blanket. "It's not like we haven't before."

"This isn't very nice of you."

"I did apologize in advance," he said, without an

ounce of atonement in his voice. "And I also pulled back yesterday when you were all green lights and thumbs up."

"I was…"

His brows shot up and he dared me to deny it.

"You sir, would never survive as a southern gentleman."

"But someone likes me anyway." He sang the words in a perfectly mocking melody.

I should leave just to show him.

We had a full house and I didn't want to make a scene. Then again, would a scene really be that big of a deal with this crew?

The idea of them all hashing this over at the breakfast table, not even caring if I could hear them or not, kept me quiet. It wasn't like I was living with a bunch of beings who would use any discretion. They'd use the opportunity to take a vote on whether I should or shouldn't, maybe start a box pool on when I'd give in and hang it on the fridge.

Then there was Mother. I'd rather deal with his teasing than have him near her.

The worst was he knew I wanted him, and he knew how good looking he was. It was written on every line of his relaxed position and the tiniest upturn of his lips. He reeked of self-confidence, and it should have made him annoying but somehow lent to his appeal.

The odds were stacked against me. I probably *would* succumb at some point. I knew it and after what he'd said, he did too.

But it wouldn't be tonight, if only for the sole purpose of keeping his ego in check. I closed my eyes and lay back down, flopping over and turning my back to him again. I'd just pretend he wasn't there.

I lay there for an hour before I admitted that it wasn't mentally possible for me. I *couldn't* pretend he wasn't there. How was I supposed to sleep like that?

To make it worse, I was fairly certain he *was* sleeping, which irritated me further. Thirty minutes after that realization, his arm snaked around my waist and he pulled me back, flush against him.

"Fate?" I whispered, trying to determine whether he was moving around in his sleep. Please, please, let him be sleeping. I had to make it through tonight for the good of the world. No one should have an ego larger than his.

"Do you always wear this much to bed?" His voice was deep and husky and vibrated through me, sending tingles everywhere.

He was not only awake but speaking to me and admitting it. Now what? "Murphy has the AC down to sixty. I get cold. What are you doing?" I asked as I started to stretch in a strategic way that, if all went right, would gain me an inch or two of separation. Somehow, he ended up fitting closer to me. Hips to hips, the back of my legs to the front of his. I'd managed to stretch myself right into an official spoon.

"Helping you sleep." His breath tickled my ear and I could hear the smile on his face.

"By spooning me?" Full body contact was not going to put me to sleep.

"Yes."

I closed my eyes. One Mississippi, two Mississippi… Maybe sheep would work better.

"It's not helping."

"Fifteen minutes." His arm didn't budge and the heat that poured off of him was starting to feel really good, dangerously so.

"This is not going to help me."

"Shhh."

This was the most ridiculous thing I'd ever agreed to but since his arm wasn't loosening, it was either get into a fully fledged battle and wake up the whole house or give him his fifteen. If I didn't, I'd practically guarantee a pool hanging on the kitchen wall by coffee time tomorrow. It wasn't like it felt bad.

The stiffness leaving me, he took it a step further as his leg nudged in between mine, dislocating my own and pushing it forward while his took its place.

"You're pushing it."

"Not the way I'd like to be."

I threw my arm over my head, knowing I'd lose this fight and closed my eyes, counting down the minutes.

I awoke four hours later in a cold sweat, in the same position I'd fallen asleep, with Fate's body wrapped around me.

"Karma?" His arm tightened around me and I didn't try to pull away. "What's wrong?"

"Nothing. Just a lousy dream." I'd woken in the middle of a nightmare. I'd been standing in the warehouse again, watching Kitty's fingers being broken, but this time I'd also seen what they had done to her legs. I'd never had an image attached to that atrocity before.

In my dream, one of the men I'd seen with Malokin had stabbed me in the hip. It was the throbbing of the tattoo leaking into my dream and I was almost grateful to the pain for interrupting it.

"You want to talk?" Fate wasn't smiling anymore.

"No." I just wanted to forget, the dream and the pain, but I couldn't. I shivered, in spite of the warmth of the blanket and his arm rubbed mine in response.

"It'll fade," he said. "The memories."

"The past will but what about the future?" It wasn't getting better; it was getting worse. Things were spinning out of control, again.

"Eventually, everything passes. The good and the bad."

I turned my head back over my shoulder and I shouldn't have. There was a look in his eyes, a concern I couldn't possibly miss and every caution or worry faded as I looked into his eyes.

His eyes shifted to my lips and I looked away quickly. One full day. I had to make it at least an entire twenty-four hours resisting Fate or I wouldn't be able to live with his ego.

CHAPTER FOURTEEN

"You killed my men." Malokin's voice, sounding guttural and nothing close to human, shook the walls of the house.

I was jumping to my feet before I was fully awake and thankful for the sweatpants and t-shirt I'd worn to bed.

"Stay put." Fate had beaten me out of the bed and was already at the door.

I grabbed the gun I'd left on the side table and ran out right after him.

Everyone in the house was heading into the living room, colliding in the predawn darkness. Luck was wearing a flimsy red thing that I guess would be considered lingerie. Mother had on some flowing diaphanous white ordeal that practically fluttered around her as she walked.

"Where did that come from?" Murphy said, still in the process of tying his smoking jacket.

Fate was suddenly deadly still as he stared through the back doors onto the beach. "He's out there. No one leave this house. No matter what." Fate caught Knox's attention and received a nod in return.

Now they were best buddies? I didn't understand the sudden cohesion between them but it didn't matter; I wasn't staying behind and I had a strong feeling that Fate's order was meant specifically for me.

Fate made for the door, me glued to his side every step of the way.

He stopped, hand on the knob. "Stay here."

"Why? This has more to do with me than you. Maybe *you* should stay in here?"

His eyes shifted behind us before he said softly, "You know why."

And then there was that vision of me, throat slit, which was always there between the two of us. "The only difference between us is we don't know what happens to you. Don't be so sure you aren't sharing the same end."

"It doesn't matter."

"Yes, it does. Unless you can say, with one hundred percent certainty that you're going to live, which I *know* you can't, I'm going out there." My eyes shifted to Malokin, where he stood on the beach waiting.

"You are so—"

"Right?" I asked, my hands coming to my hips.

"Not the word I was planning on using," he said, sounding more frustrated than anything.

"But still the correct choice."

He hesitated a few seconds while assessing me, surveyed Malokin on the beach, and finally capitulated, pushing the door open but not without a last order. "Stay within twenty feet of the house. It's protected."

I followed him out onto the deck.

"Got it." I hesitated for a split second. "Math wasn't my strong point. Where would you say twenty feet ends about?"

He looked over at me as if he were debating dragging me back into the house.

"Everyone has a weak point. It's not like we're going to be doing geometry in the sand for a math off."

"You are not making me feel better about this."

I looked out onto the beach, where Malokin was lethally quiet and staring at us like he wanted to rip us limb from limb. "I didn't know there was a way to feel better about the homicidal maniac on the beach but if you've got some secret info, please share."

Fate looked at Malokin, then the door back to the house.

"Not. A. Chance," I said, putting every ounce of steel I was feeling into those three words, making it clear this was a line he shouldn't cross. He was overbearing and bossy in a lot of his ways, and I let him get away with more than any other person I'd ever known and I didn't even know why. I still wasn't sure if it was because I had this incredible attraction to him or if he'd been the one person, since I'd started this new life, who had stuck by me over and over again when it mattered, with no regard for the risk to himself.

"Fate, I'm not the type to sit back and wait. Don't ask me to be something I can't." I didn't tell him that if he did decide to try and drag me back in the house, I'd be furious but I'd forgive him. I wasn't sure there was anything I wouldn't forgive him at that point.

But he didn't need to know that because I'd have a fight on my hands.

"Don't go farther than me."

"That I can agree to."

Once I started walking, and my eyes met Malokin's, any fear I was harboring disappeared.

Malokin stood at the edge of the ocean, the pants of his fine suit and shoes getting drenched every time the waves rolled in but he didn't seem to care. He reached out his arms and bellowed a scream that pierced the air and sent a group of thugs further down the beach scurrying in the opposite direction.

All I wanted was to get closer. The anger was boiling in me and the more I looked at him, the more the memories filled me. I hadn't realized I was capable of hate of this magnitude until now.

It might have been what Malokin desired. He fed on hate. Even now, I could see him take a deep breath, as if I was feeding his very being. I didn't care. I had plenty to fuel us both. It was thick, ran deep, and was so consuming it was shutting down every other emotion that existed.

The angrier I got, the calmer Malokin seemed to become and I knew I was the reason. I couldn't make it stop, or maybe I didn't want to.

Malokin took a step forward, looking only at me and disregarding Fate. "I knew you had this within you. If you come with me, I'll leave here; I'll leave them alone."

"I'm going to rip you apart, maul you until you don't resemble—"

"Karma, get inside," Fate barked out from beside me.

Fate sounded…weird. I vaguely registered that he'd switched gears somehow. His voice was almost brutal in its intensity. I didn't care. Something within me had clicked and I wasn't leaving this beach until Malokin was in pieces at my feet.

"Karma." Fate again. My name from his lips was a final warning but I didn't understand his problem, nor did I care. I just wanted him to shut up and stay out of my way.

I took a few more steps, not caring whether I was past the twenty feet from the house or not, my hatred still building steadily. I felt the light touch my eyes and I did nothing to hold it back. I could feel the Universe's energy bubbling around me, as chaotic as I felt and yet I did nothing to tamp it down. I fed it.

Malokin was smiling and I was about to destroy him. My fists clenched in anticipation of ripping his flesh from his bones with my bare hands.

And then Fate was in front of me, blocking my path, and I struggled to get around him. He carried me back to the house as Malokin's laughter rang in the air, taunting me, and I wanted to rip Fate apart for dragging me away from him.

He carried me through the house, past everyone as they stepped out of our way. Through the blur of rage I thought they looked shocked but it was hard to think past the emotions boiling within me. We were in the garage before he released me.

The minute he set me on my feet I turned on him. "Why did you do that? I could have had him, right then and there. All this would've been over but you stopped me," I screamed, my hands still in fists and looking to connect with his face.

He grabbed my wrists, forcing them to my sides.

"Look at me," he said.

Anger boiled within me for no reason now as I met his stare.

"Think, Karma." He shook me. "You weren't breaking him; he was breaking you."

His hands pulled me into his embrace when I would've pulled away. One hand rubbing down my back, and with each stroke, a tiny bit of rational thinking eased back into my mind.

I started shaking as I realized how badly I'd just lost myself. I was on the beach one second and then I'd barely known where I was. I'd seen nothing but red.

"How did that happen?" I ran both hands through my hair and then left them there, cupping my head, as I tried to figure out what I'd just done.

"I don't know but it can't happen again. He feeds off of you. When he does that he's stronger than me, and I'm not sure you understand the implications of that, but it's bad."

Riotous amounts of knocking sounded from the closed garage door. I met his eyes and nodded, letting him know I was normal again before I took a step back.

"Come in," Fate said.

The Jinxes were tripping over themselves as they pushed through the door. We both looked at them, knowing they were here to tell us Malokin's status and we didn't have to wait long.

"That fucked up dude tried to follow you both into the house but got stuck and started spasming every time he tried to take another step," Billy said.

"We know we aren't allowed to shoot his ass," Bobby added, "but we nailed him from the deck real good with some ketchup bombs we had saved up."

"Should've seen those balloons hit! Red shit all over his fancy suit," Buddy kicked in.

"Is he still out there?" I asked, now fearful of seeing him again.

"Nah, dude's gone. Took off after the spasms and the bombs," Bobby said. "So now what?"

The three of them looked at Fate and I like we had the answers. We said nothing.

CHAPTER FIFTEEN

The doors were locked when we got to the office building, and Fate pulled out a key I'd never seen. He jiggled it into a nearly rusted lock that looked like it had never been used.

Our footsteps echoed in the lobby, accentuating the creepy, empty feeling. No one was coming in anymore. There was no work and no purpose to report. The only purpose the building served now was as a target and this building didn't have the same luxury of being warded by Lars.

The accountant, the only human occupant, had been told we had a roach problem that was going to need strong fumigation. The fact that he hadn't even blinked an eye at that explanation just showed the dire need for some renovation.

If it hadn't been for Jockey, we wouldn't have been there either. He'd stayed behind with the Nightmares in their pasture, a place that wasn't here or there. Jockey had been confident, for untold reasons, that he was perfectly secure. I was inclined to believe him. This was the only way we could gain access.

"You ready?" Fate asked, as he stopped in front of the entrance to the hallway that would lead to the Nightmares' pasture.

I stepped forward and opened the door. It didn't matter if I was ready or not. We needed any information we could get. Digging around in Malokin's head was our best possibility of obtaining knowledge. It didn't matter who you were or what you could do in the land of dreams; the Nightmares had free reign. No one could shut them out.

As soon as we entered the dark hallway, the wind picked up and so did the screaming. It was more intense than the last time I'd walked down this hall and was reaching a screeching crescendo that made me want to cover my ears. There were a lot of scary things happening in the world, and they were leaking into people's dreams.

"Hurry up," Fate said ushering me forward with hands on my waist from behind.

"What's wrong with this place?" I asked as I moved forward, sensing something off as well.

"Not sure, but it doesn't feel right."

We reached the rustic barn door at the end and Jockey opened it before we had to knock. "Come in," he said, ushering us with his hands.

His riding boots had lost some of their shine since the last time I'd seen him. A large scuff marked his riding helmet as if he'd taken a fall recently.

"Did you do something to the hallway?" I asked as Jockey was laying a large board across the door, and Fate was walking farther into the field and appraising the situation.

"Yes. But not to worry. You weren't in there long enough to pick up any ill effects." He grasped the handle, testing his barricade before stepping away.

"What did you do?"

"Are you sure you want to know?" he asked in his factual way.

I snorted quite unbecomingly. "Yeah, after you ask like that, I have to know."

He didn't even crack a smile as he started to explain. "Uninvited guests won't have a very long life. There's a reason you wake up before you die in a dream. Anyone who comes here unwelcomed won't come again."

The possibilities clicked instantly, and I wondered if things got bad enough to risk it, was that an easy way to do away with Malokin? "What about someone like Malokin?"

"No, I'm afraid not. *I* can't, anyway. If he were to come to the hallway I could, or here in the pasture. This is my domain. But the dreams? I don't have any control of those. The mares could but that's not how they work. They stimulate nightmares but they don't create them."

"But could they?"

"They could but that isn't something I would encourage, not to save fifty worlds would I do that.

Some lessons can't be unlearned."

He was a heavy type of personality and his words were even weightier than normal. Nightmares spinning out of control and killing people? Enough said.

His eyes perused me as if I were horseflesh. "Rough night?"

I narrowed my eyes slightly. "You saw my dreams?"

"Occupational hazard. Unavoidable, at times."

"Then you know they weren't any worse than normal," I replied, making it clear that was the end of the subject. I moved to catch up with Fate.

The field was exactly as I'd remembered; perpetual nighttime with dew laden grass shimmering the reflected light of the huge moon above. The mares, more than a dozen of them with gleaming pure black coats, were gathered on the tree lined field some distance away. One nickered nervously and the rest took up the call, shrill neighs ringing across the pasture.

"What's wrong with them?" Fate asked as Jockey and I approached him.

"People are having some crazy dreams these days. It spills out onto them. They're exhausted, rundown and on edge. If this weren't important, I wouldn't risk letting you come here. They're not themselves." Jockey stood looking at his herd with his arms crossed in front of his chest. "But I know it is. If there's anything you can find that will help, it's worth it."

"What if he's not sleeping?" I asked.

"Then you wait."

***

The waiting didn't turn out to be as horrible as I'd imagined. Jockey had a saddle blanket he lent us and went about caring for the mares, leaving Fate and I laying on our backs, staring up at the starriest sky I'd ever seen.

"Is that our moon? It's so gigantic and it's always night here." The shadows formed the same face, making me think it was.

"Yes."

"You sure?" I asked as we lay shoulder to shoulder.

"Yes. I've asked him."

"Jockey?"

"No. The Man on the Moon."

I instantly envisioned a man gleaming in silver grey who winked a lot. "Why haven't I ever met him? Does he come in at all? I've never seen him at the office."

"Because you're new and he only comes by every couple of years."

New; another word for transfer. It didn't bother me the way it would have a month ago, not from him. Sometimes I felt like this Fate was a completely different person to the one I'd met when I first started.

"The other day, you said you never wanted this for me. Why did you want me gone so badly?" I asked and then waited, fearing the answer. What if he said he'd hated me or I was annoying?

"Because I know what the stakes are for us, our

kind. The dangers and the pitfalls. I knew something bad was coming, and I didn't want you to be in the middle of it. Our people, ones who weren't transfers and were born to this life, were disappearing. Friends of mine, gone. I'd have coffee with them in the morning and they'd be gone by nightfall. If they couldn't stay alive, I couldn't imagine how you would when you were at a disadvantage."

"Did you have to be such a dick about it? Couldn't you have just said that?" *And perhaps not have crushed my feelings on a daily basis?*

"You're stubborn. I thought it would be more effective to make you miserable. I didn't want to see you disappear like the others."

He fell silent, as if it was still a touchy subject to him. It was the most human I'd ever seen him act.

I tilted my head to look at his profile. "Was it hard losing them?"

"Some were harder than others. The Karma before you, we were close. It's different if you are born to this. In a human existence, you lose people suddenly for all different reasons. When it happens to us, it's shocking," his voice was softer and he didn't look at me as he spoke but remained looking up at the stars.

"After that, how could you sit across the table from him and agree to a truce?" I didn't think poorly of him for it but I couldn't understand it, either.

"Because, in that moment, it was what I needed to do," he answered. It was the answer I would've expected, and yet it contradicted what he'd done for me.

"It didn't last very long anyway," I said, thinking back to the scene in the convenience store that happened less than a week later. "Why did you do that?"

"Do what?"

And there we were, like it had just happened, back to the same question and the same avoidance.

"Stop pretending you don't know what I'm talking about."

He finally turned and looked at me and there was a challenge in his eyes. "Is that what you're saying? You're ready to talk?"

Such innocent questions, and they froze me up quicker than anything that had ever been asked of me before. This whole time, I'd thought it had been a mutual avoidance. When had things changed? Was I now the one shutting down the lines of communication and he was playing along? At least when it came to the subject of us.

And still I couldn't answer. I tried to make my brain work and my tongue move; I tried to get past the sheer panic that was gripping me more fiercely than anything I'd ever felt.

"I'll take that as a no."

He was disappointed in me, and I was shocked at how that disappointment in his voice seeped into me and saddened me in a way I hadn't expected.

I still said nothing. Why couldn't I simply tell him? *I like you with an intensity that scares the hell out of me.* After everything I'd been through, why was it so difficult? I could just say it. And then it would be out there.

And then I came full circle to the problem. What he'd say back. What he'd do. Looming rejection on a level I couldn't cope with on top of everything else going on.

We needed to talk. There were things that had to be said, however it might turn out—but not now. I couldn't deal with it right now. And I had the perfect excuse to blow the subject off as Jockey drove up in a buggy and we both sat up.

"A carriage?"

"Even I won't ride them right now. I almost wasn't able to harness her to this." We stood and Fate grabbed the blanket to hand back to him.

Jockey shook his head and motioned for him to keep it. "It's getting very cold there. You should bring it with you."

We settled in and Fate laid the blanket over us.

"Whatever you do, don't get out of the buggy, no matter how long it takes her to come back."

I nodded, even as I became concerned about this little venture, and wondered if this was the best thing to be doing.

We took off at a much more hectic pace than the last time I'd gone for a ride. This time I was prepared for the ground to disappear and the dark tunnel of visions to pop up everywhere, like riding through the largest multiplex ever created without walls. We didn't go very far before we were pulled into a nightmare. It was chaotic, people chanting and screaming all around and there, in the center of everyone, was Malokin. And me.

"Try and remember every face you see," Fate said as we circled the group, all figments of Malokin's mind.

The dream version of me stood there, docile in front of him. Like that would ever happen. The crowd jeered. Then Malokin's knife was at my throat. The blade ran across my skin, setting off a spray of blood as it did. I collapsed on the ground, red pooling around me. It was the image Fate had seen or something so close it didn't matter.

The carriage suddenly jerked around and the mare ran out of the dream as if the scene had spooked her as much as it had me. I turned, transfixed by the image of my death unfolding.

I didn't turn back around until we were so far away from the horrific scene that it was only a speck in the blackness. But the image was still there, crystal clear in my mind. I felt Fate edge closer to me, silently offering me his support. Now we both knew what my death looked like.

The carriage stopped and everything had a surreal feeling to it. I had the fuzziest recollection of Jockey asking how it went and no notion of what Fate replied, although I knew he did.

I moved in a haze, step after step, unsure how I knew where I was going.

We barely made it out of the nightmare hallway before the panic attack set in full force. Years of being a defense attorney—judges yelling at me, jurors narrowing their eyes at me as if they couldn't stand the sight of me—and not once had I had a panic attack. Now, one lousy dream and I couldn't get enough air, no matter how deeply or rapidly I breathed.

My legs decided they'd had enough once we hit the office lobby and my back slammed into sheetrock before I slid down it. It was a dream. That was all.

I scanned the hall, looking for Fate and that's when it hit me, right in the middle of my panic attack, how much I'd come to rely on him. Not great timing for a revelation like that; it notched my panic up another level of frenzy.

I'd deal with the implications of that later, after I'd reclaimed a respectable chunk of my sanity. Right now, I needed him to tell me it was going to be okay.

He was at the end of the hall, his back to me. "Fate?" My voice was pathetically weak and I detested the sound.

He didn't move for a second and I called his name again, trying to sound a bit stronger this time. He turned as if it were the first time he'd heard me and then quickly walked toward me. He stopped in front of me and knelt down, resting on his haunches.

"Look at me," he said, his hands cupped my face. "That will *not* happen to you. Do you hear me?"

It was his stubborn look that I knew so well. I nodded.

"It won't happen," he said again, and I wasn't sure which one of us he was trying to convince.

I hoped it was working for Fate because I didn't believe him. It wasn't from a lack of wanting. Still, I wished he'd repeat it over and over, hoping that maybe, if I heard it enough, somehow I would begin to believe it too.

My breathing eased, and I think he took that to mean I was buying into the whole *it would be okay* thing. In truth, it was more because I was running out of adrenaline and reality was settling in. Fate had seen it in his visions. I'd now seen it in Malokin's dream.

What I had to do was come to terms with the fact it was there, the finality of my existence, looming over me. A panic attack wasn't going to change that. Screaming and running to Fate wouldn't stop it.

For all that my coworkers put such stock in not being a transfer, we had a definite edge in one area. As a human, you were born knowing you were going to die. We visited the unlucky in the hospital and went to funerals, always remarking on the tragedy. But every time we stepped too close to it, we saw our own demises. We went with the full knowledge that we would one day die as well.

The closest humans got to immortality was the ignorance of youth, but death was always hovering nearby, even for the young. At some point our lives would end. We'd wake up one day and not go to sleep that night. We might have had warning, or it might be sudden, but from the moment we became aware of ourselves we became aware of our impending deaths.

My coworkers? Up until recently, they had been born knowing that as long as they walked the line, they could go on forever.

So yeah, I was a transfer, but that was one area where I had the edge. I had experience with mortality.

I stood, acting calmer than I thought would've been possible a few moments ago. I wiped my hands against the back of my pants. "Let's get out of here."

CHAPTER SIXTEEN

A blaring horn rang out and I saw a SUV sitting in Fate's driveway. It looked like the misfit child of a monster truck and a minivan. If I hadn't watched him get out of the driver's seat to load a bag into the back, I never would've believed Fate would drive something like that.

He was closing the back hatch, looking all sorts of rustic yumminess in his black boots and rugged gear, when I approached.

He sized up my outfit as well and found it lacking. "What's wrong with a sundress? You said we were going for a ride into the country?"

"On a *gun* run?"

"I'm sorry, but the boutique didn't have any army-girl-fabulous in stock." I walked around the ride he'd supplied. "Talking about style, where did you get this fine automobile?" I asked patting the camouflage paint job.

"There weren't too many places available to procure a vehicle for today's purpose and I know you have an aversion to borrowing." He tossed the other bag that had been sitting on the driveway into the back.

"No, I imagine not." I looked down the street and the only traffic I saw was a sedan packed to the gills, trying to get out of Dodge. If you were still normal, you didn't want to be around other people anymore. It was too dangerous.

Fate came up to me and rested his hand on my lower back as we watched the SUV drive away down the street. It took with it the last thread of deniability I'd been clinging to. People were fleeing. Campers had been flying off the lot, bank accounts had been emptying and businesses were grinding to a halt.

"This is really happening."

"Don't sound so shocked. Live long enough and there aren't too many things you don't get to see." He patted my hip in an overly friendly way but I guessed that was what happened when you snuggled in bed every night. "Come on. You ready to get some guns?"

And this was the reality now. Gun runs and ambushes. "Yep. Let's go."

The truck was rugged and high off the ground. It made sense. We were going on a run to get more guns. This truck was much more suited than a sports car. I started looking for a handle to pull myself up with but Fate came over and hoisted me up.

I waited until we were pulling out of the lot before I took the opportunity to talk about something that had been bugging me. "What's your beef with Knox?"

"I don't like him."

I waited for him to continue but he didn't. Who doesn't explain a statement like that? "Why don't you like him?"

He shrugged. "Just don't."

"You just met him for the first time, right?" I'd learned in these past months to never make any assumptions. That luxury died with my body in the train wreck.

"Yes. And you?" His eyes nailed me in a stare that had me torn between squirming and yelling.

I compromised between the two and caught a slight attitude. "I've never seen him before."

"You're sure? He was looking at you like he was pretty familiar."

"I'm *positive*." The relaxing ride into the country for guns wasn't turning out to be the pleasant afternoon getaway I'd imagined. Who'd have thought? "You were kind of rough on him at the meeting."

He shrugged. "He's the new kid and needs to learn the boundaries."

I was the new kid too, or at least I still felt like it. Wasn't a great feeling. I fell quiet, not caring to explore this conversation any further with the turn it had just taken.

We drove about forty minutes inland, and I watched as the houses became more and more spread out until we pulled down a gravel drive, surrounded by nothing but woods.

"Where is this place?" I asked, seeing nothing but trees everywhere.

"There." He pointed to a small ranch that was just starting to appear on the horizon.

I grabbed on to the handle above the door as the truck bounced all over the rough drive until we reached the house. Fate threw the truck into park and I jumped off the passenger seat.

"Here?" I hooked a thumb in the house's direction. "I thought this was going to be an armory or gun shop or...I don't know. But not this. What kind of guns are we going to possibly get here?" It was a large ranch but still a ranch. It had shutters, flowers painted on the mailbox and was that a gazebo I saw in the back?

He started walking towards the front door. "The kinds of guns we need aren't sold to the public in places that say firearms in bold lettering above the entrance."

I stared at the blue painted door with a plaque that read, "*Home Sweet Home,*" above it and the pieces clicked into place. Living in a house my grandmother would've been at home in was probably a great cover for an arms dealer, drug dealer or basically any of your run-of-the-mill nefarious types.

Fate rapped his knuckles on the glass panes of the door and someone who looked nothing like my grandpa, and had no Earthly business residing in a house like this, strode over to open it. Lanky with dark brown hair, he looked like he'd be more comfortable cruising down the highway amidst a motorcycle club of the illegal variety.

"Hey," he said, nodding his head and forgoing the

more normal custom of a handshake. "Who's she?" he asked, looking in my direction.

"None of your business," Fate said.

"This ain't no candy shop." He was looking at me when he spoke.

Okay, maybe I wasn't in gunrunner-appropriate attire but candy shop? I turned to leave, but not because I was offended. I didn't care enough to be bothered. All that was on my mind was the sunny day and how hanging outside seemed like as good—if not better—use of my time.

Fate's hand grabbed my arm when I would've left. "Why don't I just go—" I didn't get a chance to say wait in the car and explain how it was for the best, hiding my true desire to feel the warmth on my skin under my noble pretense to not cause problems.

"She's. With. Me."

The way Fate said those three words lowered my odds of a couple of minutes of sunshine down to zero.

The guy shook his head and started walking as he said, "I swear, if you weren't such a scary fuck, I'd tell you to go screw and to buy your shit somewhere else."

"You have no idea what a scary fuck I can be," Fate said as he followed Gun Guy, as I decided to call him since no other name looked like it was going to be provided.

There was something about that statement Fate had just made that sent off little warning flares in my psyche. This was my snuggle buddy at night? Another reason I shouldn't get involved on a more intimate level. If someone said they were a scary fuck, who was I to disagree?

I followed the two but not without one last longing glance at the hood of the truck. I could've lain there sunning myself instead of pondering who—or what—I slept beside every night.

"I got the stuff on the list, most of it anyways. All the AK47s, assault rifles, sniper rifles…" Gun Guy was listing off the rest of the arsenal but all the numbers and letters started sounding like a bad algebra quiz. I tuned him out as he opened a door in the small hallway that led to a basement.

He flipped on light switches, illuminating the place as we went. It looked like a typical basement, fake wood paneling, a workshop to the right, washer and dryer.

"But?" Fate asked, the break in the gun list drew my attention back.

Gun Guy hesitated, his lips compressing before he said, "I couldn't get the napalm." He stood watching Fate and I saw the slightest hesitation as if his foot was getting ready to take a step back.

Fate looked like he was doing mental gun math before he said, "The napalm might have been overkill."

Gun Guy grabbed one end of a clothes rack next to the laundry area and Fate grabbed the other as they moved it out of the way. The guy opened the paneling behind it.

Now this was what I'd expected, a room with cement blocks, lined with guns on every side. *This* was the lair of a self-respecting gunrunner, not that pansy

Home Sweet Home sign.

The guy walked over to where five large duffle bags sat on the floor. "Here's your stuff." He reached down and placed one on the table in the center, to make it easier for Fate to rifle through it. "I gotta ask you something."

"What?" Fate didn't bother looking up.

I started looking through one of the bags on the ground, not that I knew much about the serious machinery in front of me but I didn't want to look lacking.

The Gun Guy's eyes shifted to me and back to Fate as he stalled. Articulate, he was not.

"If you want to know something, ask," Fate barked out impatiently. "I'm not holding your hand or staying for a picnic out back."

The words might have sounded harsher than he'd intended while he was looking down the scope of an automatic rifle. Or maybe I was overly sensitive, not being a gunrunner.

Gun Guy's feet shuffled and I saw Fate look at them in a way that made me wonder if he was imagining target practice. Maybe I wasn't so sensitive and Gun Guy should've been more so.

Finally he spat it out. "Do you know what's going on? Is that what all this shit is for? Do you know what's coming? I mean, half the people I know in town are acting like animals."

My head shot up, waiting to see if Fate would answer. What he would say.

Fate cocked an eyebrow. "Do you really think you should be throwing stones?"

"Really, man, I need to know. Look, I'm freaked out." Gun Guy's eyes shot to me once more, as if nervous to say anything in my presence before he blurted out what he wanted to say to Fate anyway. "Whatever you are, man, I know you know things."

I looked at Gun Guy. He was scared, and for all the criminal activity he seemed to be knee deep in, considering what most people's karmas were looking like these days, he was fairing pretty well. Actually, he was doing better than I would've anticipated. He might have even been bright a few weeks ago.

I swallowed, holding back any lame explanation I could offer and was grateful Fate had to field that question. I certainly didn't know what to say. *There is some crazy non-human creature who is the epitome of anger on the loose? And he may either be the cause of this or maybe worse, a symptom of a problem we can't pinpoint?*

I saw a quick glimmer of something that might have been pity flicker over Fate's expression. I unzipped the second bag of guns, pretending to be counting them but really trying to hide my face. I didn't want Gun Guy to see the myriad of fear, dread and defeat probably written all over me.

Fate placed the rifle on the metal table in the center with a soft clank. "I don't know what's coming but maybe it wouldn't be a bad idea to lay low—really low—for a while. Get yourself stocked up and stay put.

You'll be fine if you don't go into a city, no matter how small."

The guy rested his hands on the table, looking like he was close to breakdown mode. I recognized the signs well at that point due to my own current emotional instability. He looked down and when he started talking, I wasn't sure if it was to himself or us.

"I saw a gang drag some chick into the alleyway the other day. I managed to scare them off with my gun but nobody else seemed to care. They dragged her off, kicking and screaming, in the middle of the afternoon. Everyone saw it. They just went about their business like it wasn't happening."

When Gun Guy paused, I sneaked a peek at him. He wasn't scared. He was terrified. A look of utter dread crossed his face and his next words made some of that same dread creep into me. "Man, don't you get it? If I'm the good guy, we're all fucked."

I abruptly zipped up the duffle bag I was looking through and told Fate I'd meet him outside. I didn't want to hear this today. On my way upstairs, and back to the car, all I could think of was that Gun Guy was right. We were all fucked.

I threw the bag in the backseat of the truck and waited for Fate. He showed up several minutes later and dumped the other bags alongside mine before he climbed behind the wheel.

"He's right," I said as the engine roared to life the way only an eight cylinder could.

"So that's it? You sound like you're ready to throw

in the towel."

He sounded aggravated but I'd seen the feeling he had on his face when he told Gun Guy what he thought. He could pretend none of this bothered him but it did.

"You know that's not my style. I'm more of a going down with the ship type. But I'm also realistic. I still feel the water climbing up my legs as I'm going down."

"No, that's not 'realistic', that's morbid. Realistic is having a back-up plan, which I do. Either way, we'll be okay. I meant what I said to you in the office."

I hoped he was right and he had a parachute for us.

"So let's hear about those back-ups you've got," I said, placing the sole of my sandal on the dash.

He eyed the offending strappy footwear. "I'm starting to realize why you got the work car you did."

I put the other one up next to it. "Back-up plan?"

He did the subtle shake of his head, which I took to mean he thought I was being too human at the moment and it was best to let whatever irritating thing I was currently doing go since I didn't know any better. "As to back-ups, I've got places we can go."

"Like a safe house or something?"

"More like a safe island or something."

"You've got an island?"

"A lot of people have islands."

"No, they don't. Not in the normal world, anyway. How many people can we fit on your island?"

"It's large enough to accommodate the office staff. Some employees won't need a retreat, like Jockey or Santa. They're secure."

"What about your guys?"

"They'll be staying. I've already spoken to them. This isn't bothering them much."

I thought of Cutty, Angus, Bic and Lars. Yeah, I could see how this might just be a blip on the radar for them.

"And the rest of the world?"

"I can't fit them all." He shrugged. "Eventually, they'll kill each other off until they've dwindled down to more manageable levels, and then maybe there'll be something we can do."

I didn't ask if he was joking. I knew he wasn't. And that was the difference between having a human past and watching from the loftiness of Fate's position. The idea of the world's population dwindling down until it hit *manageable levels*, whatever number that might be, wasn't the silver lining for me.

I hit the down button on the window and let the wind hit me full in the face until it was hard to breathe. I wasn't going to try and explain. He didn't get it. He wasn't a transfer. He didn't have roots here, people who've given everything they had and stood by him.

"I've got to get my parents out of here somehow."

"I've already handled it."

My head whipped in his direction. "You did?"

"Yes. As of this morning, they're on a plane to an all-inclusive resort vacation on a private island. It's a long-stay vacation they won in a raffle that a *friend* entered them in."

"Why didn't you tell me?" It was possibly one of

the nicest things anyone had ever done for me and he hadn't said a word about it?

He threw the truck into fourth gear, kicking up dust and gravel on the dirt road behind us. "I wasn't sure you wanted to discuss them but I knew that if things got worse you'd want them safe."

"Thank you."

He looked at me and his lips turned up but just slightly; nothing that would be described as a real smile or even one of his sexy smirks. But there was something there, something I felt like he wanted to say.

He didn't though and he wouldn't. He reached forward and raised the volume on the radio, the moment passing. I'd never know exactly what it was he wanted to say.

I wanted to ask. The words were already formed; I was just unable to break past the barrier of my pride that sat as thick as a cinder block wall between us.

I reached forward and changed the channel.

CHAPTER SEVENTEEN

I awoke to the feel of Fate moving around and getting up from the bed. I wasn't sure if it was on purpose or planned, but this was the second time I remembered going to sleep alone to wake up with company.

I lay there, feigning sleep, knowing he'd leave soon and not wanting to deal with the after cuddle awkwardness that came with the morning. We weren't a couple but friends didn't spoon every night. Fate and I were officially in relationship no man's land.

It took him about twenty minutes to shower, dress and leave. I could hear him come close to the bed, like he had yesterday, and he stood there for a few moments while I tried to keep my breathing even.

Then his fingers grazed my hair. He hadn't done *that* yesterday.

The door shut and I could finally breathe again. Another twenty minutes of cushion time elapsed before I felt confident he'd be truly gone. Somehow, after he left the house and came back, I could pretend everything was normal again, as if it were a reset button.

An hour later, I was on my third cup of coffee as I sat on the couch and holding a copy of the watch schedule I'd found in his papers. I'd been snooping around. My philosophy was if he didn't want me to see them, he shouldn't have left them sitting in plain view on the dresser.

"What the hell is this about?" The paper crinkled where I gripped it.

Fate, aka my nighttime cuddle buddy, had insisted on taking care of it only to completely cut me out. My name wasn't anywhere on there. Didn't spooning give me any privileges? Shouldn't there be some adjusted rate, even if there wasn't any sex, like benefits times half?

I looked around the living room, wondering where Fate—aka cuddles—had run off to this morning. Bet he'd love me calling him that next time he was about to blow some guy's head off.

I was utterly alone in the room, which was miraculous considering we were packed in like sardines. Well, except for whoever had watch duty currently and was stomping around on the roof.

I was about to grab my phone off the table, planning on alerting Fate to my disgruntlement over his scheduling, when Paddy popped up in front of me. I jerked back before my head collided with his kneecap, his cane nowhere to be found.

"You seriously need to work on your entrance. It's borderline rude." I leaned back, checking out his golfing plaid. "Late for tee time?"

"Where is he?" Paddy asked, searching the room and ignoring my critique and question.

"Fate? I don't know." I narrowed my eyes, looking up at him. "Why?"

"Get up," he said, waving his hands in an effort to hurry me.

"You haven't said why yet." I leaned back into the couch and put my feet up on the table in front of me.

"We've got to go meet people." He reached down to grab my arm, but I yanked it away.

It was an action I was coming to find more and more annoying. It was ranking right up there with being treated like an idiot because I was a transfer and Malokin making all the humans crazy. "I don't know if I want to meet those people."

"You need to meet them, and we need to go before Fate comes back."

Fate didn't want me to meet Paddy's "people," and I wasn't sure I disagreed.

"How do I know I'll walk out of there?" Wow, even having to utter that sentence aloud really sucked. That I was on a speaking basis with someone that I feared might leave me for dead would've been bizarre to me when I was human. But due to Paddy's past, he was starting at a deficit. He'd already left me hanging out to dry before. I understood why but couldn't be sure he wouldn't do it again if things got hairy.

I trusted no one with my life. Well, that wasn't exactly true. There was one person I had complete faith in to keep me alive but he was currently trying to use me for sex. Thinking of it like that made it clear I might have made some wrong turns along the way.

"You've got my word," he said, putting a hand over a heart I wasn't sure he had the anatomy for, not with all the glowy stuff going on inside.

I clucked my tongue, still doubting. "I'm not sure that counts if you're not human."

"It does."

I let a loud undecided sigh escape as I thought it through. He might have screwed me up in some places but he'd dug me out of some holes too.

"Okay," I said as I stood, and he grabbed my hand.

"But, how long…"

Is this going to take faded from my lips. One second I was standing in the living room and the next I was standing under the stars of what looked like the entire universe, complete with nebulas and gas clouds.

The floor beneath my feet had a pattern similar to marble but was unlike anything I'd ever seen on Earth. The veins running through it glowed intermittently, as if the light were coursing through it. Grecian columns ran the length of an expanse too huge for my eyes to see or my brain to comprehend. It didn't look like there was an end.

"Paddy, where are we exactly?" I tried to keep the awe in my voice to a minimum.

"Home." There was a reverence in his voice that

was so un-Paddy-like. He was standing with his head thrown back and his arms out to his sides. His eyes were closed and a smile warmed his face. I watched as he took a long deep breath. He looked like a man who'd just been let out of jail and couldn't get enough of the open air flowing through his fingers.

Watching as he stood there like that for a moment, I realized I was seeing the first hint of who Paddy was. Not what he was made of, but what made him. We weren't so much different from humans, if I thought about it. We were all simply organized energy. If you broke it down far enough, what defined everything was what mattered to you—what you cared about and what you would sacrifice for, work for, live and die for. This place was something he would die for.

His chest rose and he exhaled in a way that made me imagine him shedding some horrible weight. He opened his eyes again and turned to me, seeming somehow brighter. "Come, it's time."

I followed after him and had a feeling he was slowing his pace for my benefit. We walked and walked, and I started to wonder if this place would ever end.

At first, they were a speck of white against the stars behind them in the distance. As we got closer, I could make out a raised dais with four massive and intricately carved thrones upon it, one of which was empty. Paddy's seat.

The other three were occupied by two women and one man. I'm not sure why I assumed they'd look older, like Paddy, but I was horribly mistaken. All three had perfect forms, which appeared to be in the prime of a human life, just so much better.

I glanced over at Paddy and looked him up and down.

"What? We can't all be beauty queens," he said defensively, and it made me wonder if I'd ever really know him.

I was fairly certain Paddy wasn't his real name; I didn't think his true form was an old man at all. But whatever Paddy and these three were, that they weren't human was obvious. There was a sheen to their skin that seemed to glow slightly and a gloss to their hair that didn't seem human. Or maybe it was the exquisiteness of their features—I wasn't sure—but I knew if I'd seen them walking down a normal street in the afternoon, surrounded by a crowd of shoppers, I'd still know they weren't human. They had a certain perfection that I'd never seen.

Or maybe just not quite to this extreme. I had seen something similar on someone quite close to me, and I'd be having a chat with my cuddle buddy as soon as I got back.

The interest wasn't one sided. They seemed equally as intrigued by me but perhaps not quite as impressed. Or at least one of them wasn't.

"Closer," the woman on the far left said, vast amounts of coiled dark hair shimmering as she raised her chin with the command.

I hesitated, not really caring for the order or the tone it was delivered in. A please would've been nice.

Before I could decide whether I'd comply or not, the man seated in the center started laughing. "She's got spunk! She doesn't care what you want her to do, Fia."

"Silence, Fith!"

"I don't need to mind your wishes, Fia," the man said, not losing any of his humor, his temperament as light as his coloring.

"Come," Fia barked out toward me, a trembling undertone accompanying the order.

I felt a compulsion start to sneak up upon me then. It was odd, almost like moving my legs forward was an itch I wanted to scratch. No pain, just a feeling that I'd gain great satisfaction if I did step forward.

My legs didn't move. I didn't want to go to her. I didn't care who she was or how powerful she might be. If they were that great, the world they were in charge of wouldn't be falling apart. I wouldn't be the one dealing with Malokin. There wouldn't *be* a Malokin.

"Go forward," Paddy urged from next to me. There was something in his manner that made my senses prick. Why did he care? Wasn't he on equal footing with these three? What was his stake in me placating her?

"What's going on here?" the one called Fia demanded, as if something was very wrong and she'd just discovered it.

The laughing man suddenly stopped. Fia looked enraged, and the other woman wasn't speaking or portraying any emotion.

"Paddy, what did you do?" Fia barked across the room.

"I did what had to be done. I did what was necessary while the rest of you would've sat back and debated for another century." He slammed down the cane he was carrying again.

"You did not have our consent. Fix this! Take it back," Fia screamed.

Take it back? Things were making a little more sense now. I guessed they didn't appreciate me having some of their glory stuff in me.

"It's done," Paddy shot back.

"Now I see," the silent woman finally said, but no one seemed to be listening to her. Paddy and the woman called Fia had broken into fully-fledged argument. The man was mediating, or trying to.

The silent woman waved me over. She didn't try any funny tricks to lure me closer, just requested my presence. Her I obliged.

"I'm Farrah," she said when I got close enough to hear her speak over the yelling. When Farrah smiled, it felt like the sun coming out after a week-long snowstorm.

"Nice to meet you." And it was. I didn't know if it was some sort of magic universe voodoo that made me like her instantly but I did.

"May I touch you?" she asked, holding out a palm to me.

I laid my own on hers.

She smiled again before speaking, "Yes, it was you."

"What was?"

"A short time ago, maybe a few centuries back, I started feeling the presence of another energy. It was you I felt. I thought I recognized it the moment you stepped into our home but I wanted to be sure."

"Sorry?"

"No, don't be. You see, I'm the most sensitive of us all to fluctuations. The other two here didn't think anything of it but I felt you. I just don't understand how you came to be like this. Do *you* know?" She leaned in closer like I could offer her answers.

"You mean how Paddy did his thing to me? I was there but I'm not sure exactly how it went down, but it wasn't that long ago."

"But how did you come to be this way?" Her eyes searched my face as if I were being obtuse.

"Because of what's happening?" I had no idea what Farrah was saying, and I started to wonder if she were even sane in the sense of how I'd think of it. Maybe there was a reason she stayed quiet.

"You lied!" Paddy's voice boomed from where he was standing across the expanse, bringing everyone to silence. "You never had any intention!"

He and Fia were staring at each other in a way that made me want to back up and make a hasty exit. I had enough problems. I didn't want to get involved in their domestic dispute. Unfortunately, the old guy that looked like he was going to go nuclear was my only exit.

"This needs to end and right now!" Fia screamed at an inhuman pitch and thunder rang out like I was standing right beside a bolt of lightning.

"You can't! I'm not sure *I* can anymore," Paddy lashed out, no longer sounding like Paddy at all; the voice was of a younger form that I was certain lay beneath.

Yeah, definitely time for my exit. This was the last time I was accepting one of his invites.

I looked over at Farrah. "Is there any way you could give me a lift?"

"Certainly."

CHAPTER EIGHTEEN

Farrah popped me into Fate's garage alone. I didn't want to broadcast where I'd been to the occupants of the house and doubted I'd be so lucky as to find the living room empty again.

I cracked the door open as quietly as possible, hoping to situate myself out on the deck like I'd been reading all morning. I tiptoed into the hall and the first thing I noticed was it was dark out. How long had I been gone?

There was still hope. The house sounded quiet, the only noise was the AC kicking on.

I took another step in and saw why. Everyone in the house was sitting either on the dining room chairs or the couch. No one was speaking or so much as moving in their seat. Alarm bells rang. They all were transfixed on a spot I couldn't see. Was Malokin there? Had he breached the wards? My adrenaline cranked into full output. I needed a gun.

I turned, planning on going back to the makeshift armory in the garage, when I heard Fate's voice, "And no one saw anything?" Indignation, impatience, agitation and anger were all neatly packed into his tone. It wasn't Malokin; it was even worse. It was a furious Fate and I knew what had pissed him off. I'd been gone way longer than a few minutes this time and hadn't left word with anyone, which were the house rules.

One by one, their heads turned towards me as I entered the room. I saw eyes widen as their gaze split between the two of us.

"What's going on?" I asked in a light, *hey, everything's good here* voice.

I could see Fate's chest rise and fall as he looked at me. Oh boy, this was definitely about me going missing. "Murphy? You turn the AC up again? It's freezing in here. Going to go grab a sweater," I said, looking for any excuse to move the brawl, which was sure to come, out of the gladiator arena and away from the spectators.

No one said anything as I walked past, not even a stutter of a reply from Murphy. But I had everyone's rapt attention as I moved toward the hallway that led to the bedroom.

I hadn't taken more than two steps down the hall before I felt Fate breathing down my neck behind me. His hand landed on my back, hurrying my step as I walked into the bedroom. He shut the door firmly but I didn't care how upset he was. I had my own issues.

"Where have you been?" He crossed the room and was in my personal space, hands on my arms, pulling me to my toes.

I looked directly into his eyes, wanting to make sure I didn't miss even the tiniest part of his reaction. "I've been visiting with your *relatives*. Who, by the way, seem to live a few miles short of Sanityville."

"You went to see them without me?" he asked. His words were softly quiet but not what I'd describe as a gentle whisper. It was more along the lines of *let me get this straight before I really lose my shit.*

"Yes. You don't deny that you're somehow related? Were you ever going to let me in on that?" Looking at him now, I was positive I was right. There was a connection, whether he admitted it or not. Maybe not enough to make him a glow stick on the inside, but it was there.

"Do you realize what could've happened?"

I didn't think he realized but his fingers dug into me as he said it.

"I had Paddy's word." I pushed off of him with my palms on his chest and he released me, both of us going to opposite corners, not sure who'd won the first round.

"Because he's been so reliable in the past?" he threw back at me, gearing up for round two as he stood beside the dresser.

I swallowed as he threw my own fear back at me but decided that I wasn't going to let that divert me from the subject of his deception so easily. "What about the fact that you never told me you're somehow like them?"

I was across the room, arms folded over my chest as I stared him down.

His jaw tensed; one hand was on his hip and the other lay fisted on the top of the dresser. The air in the room seemed to be filling with his anger.

He finally looked at me again, and I saw in his eyes the same thing I'd seen at the convenience store, the same thing that had probably made Gun Guy call him a scary fuck. Knowing with surety that he wouldn't hurt me was the only thing that kept me in place when that stare was leveled at me.

He finally spoke. "Do you know that just going there could've killed you?"

"And you know that because you've been there how many times?" I pointed my finger in the biggest aha movement ever, refusing to bow down to him.

He scowled and shook his head. "You know nothing."

"Then you're denying it?" I asked as we officially entered round two.

"No, I'm not. It doesn't matter. What matters is you could've died."

"And all that pretending you didn't know anything."

"When did I ever pretend?"

I squinted my eyes in disbelief. "Who's the old man? Remember saying that?"

He leaned forward. "Because the man I knew wasn't called Paddy and he didn't look old."

"You've held out."

"And you haven't?" He crossed the room again, stopping just shy of literally stepping on me. "Don't go off like that again."

My hands instinctively went to my hips. "Or. What."

"I'm telling you, don't."

"Telling me? And when I do 'do that again' what are you going to do?" It was complete bullshit on my part. I had no desire to see those crazy Universe people again, and certainly not without backup, but his words hit the one button that could make me willingly self-destruct. I'd sworn to myself that Malokin's had been the last orders I'd ever take again. I didn't care if it was an angel from God asking me to do something. Never again.

He didn't speak the words but his face said *you'll see.*

"This conversation is over." I walked out of the room, knowing I was about to snap. It was too much stress in too short of a time, and I wasn't thinking clearly anymore.

I'd expected him to try and stop me but he didn't.

He did follow me.

I'd barely made it into the hall before Knox was there, completing our happy trio. "I was just coming to make sure everything was okay," he said as I was forced to stop where he stood in front of me in the hall, Fate at my back.

"It's fine," I said, trying to keep my agitation from leaking out into my words.

Fate also answered the question directed at me. "Mind your own business."

Knox's eyes shot to Fate. "Everything that happens is my business."

"Nothing here is your business. You're here because I *allow* you to be. Go back to the office if you want to play at boss. As long as I let you, that is." Fate stepped around me then and literally bumped into Knox as he walked, adding, "Don't piss me off," as he passed.

I shook my head and went straight for the bar myself, praying to the god of booze there was a bottle of Maker's Mark there. I really needed to have that chat about playing nice that I hadn't gotten around to yet but I needed a shot of something strong first.

No Maker's Mark? Last time I'd had some, the bottle had been half full. How could it be gone? My eyes searched the still occupied living room for the Jinxes, who were cleaning their guns on the dining room table.

"I'm sorry, was the case of scotch not enough?" I asked, ready to bang their little skulls together.

"Oh, that? We decided to add it to emergency booze fund," Bobby graciously explained and put his head back down to oiling and cleaning.

Mother came sweeping by, making tsking noises as she did. "Ladies don't overly imbibe," she said as she passed.

She was lucky she was quick on those skinny little legs of hers or I might have grabbed a piece of that fabric floating behind her and strangled her in her own frills.

Fate stepped forward and silly me assumed he was going to make amends for being such an overbearing ass

187

by pulling out a hidden bottle from somewhere I hadn't seen. Then we could pretend that we weren't in the middle of a drag out and dirty fight and all was good again.

He stepped close but offered no bottle. "I asked you a question that you haven't answered."

And typical Fate, he wasn't going to play the game that said you didn't fight in front of a room of onlookers. Why would he? He didn't follow any rules he hadn't made up.

It took me a half a second to comprehend that he really *was* going to do this—make this an issue when he knew everyone was listening to every word. He'd force my hand and I hadn't come this far to take orders from anyone. And if I knew his ego like I thought I did, it would become an all-out brawl because neither of us were going to back down.

Fine. He wanted to do it here? So be it.

"I answered you loud and clear." I grabbed a bottle of Grey Goose from the ones left. I guess the Jinxes didn't like vodka but it would do just fine for me. I'd probably do a straight shot of gasoline right now.

"You don't have to answer to him." Knox's voice came from right behind me and I dropped my face so no one could see me roll my eyes. Fate wouldn't kill me. It might get ugly, and we might put a loud enough show on for the whole neighborhood, but I'd make it. Knox, I wasn't so sure.

I appreciated the support, but oh God was his timing complete shit. Now instead of handling my own issues, I had to handle his. I wanted to smack my hand onto my forehead and ask the Universe what the hell it was doing but I'd come to the conclusion, after that last meeting, it had no real idea either.

I didn't even have to look at Fate to know he was now in full fight mode with a vengeance and a new target. I wasn't sure any pleading on my part would keep those two from going at it now. There was some instinctual dislike there, which baffled me. Fate hadn't seemed to particularly care for Harold either but yet he'd managed to get along with him just fine. Not so with Knox. And now we were all living together like a big dysfunctional family.

"I warned you to stay out of my business." Fate started closing the already small distance between him and Knox, and I tried to keep pace, getting sandwiched between the two of them. Advice my mother had given me years ago chimed in my head; *a woman stepping in between two fighting men sometimes adds gas to their engines*.

Usually, I agreed.

Not with these two. They came fully loaded already. If I stepped out of the way, their egos weren't going to calm down and they weren't going to magically hug it out. They'd brawl.

"Why? So you can try and tell her what to do?" Knox's chest was puffed out.

"I can. She's mine."

Mine? He said I was his? It was all sorts of cave man but it sent the most delicious tingle down my spine.

I really wanted to wallow in that feeling but they were going to beat each other up in about two seconds. *And it wasn't like it was a declaration of love, you sappy girl. He thought he owned everything, and now that included you. Snap out of it!*

I pushed the soft fuzzy feelings from my psyche and focused on Fate and Knox. The only thing they seemed to agree upon was that they didn't want me in between them. They moved left, I went left. They dodged right and so did I. This went on until a large pair of hands lifted me up and placed me slightly to the side and partially behind Knox.

"What. Did. You. Just. Do?" Each word out of Fate's mouth was like a bullet into the air. Since the first time I'd met him, he looked like he was on the brink of losing control. I'd seen him mad. I'd seen him threatening. Hell, I'd seen him look like the Devil, fresh with burn marks on his clothes. But never had I seen him about to lose his shit.

Without my soft padding in the center, their chests were almost touching, they were so close.

"You don't own her," Knox replied.

"I'm going to warn you once. And you don't know how lucky you are to get that. Do not touch her again. The last people who did lost their heads." Fate's voice seemed to get deeper and quieter with each word.

"And you think you can do that to me?" Knox asked, still hanging in there with equal bravado.

Had to hand it to Knox; he was the only person I'd ever seen stand up to Fate. The new guy had some balls for sure—or perhaps he wasn't as bright as I'd thought. I just hoped he had some spares because Fate looked like he was going to rip them from his body at any second. The tides had turned and it was time to edge back, wanting to get out of the line of fire in case there was an accidental discharge in my direction while I debated different tactics to calm this down.

Suddenly, they both turned their gazes to me like two Rottweilers about to go after a favorite chew toy.

I threw up both my hands to fend off a possible grab as I took several more steps backward. I'd decided today, this minute, that I wouldn't allow anymore grabbing to occur. This one pulling me here, that one picking me up and moving me there, the manhandling had officially come to an end. "I don't know what your problem is with each other but leave me out of it."

The room was so quiet that I could hear some shifting on the couch behind us before Murphy, who must have been speaking to Luck, said, "Did she really say she didn't know what their problem was? I know she's a transfer but isn't that a little slow even for a human?"

Murphy's words, although aggravating me more, seemed to have the opposite effect on Knox. He looked up and over like he was surprised we had an audience. I watched as the fight drained from him, and he made some excuse about having to go in the office for something or other.

Fate watched him leave, looking satisfied enough with the departure to not pursue him. He pulled out his phone, which part of my brain had realized had been ringing for quite some time, then shoved it back in his pocket.

He looked at me, all our unresolved issues hanging in the air between us. "I have to go."

I shrugged. "So go."

He stood there for a couple more seconds before he finally turned and left without saying another word to any of us.

The living room emptied out pretty quickly now that the show was over, leaving only Luck, Murphy and me.

Luck punched Murphy in the arm. "Murphy, I can't believe you said that before. They all heard you and it was so uncomfortable they left."

"You're right, Luck." Murphy cleared his throat and his next words came out considerably louder. "Karma, I'm sorry I said that. It's not your fault you're stupid sometimes. You can't help it."

She sighed loudly at him. "No, you're the stupid one. What are we supposed to do now? There's nothing on TV."

There they sat on the couch, each with a cup of tea in their hands and some cookies on the table in front of them.

"What is going on here?" I said, motioning to the snacks. No TV playing in the background, just the two of them sitting and waiting for a show that didn't air on cable.

"I know," Luck said, making me think that she felt

some shame about them using my life as a spectator sport, until she continued. "But whoever went shopping bought the wrong popcorn." She shrugged.

Murphy nodded his head as he tapped his watch. "I have to agree. Even when the world is falling apart, you need to have standards to live by."

"Get up," I said to the two of them.

"Why? Are we going to go follow him into the office?" Luck asked, clearly intrigued by the possibility of more show time. Murphy's animated head nodded vigorously in encouragement.

I sighed but didn't bother to correct them. That was who they were and, as much as it annoyed me at times, they were my family. "No. We're going out."

Two disappointed ohs came out in unison.

"I guess if the show's over," Luck said. "Plus *she's* upstairs in my room."

Murphy let out a prolonged sigh. "I didn't have any other plans, did you?"

Luck shook her head. "No. I guess we should go."

CHAPTER NINETEEN

It was after midnight when we got back from the dive bar Luck, Murphy and I went to. I'd chosen to frequent many of them in the recent past but it hadn't been a deliberate choice this time around. There hadn't been much of a selection of places to pick from. Most of the respectable establishments had shut down or were only opening during the daylight hours, when things were a notch calmer. The places open at night catered to the seediest crowds and you paid a premium to be in such esteemed company.

Tonight might have been the first time ever that Luck hadn't found herself a boy toy she wanted to take home. It wasn't for lack of trying. She'd been armed to the teeth with her best red lipstick and highest heels but the selection had been dismal and not up to even her low standards.

The stench from the foul karma people had been throwing off choked me almost as badly as the shots of cheap tequila I had thrown back. Still, Luck and Murphy stuck it out there with me until the wee hours of the morning. I'd needed some time away from the tension of the house, and Murphy was having a good time furthering the woes of our fellow customers, while Luck enjoyed watching.

Luck and Murphy stumbled their way upstairs once we got back as I headed toward Fate's room—now mine. Even though I'd resented being put on the spot, I was glad I wasn't walking past a room Fate was sharing with Mother.

My hand hesitated on the knob but not for long. Even with the argument today, I always wanted to see him. Too much so.

I pushed open the door to an empty room and looked at the clock on the table. Two a.m. and he wasn't here.

I got ready for bed as I listened for the door. I crawled under the covers and lay there, watching the minutes tick by. Two thirty. Maybe between telling him I didn't want to stay with him and our fight earlier, he'd finally given up.

This was what I'd wanted. I pulled a pillow over my head to block my sight and deaden my ears, forcing myself to stop waiting. It didn't matter if he showed or not. In fact, it was good if he didn't.

I threw the pillow to the side and got up, walked a few steps. Maybe I should check and see if Luck was okay since she drank a lot. It's not like I cared if Mother was in her bed or anything.

No. If that was what he wanted, then it would never have been worth anything anyway. I knew eventually he would tire of wanting me. It was for the best. Getting attached as much as I already had wasn't good. I wasn't even sleeping with him and I was becoming a clingy mess. I turned around and got back in my bed again.

Fuck him. He was a dick. Who cuddles with someone every night and then disappears because of a couple fights? Cuddle and dump might be worse than a one-night stand. This was harder than when he'd asked me if I was still planning on leaving after we had sex. No, this might even be worse than when he stole my piece of birthday cake. God, he'd been such a dick to me. Come to think of it, I didn't know why I was speaking to him at all.

Fate? No—Dick. That was his new name. He'd see who didn't give a shit next time I saw him.

***

"You're looking kind of tired," Fate said the next morning.

"Nope. I slept like a baby, better than I have in weeks." *Dick.*

We stood, side by side, about fifty feet from the entrance of the local supermarket that I'd shopped in less than a month ago, when it had been brand new. I'd been so excited to have a new market, free of all sorts of human reminders left over from my mortal days. I'd go in and not have to pretend that I didn't know the cashier at the checkout or that I didn't know the manager played poker with my dad on Thursday evenings, that I hadn't babysat the kid collecting the carts from the parking lot.

Now I stood there, forcing myself to look at the transformation. One of the front windows had been knocked out completely, and a steady stream of people were going in and out through the gap like it was the main entrance to a store on a Black Friday sales bonanza.

How things had fallen so quickly was baffling to me. They were still human beings—unlike the bastard next to me, who I wanted to hit over the head with the hilt of the gun strapped to my ankle. Malokin was like a virus spreading through the human race, or maybe he was simply the by-product of a world heading downward that fed his birth. It was hard to know which came first, just that a coincidence this strong wasn't usually chance.

Either way, this was what life was now, and if we needed supplies, that's where we had to go. I glanced over at Fate, keeping a stony expression plastered on my face.

I'd woken up as alone as I'd gone to sleep. He'd been up and as cheery as a cherry on an ice cream sundae this morning. He was having coffee and saying something about how we needed to make a run today and some bullshit about how I had to be the one to go with him. I guess he liked variety. He'd have to look somewhere else if he thought he was going to add me to the mares on his carousel.

"Ask." He let out a disgruntled sigh and I wondered

if my mask had slipped. "God, if I'd known you were going to be like this, I would've left a note."

He was annoyed? I wanted to ask him if being a dick and bed hopping inconvenienced him but then he'd know it bugged me for sure instead of assuming. "Ask what? I don't have any questions." Not for him. Not anymore. Every question and doubt had been answered last night, confirming everything I'd thought when the philandering pig who insisted I stay in his room did a no show. *Cuddling dick.*

I took a step forward and he wrapped a hand around my upper arm.

"I'm sorry you missed the memo, but I've struck manhandling from my list of acceptable behaviors." I looked down my nose at the offending hold, "If you wouldn't mind?"

"How did you plan on enforcing this new list of rules?" he asked, offending hand still in place.

"If you were a gentlemen, like some others I know, I wouldn't need to enforce it." I let the implication of Knox hover in the air, waiting to see if it would hit the target.

His jaw clenched and his grip firmed. I'd call that a bull's-eye.

"Ask."

I turned away from him. He could keep me standing in this parking lot all day and night. I still wouldn't ask. "I told you. I don't care."

"That's it? You don't even ask? You know, I knew you had a lot of pride but don't you think this is a bit ridiculous?" he asked, his hand not budging from my arm.

"I haven't the foggiest idea of what you're referring to," I replied, refusing to even look at him.

"Fine. I'll tell you anyway, since someone needs to save you from your whopping ego."

"*My* ego?"

"I was at Lars's last night. They had a problem over there."

He dropped his hand. It was probably because he couldn't achieve the smug look he was going for without being able to add the final touch of crossing his arms in front of his chest.

His hand was no longer forcing me to stay there and listen; I was forced to stay of my own volition. But damned if I'd make it that easy. "You could be making it up."

"That's the best you've got?" He raised his eyebrows while managing to squint his eyes at the same time.

He wouldn't be able to pull off a lie like that with the way our co-workers gossiped. If he'd been with Mother last night, someone would have been spilling the beans by morning. I would have heard about it over breakfast. I could hear them now, *Can you pass the bacon, Fate slept with Mother and I'd like the syrup as well.*

I shrugged in acknowledgment as the toe of my boot sent a pebble flying. "I didn't ask because it wasn't a big deal either way."

"I could tell. I love listening to the music so loud that I can't hear my voice."

Every time he'd tried to speak on the way over, I'd turned the volume on the radio up a couple of notches. My back to him, I looked at the supermarket because I had this goddamn smile trying to burst out on my face and it was stubbornly fighting all resistance. A subject change before he caught onto how relieved and giddy I was feeling wasn't a bad idea. This was pathetic. It was like dying had set me back ten years of emotional maturity, right smack into the awkward teens again.

"I just don't get it. How's Malokin making everyone crazy?" It was a stupid question, in the sense that Fate didn't have any more answers than I did. I knew he didn't. We'd discussed this several times. But it didn't matter, because that wasn't the point. I had to get us back on work talk.

Unfortunately, I was worried the smile on my face tainted the tone I'd asked in. It was a somber question and I'd made it sound like I'd asked for my favorite flavor of ice cream. Hopefully he hadn't noticed that my question about world disorder sounded a lot like the way I'd say *can I have extra whip and rainbow sprinkles*.

"That question is really eating you up." I'd never heard Fate quite so sarcastic.

I put my hands to my cheeks, trying to manually pull the smile down. "It is." Nah, that couldn't have sounded as weird as I thought.

I heard Fate shuffling things around as he grabbed several duffle bags before he started walking toward the place. He was moving forward into the store. Back to death and destruction. Oh good, comfortable footing again.

The awkwardness was past, along with the honest moment. A lot of those seemed to be slipping by lately, with my encouragement, and I was starting to get sad about watching them go. But I still wasn't ready to try and stop them leaving. I always had the excuse of unfortunate timing to fall back on.

I watched his back and the surroundings sucked up all my attention again. Destruction had a tendency to ground you in reality when it was smacked in your face.

He stopped and turned back to see I hadn't moved. His eyes narrowed as he took in my still form.

I shook my head. "I don't know about this."

I'd spent years of my life defending criminals but always holding myself to a higher standard. Was I really going to contribute to a business being looted? Nothing about it felt right.

"Do you know the last time I had to do my own shopping? At least this is something you're used to doing." He pushed the sliding duffle bag back onto his shoulder.

"I'm not talking about shopping. I'm not comfortable contributing to this." I pointed at the store.

He pointed toward our destination. "At this point, it's either loot or don't eat. I've had to not eat before. We won't die but it sucks. As far as stealing, I'm going to send the corporation that owns this store a nice check as soon as the postal service is up and running again. I'll round up if it makes you feel better but I'm eating tonight."

I gripped my own duffle bag and forced myself to follow him. Those were terms I could live with.

"Stay close to me," he said, as we headed toward the broken window.

"You have seen me fight, right?" I wasn't a slouch when it came to hand to hand combat, as I'd proved in the past.

"Stay close anyway," he repeated, and I knew what scene his mind was replaying. The almost rape. Why was it I could walk around kicking ass for months but get overpowered one time and I was the weak loser? Reputations suck like that. Hell to build and so easy to destroy.

"You know, there was something off about that guy. He was really strong. These are only scattered humans. Not even a true mob." Not like what I'd seen heading down the beach the other night. It had been a group of twenty or so. They'd taken one look at Fate, machinegun in hand, and had kept walking.

Although word was getting around, even with the crazies, that there was a gang of three thirteen-year-old boys that liked to use pedestrians as target practice. They aimed to miss but they weren't great shots. Our block was getting more and more peaceful.

"They aren't a mob right now but in times like these, you don't take anything for granted." What he didn't say was *like how I let you walk into a convenience store alone.*

I knew it was eating him up, because he felt some strange responsibility for me, so I let the subject drop. I didn't care for the reminder myself.

We stepped over the low clearing of the empty window frame. The building was worse inside than I'd imagined.

"This is horrible." People were dashing in here and there, grabbing foodstuff that they thought would last and getting out before a real gang showed up. Everyone who saw us walked in the other direction. I sometimes found it amazing how, after so many years of living in a civilized society, people still instinctually knew a threat.

"I know. It's worse than a weekend." Fate sounded disgusted for his own reasons. He moved confidently through the aisles, clearly more irritated about having to shop for himself at all than the manner in which he was being forced to do it. "I can't believe my shopper disappeared. It's impossible to get good help anymore."

I grabbed a jar of kosher dills and put them in my bag, wondering if we should've searched for a cart.

"What happened yesterday with Paddy?" he finally asked. I'd been waiting for him to revisit the subject since I'd seen him.

"Nothing much new to report other than your relatives are crazy. As to that, are we talking cousins? Siblings?"

He stopped in the middle of the aisle. "Don't go there again," he said, ignoring my question.

I stopped with him, wanting to hash this out as well. Better in the middle of a bunch of crazies in the grocery store than the bunch of crazies at the house.

I stiffened my spine and prepared for battle. "I have no desire to go there again. But you need to know—I'm not going because *I* don't want to. Not because you told me not to."

"Fine." He shrugged and started walking again, as if the subject were no big deal and it hadn't been a huge fight last night.

"Fine?"

"Yes."

"Because you're still getting your way?"

"Yes."

"Only this time and because it's what I want."

"We'll see." He picked up a can of black olives. "Do you like Puttanesca?"

"So, how are you linked to them?"

He stuffed the can of olives into the duffle bag on his shoulder along with another one. "I think that's what I'm going to make tonight."

"Why do I even try?" I asked, looking upward, more to myself than him.

"Good question," Fate answered anyway.

"Where have the guys been, by the way? What was the emergency last night?" I asked, seeing if I could get him to crack somewhere else.

He stiffened just the tiniest bit, and if I hadn't been staring at his back like a lovesick teenager I would've completely missed the slip.

"Minor incident with some humans. Not a big deal."

He was lying and I was going to grill him over it as soon as I got past my shock. Why, after all this time, was I able to read him when I never could before? I'd always been able to read people but never Fate. Unless it wasn't me. Maybe it was such a whopper that even he slipped a little?

"What happened exactly?"

"Nothing major."

Oh yeah, this was a biggie. Picking up my pace, I dodged in front of him, out past the end of the aisle. I wanted to make sure I could see his lying face when I hit him with my next question.

"Shit," I said, instead of my planned inquisition.

I yanked on Fate's arm and tugged him deeper, back into the aisle with me.

"What?"

"The guy I saved on the yacht, the one we couldn't find for my bucket list? The one Malokin had already gotten? He's here." I motioned to the right of where we were.

Fate eased forward slightly and then ducked back. "And he's leaving."

My response was immediate. "Let's go."

"Agreed."

With everything going on, I'd forgotten that there was one bright point. My bucket list was back on, and this time I wouldn't hesitate.

CHAPTER TWENTY

We'd managed to track the guy ten blocks. The entire time I wondered why Malokin didn't supply cars to all of his people. Not that I cared about their convenience; it was just that destruction was hard enough to look at when you were whizzing by at sixty miles per hour. At walking pace, it was too much to take in. Broken windows, burned buildings, looting—I was watching my home town fall apart piece by piece, my childhood memories slowly being torn down.

There was also the issue of other foot traffic. We'd gotten into it with a gang on the walk over when we'd had to duck into an alley. Watching Fate kick the shit out of five guys at the same time didn't help my crush one little iota. I felt myself slacking off just to see him in action.

He'd given me a look after the fight that had me making excuses about not sleeping well last night and contradicting my earlier story of a great night. This crush

I had on him was really screwing up my credibility. Fortunately, he hadn't had enough time to dwell on my lack of performance, since we'd had to catch up to our target.

We followed the guy to a run down building, with no signs or markers that claimed the place other than a for rent sign that looked like it had been hanging there with no takers for quite some time. It looked like it might have been a strip mall at some point but had lost its purpose during an economic downturn because it was too far off the beaten path to sustain itself in anything less than a booming economy. The steady flow of humans walking in and out was probably the most foot traffic it had seen in years, possibly ever.

We got as close as we could without anyone seeing us before having to duck behind a partially broken brick wall. From there I watched the craziest and most degenerate of our current population enter and exit. "What is this?"

He pointed to the flow of people leaving. "They're all armed. See the way some of them are testing the weight of their guns? It's because they just got them. This place was empty a couple of days ago. Malokin must be setting up pop-up armories."

"I guess we know where everyone is getting their guns these days." Almost all of the people leaving were brandishing smaller arms. I was thankful that at least they weren't arming them with automatic rifles and the heavy stuff, like we had.

"This doesn't make sense. Why not keep the guns?"

I answered my own question before Fate did. "Unless you want complete anarchy. You want the world to hit a point of no return, or at least be so far gone that you have such a steep climb back it could take decades. A world of such chaos and disorder it would be easy to step into the gap if you have even a modicum of planning and resources. He wants to be a dictator."

"Some of the most horrific dictators rose to power amidst chaos."

I surveyed the building again, taking in all the possible access points. "We've got to give it a try. We might not get a better chance. Even if we don't find any information on Malokin, worst case, we take out some of his people. It certainly isn't going to *hurt* our cause."

Not often are Fate and I on the exact same page with things but when we both turned and looked at each other, in that moment we were utterly in sync. I could see the muscles tensing already and bloodlust in his eyes.

His hand lay on top of where mine was over my gun, holstered at my side. "Before we do this, just know it could amp up this fight. The official truce might be over, but neither of us has pulled the trigger since the condo burning down. I killed his people. He retaliated. We do this, we might be inviting direct open warfare."

"Open warfare is coming whether we do this or not. It's simply a choice of whether we wait for it to come to us or we meet it head on." Even as I said the words, I knew he was probably more aware of it than I was. His statement had been for my benefit. My next words were for his. "I'm going into this with eyes wide open. I get it."

"This was one of those things I was hoping you'd miss," he said, looking straight ahead at the building.

It was another one of those honest moments that seemed to be sneaking up more and more often, and the effect wasn't lessening per exposure.

"You ready to do this?" he asked, snapping out of whatever glimpse I'd just seen.

I nodded my head and tightened my ponytail.

"We get as close as we can without being seen. Anything iffy, we leave. If we can take a shot, we do. Agreed?"

I grabbed my gun from its holster and gripped it. "Sounds good to me."

"If something goes badly, the other one gets out."

Now I paused. "We just leave the other person there, knowing Malokin's propensity for torture? You want me to agree to possibly leaving you in a pool of your own blood?"

"Yes." His face was set.

There was only one answer that would do to get this show on the road.

"Fine." I shrugged as I lied. I'd never be able to leave him for dead. The idea was as abhorrent to me as dying myself. Maybe more so and that was scarier than the building of gun toting crazy humans.

I tested the weight of my gun, knowing he wouldn't really leave me either. He'd already had the opportunity and hadn't.

I peered back over the wall, eyeing up our best chance to get close enough to do damage.

Fate edged closer and said, "Our only shot is approaching from the back of the building where no one seems to be going. The trees will give us some cover."

"Agreed."

Crouching down under the cover of the wall we headed off, taking several minutes to wind our way around to the back of the building without anyone catching sight of us. We made it to the tree line and then right up against the stucco side of the building where we could peer in the back windows unobstructed.

The room was packed with people. They appeared to be forming a huge line, all waiting to get arsenal from a made up concession stand where handguns were being passed out like hotdogs and peanuts at a ballgame.

He tilted his head toward the inside. "Do you recognize any of them?"

I looked back through the dirty window, happy for the layer of grime shielding us somewhat and the overcast day helping out. There were five nonhumans in there. It was easy to spot them among the others, who all had karma in varying shades of dingy to almost black. Two of Malokin's men were at the table and the other three were closer to the door, monitoring the traffic in and out. I scanned each face "I only recognize the one. Do you think we can get all five?"

Fate took my place at the window as I moved to the side again, my back against the wall.

He pulled back. "I'm not sure. The humans toting

guns aren't going to want their party crashed or their free goodies taken away. They'll probably join the fight."

"We have to shut this down," I said.

"We might be better off letting it run its course, then seeing if Malokin's guys lead us back to where he's holed up."

"What if they don't go back to Malokin for weeks? Meanwhile, all these new guns are hitting the street and we did nothing? I'm tired of doing nothing."

"It's not the smart move."

"I can't let this go on, not knowing if one of those crazy people is going to take one of those guns and shoot someone I know later on today."

I held my breath, wondering if I was going to have to do this alone, until I saw his eyes shoot to the gun in my hand. "How much practice have you had lately?"

The air slowly leaked out of my lungs. "I'm decent. Not as good as I am with knives but I can hit what I'm aiming for."

"Do you think you could take two of them out while I take the other three?"

I smiled. "Depends on how quick the second one moves after I shoot the first. I'm game if you are."

"It's cold blood," he said, reminding me of my past shortcomings.

"Watching them pass out guns like that to a crazy horde that's going to rip apart the only place I've called home? Trust me, there's nothing chilly about my blood right now." It was the exact opposite. I was gripping the gun hard in order to mask the anger shaking in my hands.

He motioned for me to look through the window with him and then signaled to the left. "I'll take those three. You take the two on the right."

My yacht guy was in his three. "No, I need to take out the guy we followed."

"Bucket list." He nodded.

"Bucket list," I confirmed.

"Going to make it a little trickier, spread out like that, but I respect the list. Take the three and I'll try and pick up your slack."

"You respect the list?" My voiced hitched progressively higher until I didn't recognize it by the last word.

His eyes scanned mine before they squinted and he scowled. "Now you're going to get all soft on me?"

"No! I don't know what you're talking about," I said brushing off the fact that him respecting my bucket list felt like the first time a boy had handed me a stuffed animal at a carnival.

He took one look at me and sighed aloud. "I save you from gang rape? No big deal. I tell you I respect your sicko murder list and you turn into a puddle of mush?"

"You can mock the list all you want now. I know you respect it." I squinted back at him.

"Just get ready. You aim left. I aim right. We're about to hit a hive with a stick. Take your best shot. Once they spot us, we run like hell before all those guns turn on us."

"I ever tell you I like your style?"

"Actually, yes, you have."

"I have?"

"Think really hard."

Oh God, it must have slipped out one of the times we'd had sex because the guy did know how to move.

"There are two cracks in the glass. You take the lower, I'll take the upper. We go on the count of three."

I moved into position and leveled my gun at the guy on my bucket list. "Count away."

Three came quickly. I pulled the trigger and the first name on my bucket list could officially be marked off. Everything after that was a blur. I took the next shot and clipped the second guy in the leg. After that, a clear shot become impossible. The inside of the building looked exactly like Fate had warned, a swarm buzzing around chaotically.

We started receiving return fire at a rapid rate and I ducked just as a bullet shattered the rest of the glass. Just as I squatted down, the ache in my tattoo, which had been leaving me alone recently, decided to rear its head and stick out its teeth. The pain sucked the air from my chest and the strength from my legs.

"Fun's over. Time to go," Fate said, not looking at me but at the ensuing chaos. He reached over and grabbed my hand, tugging me after him.

Instead of following, I stumbled.

"Are you hit?" His eyes were scanning me quickly.

"No. Just a cramp or something."

He pulled me to my feet and tossed me over his

shoulder, taking off with me in tow. The humans didn't put up much of a chase. Even with my weight, Fate was too quick for them anyway. Plus, they'd already got their free guns.

We were several blocks away when the pain finally started to subside.

"I'm good," I said, breathless and still recouping from the pain and bouncy ride.

"What the hell happened to you?" he said once we slowed down.

"I got a cramp," I said defensively.

He bent toward me and his face scrunched up. "You got a *cramp*?" he asked in disbelief.

"Yes. Sometimes the tattoo cramps." I knew I was underselling the situation but I didn't know how else to describe it. It was a cramp, and I didn't want to blow it out of proportion.

His expression was already changing from annoyance to something I didn't want to deal with. I'd known the mention of the pain originating near the tattoo was going to give it a different meaning.

"Let me see it." He pointed toward my hip and stepped closer, forcing me to back up. He was following me, an intent look on his face.

"Why? You want me to light up the alley like the Fourth of July?"

"I want to see it."

"Fine. Look." I tugged down the side of my pants and pulled back the bandaging. "See? No freakier than normal," I said as I pressed the tape back, hoping it had enough sticky left in it to hold.

"Lars is going to look at it."

I nodded. Lars did the tattoo but I had a sinking feeling he wasn't going to be able to fix what was going wrong.

I hopped around on my feet a bit, trying to infuse my appearance with good health and excitement, only partially faked. "How many did we get back there?"

"We got them all," he said, and I could see my excitement chipping away at his doubts over my tattoo.

"All? What about the guy I clipped in the leg?"

"He was an easy shot, limping as he was."

Now I really was jumping around the alley and Fate was openly smiling at my enthusiasm. "I wish I could see Malokin's face when he finds out we got five of his people! And my bucket list officially has a check!"

I was almost skipping as we started to walk back to where we'd left our car at the market. "Five of Malokin's men down. Four for you and one for me. Maybe three and a half from you. I did make that one guy easier. I think I deserve partial credit on him."

In the middle of my elation and recent achievement, I didn't expect the smile to slip from Fate's face.

"I think we need to have a talk."

CHAPTER TWENTY-ONE

"There's something I need to tell you about last night," Fate said.

"What?" I said aloud, while internally I was shouting *I knew it*. He had slept with someone, goddamn gigolo. I knew I shouldn't have trusted him.

"That's not fair." There was a gravelly quality to his.

"What's not fair?" *He wanted to talk fair?*

"What you're thinking." His voice went from gravel to stone. "It's written all over your face."

"What's written on my face is what I heard in your tone. Obviously I'm not going to like whatever it is you have to say, which I'm withholding opinion on until I hear all the facts."

His eyes called me a liar but when his mouth opened, he said, "I want you to meet someone who was converted by Malokin who's staying with Lars—who, by the way, I didn't sleep with, even though, according

216

to you, I can't keep my dick in my pants. And you can't kill her."

"You do know how odd that sounded, right? Putting that whole speech about your penis in the middle of that statement?" On the positive side of things, Fate wouldn't sleep with someone involved with Malokin in any way. It still didn't mean I was going to like this.

"Having to ask you not to kill someone is utterly normal? Your bucket list? Again, completely normal shit you've got going on. And yet I don't accuse you of being a murdering lunatic."

Spotting a gang on the horizon, Fate and I ducked into a partially burned out self-serve laundry place. After all, we couldn't kill every lunatic on the street or there wouldn't be enough people left when things hopefully righted themselves.

I hopped on top of a somewhat clean washing machine and continued my argument. "Only because I haven't been doing very well with it. You, on the other hand, have had quite a bit of success with your numbers, from what I've heard. I know your batting stats are up there. Don't forget, our coworkers talk. A lot." I leaned back and immediately thought better of it as my palm landed in a mixture of spilled detergent and ash.

"Do you realize how long I've lived? I wasn't a priest, for God's sake." He handed me a rag that was lying on the counter.

I took it and jumped off the machine, trying to keep a few feet of distance between us. If I was three feet away at all times, it would be psychically impossible to have sex. "No, I have no idea how long, because you've never told me that either. Who is this person and why are they with Lars?"

"It's some girl who showed up at his shop. She's under his protection." He hopped up on a folding table to sit, leaning forward with his hands braced on either side of him.

"I'm not saying I would kill her, but why can't I?" I clanged a dryer door shut. "Since when did we start caring about keeping his people alive? Is this some sort of pity deal?"

"She came to him for help. She claims she's not a bad person. Lars is a bit on edge about her."

It took a second for all the pieces to click together. When things moved as fast, as they did these days, it was hard to be sharp at all times. But whoa, when they did click, I was speechless, at least for a second before I blurted out, "He's fucking one of Malokin's converts? I can't believe this. And I'm supposed to not kill her so he can keep his sex toy?"

"I didn't say you wouldn't want to." He leaned back, resting an arm along the machine next to him, somehow finding the only clean space in the joint. "I'm telling you, you can't."

"And you're fine with this?"

"I'm giving him space to figure it out."

"Figure it out?" I snorted. Lars screamed sex. "If he hasn't figured it out yet, he should probably give up hope. Like Lars needs another crazy girl to fuck? You boys are unbelievable. Hey, why try and stop this at all?

Hell, more crazy chicks to bang." His eyes followed me around the place as I thought out the situation on my feet. "And don't look at me like I don't know. I've heard all the stories."

He shook his head. "This one's different."

"Oh yeah, I agree there. Most of the girls he fucks aren't part of Malokin's Army of Evil."

"You're making assumptions. I met her. I'm not so sure she's bad."

"Let me guess, you want to fuck her too?"

"Nope. Not even a little." His gaze locked on me like a homing signal and sent me scurrying to my next pointless thing of observation, a detergent dispenser.

"Why wasn't I invited last night?"

"Bucket list."

"Oh yeah. I forgot." These people made an awful big thing out of a list I hadn't been able to execute very well. "When do I get to meet her?"

"Leaving the timing up to Lars." Fate jumped down from his seat, ducked his head out of the building and then waved me forward.

***

The house was peaceful and quiet. Fate was out looking for more pop-up armories with the Jinxes, and everyone else was asleep. The moonlight spilled in through the doors.

At night, when it went silent like this and the crazies had all finally succumbed to exhaustion, I could almost pretend everything was normal.

The warmth of the mug seeped into my palms, where they wrapped around it, as I walked over to the couch. I'd curl up in the corner and watch the waves break on the ocean. Sipping my tea, I'd dream of normal everyday bliss while I waited for exhaustion to claim me as well.

I'd imagine that the world wouldn't be falling apart. Maybe I'd never died and was at a friend's beach house, making a late night cup of tea because I was up and worried about a trial next week or some other matter that now seemed trivial.

Only hiccup was, in my dreams, Lars was never sitting on the deck with a machine gun resting on his lap.

I moved past the couch and opened the door to the deck instead. He looked over at me as I took the seat beside him. His boots were kicked up on the railing as the moonlight bounced off his hair. He was a handsome guy if you could get past the fact he'd been the Grim Reaper in a past life and he looked like he was still willing to lend a helping hand to anyone who wanted to pass over.

"How are you?" he asked.

His eyes scanned me, searching for some visible display of my messed up psyche. That's when I knew for certain he'd not only had the entire story of everything that had gone down recently, but all the nitty gritty details as well.

"I'm fine," I replied. And I was but I could have been a walking train wreck and still wouldn't have admitted it. Looks of pity had that effect on me.

He nodded, like someone who understood on a personal level what it was like to keep your own counsel.

"Live long enough and bad shit tends to happen. More often than usual with you, but it's unavoidable." He smiled, taking the unintentional sting out of his words. "Take enough steps and sooner or later one of them is going to be in dog shit."

"I guess I'm lucky like that." I looked down the beach, seeing a few stragglers but not much else. "Quiet tonight."

"Enjoy it. We might not get too many more of these." He crossed his ankles where they rested on the railing, the heavy boots making a thudding noise in the quiet of the night as he repositioned them.

I buffed my nails on the pajama shorts I was wearing. "I wasn't going to ask but since the world's going to shit and I'm at a lack for more appropriate small talk—"

"Figured he'd tell you about her," he said with no surprise in his voice.

"Yes."

"You can't kill her and add her to your bucket list."

Fate was right. He was edgy. This girl was getting to him and that could be very, very bad. "I can't believe you're sleeping with one of Malokin's people. If you haven't noticed, we're at war with him. What are you thinking?"

"She's not with him," Lars's voice was firm and

more than a little defensive. His hand ran through his long black hair as he sighed. It took a full minute before he spoke again, less decisive this time. "At least I don't think she is. Talking about fucked up relationships, how's yours?"

"I don't have a relationship."

"*Sure* you don't. You two walk around saying nothing about anything and pretend it's completely normal. Worry about your own issues."

He resettled the rifle in his lap as I stared at the chips in my nail polish in the heavy silence.

"We're both screwed up. But your situation is still worse." All I needed to do was stick my tongue out to make that statement complete.

He turned his head toward me and raised his eyebrows. "Care to debate that?"

I stared down at my nails again, thinking that having them plucked off one by one would be preferable. "I won't talk about yours, if you don't talk about mine."

"Done. That was significantly easier than I had imagined." He waved a finger toward my hip. "On to other subjects, I'm supposed to take a peek at that."

"Sure." I kicked my feet up on the railing beside his but with not nearly the same satisfying thud.

"I'm not going to see anything wrong with the tattoo, am I?" he asked as neither of us made an effort toward show and tell.

"Nope."

"Care to share what the issue is?"

"Nope."

"Understood."

I stood and stretched out my arms with a yawn. "It's been nice chatting with you, Lars. Sort of, anyway."

"Back at ya, babe," he said, using the top of the gun to salute me.

CHAPTER TWENTY-TWO

We all watched The Matrix the next night—for our own individual reasons. I'd seen the movie more times than I could remember and was looking for a mindless diversion while I waited to see if there would be retaliation from the recent hit on Malokin's men. Luck would do anything that avoided being in the room she shared with Mother. I swore Mother was just there to annoy Luck. The Jinxes thought Neo was almost as cool as Fate and Murphy—well, he just went along with the plans usually.

When the doorbell chimed, every head popped up. People came and went constantly now. The only oddity about getting company was who would bother to ring before entering?

Fate rose and headed over to the door as if he'd expected guests.

"Hey, good to see you. Come on in," Fate said to someone still out of sight.

"Thanks!"

No, that couldn't be who I thought it was. Then he stepped in and I saw him with my own eyes. Cupid, dressed in his signature silk, a Louie Vuitton suitcase on wheels trailing behind him.

I stopped chewing mid-popcorn bite and looked around the room, gauging everyone's reaction. I couldn't be the only one freaked out about living with Cupid. When I hadn't seen him recently, I'd figured he had some cloud to go hang out on. When he hadn't made the meeting, I figured said cloud was a bitch of a commute. Not so lucky.

Taking in the expressions, it looked like we were all frozen in a moment of silent panic. The only thing keeping me in my seat was Fate's warm greeting. He'd known he was coming. What was this about?

Fate stood next to him—not just close to him but he actually patted him on the back. "Cupid is going to be staying with us. He's promised to be on his very best behavior."

Cupid couldn't have looked happier about it. So much so, I felt a twinge of guilt over the fact that I was fighting tooth and nail to not run from the room.

All of us tried to utter greetings in varying degrees of forced enthusiasm while keeping our distance. Knox, poor shmuck, rose and went to greet Cupid and shook his hand. Clearly no one had bothered to warn him.

While Cupid was distracted by Knox, and everyone else was distracted by Cupid, I got up, and this time it was me grabbing Fate's arm and dragging him behind me. I didn't stop until I got into the bedroom and shut the door behind us.

"What are you doing?" I nailed him with the question before the lock clicked into place. I waited for his answer even though I had my own suspicions. Fate had declared war on my libido. He'd said no more messing around, and this had to be part of his master plan. Cupid was full proof. He could get a girl in bed quicker than a bottle of tequila and Brad Pitt on bended knee.

He relaxed back against the dresser, not a hair out of place. "He needed somewhere to stay."

"And he couldn't stay with his people? Those little flying cherubs couldn't whisk him away to safety somewhere?"

"He wanted to feel included."

Yes, that was the Fate I knew. So worried about people feeling like they were part of the gang. I was having a hard time not choking on the bull he was spewing. "I will not stay here with him."

"You can't leave. You made a deal." Fate plopped down on the bed as if he were preparing to take a nap.

"I didn't agree to stay here with him."

"Then tell him to leave." He stretched out his arms and tucked them behind his head and then had the nerve to yawn.

"You invited him here to..."

"To what?"

"Why me? Can't you find someone else to sleep with to amuse yourself?" Someone that wouldn't be torn apart when you moved on from her.

"Because I don't want anyone else."

If he had just stopped speaking then, I might have grabbed on to him with both hands and thrown caution to the wind, but he didn't.

"I want to amuse myself with you."

All the warm and fuzzy feelings from a moment ago were now cold, wet and soggy. I'd gone from warm plush teddy bear kind of feelings to something you found at the curb, discarded after a flood.

"Where are you going?" he asked.

"I'm going to go ask Cupid to stay somewhere else."

"Really? You're going to tell Cupid to go?" He acted like I'd said I was going to get the Jinxes to stop drinking. Then he started laughing.

"Yes. In the nicest way possible, I'm going to explain that due to his past behavior, it isn't a comfortable situation."

He got up from the bed and walked toward the door. I thought he was going to try and stop me but he opened it and took a step back. "It'll never happen. That southern girl is going to rear her polite little head, but I can't wait to watch you try."

"You'll see."

"Please, I'm dying to."

It took me a minute or two to track Cupid down in Fate's office, while Fate himself dogged my steps. The door was ajar when I got there. The furniture had been moved to the side and an air mattress was in the middle.

I was still nervous about getting too close but this had to be done. I could do this and be uncomfortable for a few minutes, or not and be waiting for a sex bomb to blow at any moment.

I tapped on the wood of the open door as I watched him unpacking his clothes onto a freestanding rack along the back wall. "Cupid? Do you have a minute?"

"For my favorite couple? Of course I do! Come in," he said, smiling a hundred-watt smile and waving us both in. "Sit!"

I took the office chair and Fate perched a hip by my side.

"Cupid—"

"Please," he held up his hands, "before you speak, I have to get something off my chest."

I nodded, hoping it had something to do with how he wouldn't be able to stay long.

"When Fate asked me to come here, I can't tell you how happy I was. My job, well, it hasn't always made me the most popular. There have been many a night I've lain awake, pining to be one of the *gang*. To now have you embrace me, along with Fate, it really means the universe to me." He laid a manicured hand above his heart.

I was torn between wanting to ask him where he was still able to get his nails done or what exactly had Fate told him. This was going to be trickier than I'd initially thought. Still, if I dug deep, I had the social graces buried somewhere inside that would be able to pull this off without him being completely insulted.

"Cupid... I—"

"You know, I really thought after that last little nudge I gave the two of you that you were very upset with me. I only did it because I felt it was for the best. I'm so thrilled you aren't holding a grudge."

"I... You know, um... " My words died and I forced a smile onto my lips. Looked like I was going to use those southern manners to go down gracefully instead.

I felt Fate's hand land on my shoulder. "She's trying to say she's so happy you're here, too."

I let out a long sigh and then agreed; all the while my brain was silently screaming *shit, shit, shit* in my head.

CHAPTER TWENTY-THREE

"Are you sure it was safe to come by yourself?" Kitty asked as I sat beside her on the couch. A large throw with the image of a cat, which went with the rest of her décor, lay over her legs. I knew her legs were still weak from when Malokin had broken them. The reminder of her torture, some of which I'd witnessed firsthand, was one of many that still haunted me from the time Kitty had been held hostage. She still seemed hesitant to stand even though there was a healthy looking flush to her skin.

"Yes, it's fine." I peeked out her back window and saw Paddy rummaging through her garden and hitting her tomato plants with his cane. When he'd stopped by for coffee this morning, I'd told him he owed me after the meeting the other day. He'd agreed to come but preferred to remain outside and unseen. I could understand all that but I wasn't sure what was so offensive about the red fruit.

"Sorry I haven't been by that much lately." I could fool myself by thinking there hadn't been time. It wasn't like I couldn't find a rational excuse, with the world was going to hell. No one would think twice about it and Kitty wasn't one of those people who looked for hand holding.

The truth was I'd been avoiding this visit. She had suffered greatly, still bearing the emotional and physical wounds, while I'd floundered. I was ashamed that she had gone through so much because of me. Logically I understood Malokin was the one who carried the blame, but emotions didn't work in a logical way. I'd finally gotten her out of there but not before she'd paid the price for both of us, and now I was paying my share in guilt.

She didn't speak about what she had been though. There were large slots of time that were unaccounted for and probably always would be. That's how, even if I hadn't seen any of it, I still would've known how bad it had been. Some pain went too deeply to speak of.

"How are you doing?" I asked as I petted one of the many black cats roaming her house.

"It's been so nice seeing the guys again." She smiled toward the back of the house, where Bic was putting groceries in her refrigerator, before she looked back to me and redirected the topic away from her. "How's it going with you?"

"Pretty good," I lied, not wanting to dump anything else on her plate.

She snorted loudly. "That's not what I hear. Your fights with Fate are like the daily soaps these days.

"You're two of a kind, stubborn as all hell. That can be good or bad. It's easier with two different types of people, when one is soft where the other is hard. You don't have the clashes, the constant blows.

"But you two? No. You won't come together easy. You knock into the other, setting off sparks with each collision. But eventually, after you've knocked and rubbed away all the hard edges, you'll come together stronger for it."

"We aren't coming together," I said, sipping my tea.

Her eyes rolled. "Yeah, I heard you were in denial too. Don't worry, I wasn't planning on harassing you today. I had something else I wanted to talk to you about. That Knox boy came by. He's not a bad sort, and he's agreed to put me in for early retirement."

"You're leaving?" I understood the desire and shouldn't have been surprised but I was.

"It's been a long road and I think it's time to call it quits. It's just…" Her voice died off as I watched her eyes fill with memories.

"Different now," I said, finishing her sentence.

She nodded. "Bernie is going to watch after the cats until they get my replacement."

"When?" I didn't realize I'd grabbed her hand and was squeezing it until she squeezed back.

"As soon as I say all my goodbyes."

My smile was weak. As much as I tried to muster up how good it would be for her to move on, the words didn't want to come out.

"Sometimes endings are good," she said, patting my hand.

"Do you know where you're going to end up?" I'd heard stories of reincarnation that ranged from Indian princesses to Hollywood stars but I had a feeling that wouldn't be Kitty's path.

"Nothing grand." Her eyes looked skyward and a look of whimsy appeared. "Maybe a florist. I think I want bright beautiful colors around me all the time, even in the winter when it's the bleakest."

"Will I see you again?"

She smiled. "I'd bet on it. Just maybe in another life."

***

My step was heavier when I walked out of Kitty's house, knowing that I'd probably never see her again. As much as I wanted to be happy for her, I couldn't help but mourn her already.

"Paddy, thanks for coming with me today," I said, as he came around from the side of the house.

"I was in the mood for some fresh air." He took a breath so deep I could see his chest rise dramatically. "By the way, she'll be okay," he said as he exhaled slowly.

The pain hit without warning. I gripped the railing on the second set of stairs that led to the sidewalk in front of Kitty's house, my hip on fire. The metal was hard in my hand as I squeezed, waiting for it to subside.

One of the most intense bouts I'd had, it finally started to abate after almost a minute of pure agony. My lungs were able to expand. I looked over at Paddy, dreading the questions he was sure to have.

Paddy wasn't there anymore, or not a Paddy I recognized. A handsome male in his prime stood in his place, almost angelic in his fairness and beautiful features. Even his eyes squinted shut and his compressed lips didn't detract from his beauty.

Then he was gone and the Paddy I knew was next to me again, looking much more frazzled than he had this morning. His eyes shot to where my hand had unconsciously come to rest over the area of my tattoo. There was something about his expression that made me uncomfortable, but I brushed it off due to the recent pain.

"How long?" he asked.

"A few weeks, give or take. You?" I asked, afraid I'd know what the answer would be but having no clue what it meant.

"Same."

"Sharp pain?"

He shook his head but didn't offer a description of what he felt. I took the hint and moved on to my next question.

"Do you know why it's happening?"

"No. Like I said, when I gave you a piece of me, it was a first."

We stood silently for a minute before I suggested we leave. The walk to the car was as quiet as the ride, and my unease in his presence was slowly gathering steam.

I wasn't sure if the awkwardness was created by him, me or both of us. It might have been that I'd seen Paddy for who he really was. Somehow knowing him as one of them, in such a tangible way, and not the old man I'd come to know, made him more alarming.

Paddy disappeared a block before I pulled up in front of Fate's, the only thing he'd said before vanishing repeating itself in my head as I sat there for a moment before getting out.

"When they don't understand why I would choose the form of an old man, this is what I tell them. Most don't see the old, they don't stop and stare and say, 'Who's that?' They hold the door for them and help them on their way. Why? Because the old aren't a threat. They're just something to be pitied. But it is the young who deserve the pity, for they have no clue what is heading their way."

And then he was gone.

CHAPTER TWENTY-FOUR

I'd been lying on our bed as I tried to convince myself that the pain I'd been feeling was nothing. That Paddy, or whoever that thing was, feeling unwell at the same time was merely a coincidence. After all, it didn't hurt right now. It was simply growing pains.

But still, it might be time to voice my concerns.

The bedroom door swung open and Fate, the man I needed to talk to, was standing in the threshold looking like he'd just shot a Givenchy print ad. Black suit, black shirt and sunglasses; you had to wonder what it would be like to walk around the Earth looking that perfect.

"Where are you heading?" I asked, once I remembered not to stare and then took another several seconds forcing my eyes to stop doing exactly that.

"Where are *we* heading." He laid a garment bag down beside me on the bed where I'd been hiding, or for appearances' sake, pretending to read a book. "We need to meet an old acquaintance of mine. Put this on."

"I've got clothes."

He shook his head. "Not the kind you need."

"Who cares what I wear?" I asked as I sat up, eyeing the bag and wondering what delicious outfit lay inside while pretending I didn't care. Fate had good taste, maybe even great. Whatever was in there was probably really pretty.

"The people at the place we're going, they'll be insulted and less likely to help if you aren't dressed to a certain standard."

"Who are they?" I asked as my fingers ran over the garment bag. Fate didn't run fools' errands and he definitely never cared what anyone wanted. The fact that he'd just supplied me with a dress for this? It was important.

"Some old acquaintances. People you'll want to meet. Be ready in thirty minutes." He turned and left.

Old acquaintances. It was hard not to be curious. I was fairly certain old to Fate didn't mean something as frivolous as twenty or thirty years.

A piece of Fate's past hovering within reach?

I unzipped the bag as soon as he left the room and only because he walked quickly was I even able to wait that long. Once I'd decided to go I couldn't wait to see what pretty things I was getting to play dress up in.

I looked down at the dress that was now fully out of the bag. There was nothing I could outright complain about. It wasn't ridiculously low cut or short in the hem. It was only that I knew what it would look like on. I wasn't built the way I used to be. This new body had come with some curves that my self-esteem didn't quite know what to do with yet.

I looked at the clock and knew I had to get moving.

I stripped off my shorts and t-shirt and the fabric of the new dress practically slithered over my skin. I didn't need to look in a mirror to know it was clinging to every nook, hollow and curve I had.

Solid black, and with a hem just shy of indecent, it had a high neck but it clung to the point that cleavage wasn't necessary. My low-heeled sandals looked ridiculous so I swapped them out for a pair of strappy heels I hadn't been able to resist at the boutique.

I threw on some make up, ran a brush through my dark hair until it was lying in some semblance of thick waves around my shoulders and then hesitated. I wanted to look good but I didn't want to look like I'd *tried* to look good.

The house was quiet a half hour later when I stepped out of the bedroom, somewhere in between natural and glam girl. Fate was standing by the glass doors, staring out at the ocean. His arm rested above his head and his back was to me.

"Where is everyone?" I asked, as I click-clacked into the silent room and stopped by the couch. Fate hadn't moved yet.

"Everyone went scouting for more pop-up armories or a lead on Malokin's base. The Jinxes are on the roof keeping watch," he answered.

He hadn't bothered turning around yet, which made me feel slightly lighter and took the edge off. I'd been getting ready as if this had been a date but it wasn't. The tension eased from my shoulders and I walked over to the bar and poured myself a drink.

"Who are we going to meet? You didn't tell me."

"Some old…" I heard Fate start to say before his words trailed off.

"Some old?" I took a sip and turned, glass in hand and nearly choked on the whiskey.

His arm still rested on the door but his face was turned toward me. Sometimes I thought I imagined the amount of heat this man could generate until I saw it again. His arm dropped and his eyes took in every bit of me. He started toward me, and I wasn't sure what he was going to do once he reached me but I had hopes.

And then he stopped halfway and I had to force my legs not to close the gap.

"We have to make dinner," he said and the heat I'd seen written all over him seemed to be retreating, or was at least being held in check.

"I'm ready." My voice came out breathier than normal, and my lips felt incredibly dry as I stood there, wondering what might have happened if he hadn't pulled back at the last moment.

"So am I but we have to go anyway." He was back under control again and closing the final distance between us.

His hand went to the small of my back and the pressure there brought me closer, just shy of full contact with him. We could all be gone next month, next week, or maybe even tomorrow. Why was I avoiding this?

I tilted my head back as my lips parted.

"Don't do this to me right now," he said, his voice much deeper and softer than normal.

"Do what?" I asked, and I couldn't stop thinking about what it would feel like if he took me right now.

His lips closed over mine. His hands cupped my ass, dragging me against him and showing me just how ready he still was. And then he was pulling my arms down from where I'd wrapped them around his neck.

"If it was any time but tonight," he said, with a deep timbre pulling away and taking a few steps back. "Stop looking at me like that or we won't make it anywhere." He motioned toward the beach. "I ordered a door. We should go."

After a slight hesitation he started heading toward the back of the house, which would lead us to the beach. I looked out and beyond him to see the door starting to glitter in the distance, along with the guards on either side.

The sight of the doors drove the hormones from my brain like a broom to a cobweb. "Oh no." I took off in the direction of the kitchen and started frantically opening the lower cabinets.

"What are you doing?" he said. "We've got to go."

"Don't you have any metal polish?" I asked, digging out every bottle he had and dumping them on the floor.

"I don't know. I've always had a crew that came in and did everything up until they all went crazy."

I groaned and loudly. "This is very bad."

"Is this about the guards? They aren't going to care." He stood at the end of the kitchen, looking at me as if *I* were mentally deranged.

"Oh yes, they are. I might get relegated back to swamps if I see them empty handed after all these weeks." I got to my feet, scanning the kitchen for any other possible offering. "Towels, at least let me take them towels," I rushed past him to the hall closet.

Fate watched, leaning on the breakfast bar as I moved around in a panic. "They barely talk, and they only started that when you came around. I think you're putting too much thought into this."

"You know, for being the almighty Fate, who's lived forever, sometimes you seem scarily like every other male I've known in my human life."

His hands went to hips as his chin took on a stubborn tilt. "We don't have time for this silly stuff."

I grabbed half the stack of towels he owned and motioned for him to precede to the beach, all the while hoping for the best. There I was, heels sinking into the sand and barely able to see over the heap of towels, as we headed toward the door.

I knew it was going to be bad as soon as I approached by the way I could see their heads turn away from me as we got close.

It was worse than I'd expected.

The visor slot of one helmet head shot to my hands, full of towels but devoid of polish, and turned back quickly.

"I brought you rags." I held my hands out towards

241

them, half a stack of designer towels in each. They took the offering while Fate grumbled something about them costing a lot more than "rags" would have.

And then I waited. Their heads swiveled to my hands again, as if trying to find polish that might have been concealed beneath, and my palms grew sweaty. I took a breath and decided to get it over with quickly.

"I don't have any." They turned their backs on me before I got the entire sentence out but I kept going. "I'm sorry. I wasn't prepared for this trip. I know I haven't seen you guys in a while but it's not like we've been doing many jobs and—"

"You're rambling and they aren't listening," Fate said as he rocked back on his heels.

He was wrong. They were listening. They were just pretending to ignore me. "I promise, I will get you polish this week."

Guard on the Right's head turned back to me by a millimeter. He was the softy of the two.

"Come on, guys, don't be like this. I swear, I will get you polish."

Guard on the left turned the teeniest bit and then looked away again, rethinking his action.

"I'll get the really good stuff I said was too expensive to buy." I watched and waited. Nothing. "I'll make Fate buy you an entire case," I threw out desperately.

"Where am I going to get a—"

I shushed Fate violently and gave him the eye.

"Fine. I'll get a case…somewhere," he said loudly.

Finally, they both turned back to me. They gave curt little nods I interpreted to mean I was on probation.

"Thank you! I will come through for you! Or more accurately, I'll make him come through for you, but it will happen."

They looked at each other and in unison, turned forward and nodded a bit more enthusiastically, or as much as a suit of armor could.

We walked through the door and I was thrilled to not step out into a swamp.

"You have the oddest relationship with them I've ever seen," Fate said as he followed me through.

My eyes adjusted quickly as we went from the beach in full daylight to starry skies on a cliff overlooking the ocean. A pavilion stood twenty feet away, which held several very long tables, all with people seated at them. There were several smaller ones as well but one particular table closest to the cliff, where a single man sat alone, caught my attention.

"Where are we?"

"An uninhabited isle off the coast of Greece."

"Who are the people?"

"Those are the Greek gods."

Slowly, one by one, heads swiveled in our direction and nerves started to burst within me, exploding with each new stare.

"I'm not sure I'm ready to meet gods."

"You're Karma. Don't forget that. It's a pretty potent position. They won't mess with you." Fate's hand came to rest reassuringly on the small of my back as we made our way through the crowd, each god looking more beautiful than the last.

"What are they doing here? Is this some sort of god party?" I whispered, relieved that I'd worn the nice dress.

"They gather here once a year under the last full moon of spring. That's Zeus, in the corner in the tuxedo, getting a glass of champagne from the waitress." He motioned to the gorgeous woman sitting next to him. "That's Hera, his wife. They've got a complicated relationship. Fight constantly but looks like a good night though." He urged me with his hand toward the table where the man was seated by himself. "And that's who we're here to see."

"Who is it?" I smoothed my dress down and ran a hand through my hair.

"Ares, God of War and Violence."

"Ahhh, good call." If there were anyone who might know about Malokin, it would be someone with the same goals and motivations. "How do you know him and the other gods?"

"Hang around long enough, you tend to rub elbows with all sorts."

Ares rose from the white linen table he sat at as Fate pulled out a chair for me.

"Ares, this is Karma."

"A pleasure to meet you." He smiled and then leaned over my hand and brushed a kiss across the knuckles. I would've thought he'd be instantly dislikeable. He was violence and war, and he had dark good looks that seemed to suit his position perfectly. He also had this charisma that was pouring off him effortlessly. It was the way he smiled, but just slightly, and the way his eyes narrowed as if he knew just what I was thinking and agreed with every thought.

Yeah, I confess, I liked the God of War. I'd done worse things in my life.

"She's just as you described," Ares said, still looking at me.

My eyes shot to Fate, who had taken a seat and was staring off at the horizon as if Ares hadn't outed him. I would've loved to have heard those comments. I was positive he must have included the word transfer in there a few times.

A waitress in a flimsy white slip dress came by and placed two glasses of champagne in front of Fate and me. When I would've reached for the glass, Fate's hand came and rested on mine, as if to casually hold hands. My eyes shot to his as he looked at the glass and then back to me.

"Kill joy." Ares said before he raised his own glass and took a healthy sip.

"After that lost year in the crusades, I find it better to abstain," Fate said. "What do you know of the person I was inquiring about?"

"I know he's stepping on my toes and that he shouldn't be here. He shouldn't exist at all." The true potential of Ares poked its head out as he spoke and I could literally feel the violence churning in the air around me. A sheen of sweat started to coat my skin.

"There's always been some overlap, here and there. You know this well yourself as you've occasionally had to make your way into our domain and have stepped on Moirai's toes, you both handling fate. But this one, he has no couth, no manners. And he's a glutton. No thought for balance and yet he moves about in my territory as if he has every right. I want him gone." His fist slammed into the table we were seated at, leaving a burn mark in its wake.

The only thing that kept me in my seat was Fate's relaxed demeanor, as he was still reclined in his own.

"But did you come up with anything to help us?" Fate asked.

"No." Ares stood abruptly, barely containing the anger boiling and swirling around him. "But I want him gone."

"Then give us something we can work with." Fate rose as well, and that was the only cue I needed to leave.

"Don't you think I'm trying?"

I dipped my head, thinking this felt awfully familiar. Another god having a temper tantrum in less than a week? I'd either been created at a bad time or these folks needed some anger management classes.

"Try harder," Fate continued. "Let me know if you get anything."

Fated moved to leave and I didn't need a signal to join him. The waves of anger swirling around Ares were getting stronger by the second as we headed toward the doors that had remained open and waiting.

This obviously was not Ares's first meltdown.

"Now what?"

"I know a great restaurant over in Mykonos. You hungry?"

CHAPTER TWENTY-FIVE

We didn't get back to the house until after eleven p.m. and a couple of bottles of wine. I walked in the bedroom and dropped my heels to the floor while a wine buzz still clung just enough to lower my inhibitions to the other side of not caring.

I didn't know what this was between us and I didn't care anymore. It wasn't the time for logic and rules. Everything else was going crazy, why did I have to hold myself to a higher standard? It was time to feel, not think, and that's what I was going to do.

Stopping in the middle of the room, I turned towards Fate. My fingers went to the shoulders of my dress and tugged them down while he stood there watching me. Another pull and I had it stripped down past the lacy black bra and panties I'd chosen to wear today because, from the moment I'd seen him earlier, part of me had known it would end like this.

His hands were on me as my dress was falling in a

pool at my feet. His lips came to mine, greedily taking what was offered. My hands reached up over his shoulders, pushing his jacket down. His clothes were shed until the heat of his bare torso was melding with mine. He grabbed a thigh in each hand and hoisted me up effortlessly as I wrapped my legs around him.

His tongue sparred with mine and I could feel the change instantly. When Fate did something—anything—he didn't hold back.

I fell backward onto the bed with him landing on top of me, fitting in between my legs. The rest of his clothes were shed in between kisses and love bites and then I had nothing but his hard flesh pressing me into the mattress.

I locked my legs around him, urging him inside me.

"Not yet. Not again. This time we're taking it slow, even if it fucking kills me," but his voice sounded as pained as I felt frustrated.

I gripped his head in my hands. "I want to feel you in me. Now." And I did. I was almost crazed with the need to have him joined to me.

He let out a low groan as if my request had completely undone him.

"Get on your knees," he said and then flipped me over before I could comply.

And then he was pressing into me from behind, a hand on my shoulder holding me in place as he thrust forward. His penis pulled out almost completely before thrusting deeply back in. I arched into him, urging him to pick up his speed as I lost myself to the moment.

He was growling as he pressed into me before we were collapsing on the bed. We fell apart and there was something heavy in the silence that followed which had me looking at him. He didn't appear very happy. It's not that I expected him to jump up and down or spring into cartwheels but I wasn't expecting a pissed off expression either.

My hand trailed down his chest. "What's wrong?"

He turned and leaned over me with his weight resting on his arms. Staring down at me, his eyes narrowed. "I'm not the problem. What's wrong with you?"

"Nothing," I said, definitely not wanting to talk. Talking could lead to thinking, and I didn't want to do that. I was tired of thinking. I raised my fingers to curl into his hair, trying to tug his head down and bring his lips to mine as a distraction. He initially obliged but then pulled back against the pressure of my hand.

He grabbed my wrist and pressed it to the bed, not cooperating with my demand.

"You're even kissing differently." It was an accusation.

"So what? Maybe it seems different because of Cupid's spell."

"No. There's something wrong but that's not it. Both of those times you were here with me." He leaned back further. "I don't know what this is."

He leaned down and I thought he was going to drop it but instead of our lips touching, he leaned his forehead against mine. He let out a groan that sounded almost painful before he pushed off of me.

My jaw dropped open. "Didn't you tell me recently you were going to get me in bed by hook or by crook? Well, you got me in bed and now you're complaining?"

He didn't answer in words but made more growling sounds that I decided to interpret as an insult.

"I've thrown up my hands and said what the hell, why not, and you're still not happy?"

"'What the hell. Why. Not.'" Each word was repeated crisply.

"Yes, exactly." I stared at him in disbelief as he walked across the room as if he wanted distance from me.

He sighed and then that turned into a growling sound of sorts too. When that was finally over, he still wasn't done and let out a string of curses.

"Where are you going?" I watched as his back retreated toward the adjoining bathroom.

"Shower."

"You've got to be kidding me." I put my fist over my mouth to hold back from screaming.

"Nope." His lips popping on the P as he pronounced it.

"Why?"

"Because you gave me the wrong answer."

"Do you normally quiz women when you sleep with them or am I just special?"

"Just you." Each word was coming out of a clenched jaw as if he were as annoyed as I was.

"This is ridiculous. You're really going to go take a

shower?"

He stopped and moved closer and for a second my heart flared as I thought perhaps he was coming to his senses and would stop making such a big deal out of this.

He stopped short of me and ruined it by starting to talk again.

"I think tonight was all about having a warm body."

"And what would be so horrible about that?"

"Because right now I'm wondering if it could've been Knox in here and you'd have acted the same way."

"I can't believe you just said that." I yanked the blanket over me.

"Yeah, well, I'm pissed off that I give a shit too but I do. When I fuck you, I want you to know it's me, I want you to need *me* there with the very core of your being, clinging to me as if you'd die without it. I want it to be raw and real. Hell, even when Cupid was involved, at least I knew it was about us and not because I happened to be there when you were having a bad week." He straightened and starting walking toward the bathroom.

"Maybe if you hadn't been such a dick the first couple times I wouldn't be like this," I yelled at his retreating back, not caring if the whole house heard me.

He slammed the door.

He dumped me twice, and I was still willing to sleep with him and it wasn't good enough? I flopped back down on the bed. Why did everything in life have to be so goddamn complicated these days?

CHAPTER TWENTY-SIX

Fate wasn't in bed when I got up the next morning and I was glad of it. The morning after rejection might be even more uncomfortable than the morning after a good cuddle. What was most annoying was he walked out just as I thought we were warming up. I finally slept with him and got cut off for the effort. Last night was like having one spoonful of ice cream. I know there's people out there who have that kind of restraint but I wasn't feeling like one of them. Things were getting ugly. I needed some comfort and I was gearing up for a binge on it.

Cupid was standing at the counter in the kitchen as I shuffled in, looking for coffee. I paused beside him and poured myself a cup. Leaning against the cabinets, I took in his silk pajamas and suave ways. Maybe I should have a little chat with Cupid. He did have his uses, after all.

I measured his mood and angled myself in front of the nearest exit. He tried to smile at me but the corners of his lips were struggling to keep an upraised position. How the roles had changed. It wasn't long ago that I was running from the room from him. Now look at me, blocking his path.

I smiled, sipping my coffee, watching him watch me. Small talk, that was a good start. "So, how have you been?"

"Good. And you?" His eyes narrowed in contrast to the warmth of his tone but he always had a voice that sounded like he'd just had sex.

"Same. Thanks."

His lips started to twitch under the strain before he finally gave up the fight and dropped the hammer. "No."

Now he said no? Oh, I didn't think so. I grabbed the coffee pot and topped of his mug for him. "No?" I asked, playing dumb.

"Yes," he said.

"Wait, no or yes?" Life was so confusing when you didn't actually ever say anything. How had I come to this place? This no man's land of non-speaking?

"Yes, I said no, I will not do it." His chin went up.

He was going to act like he was above it all? Now? After all the stunts he'd pulled and two more notches on his belt? No, he wasn't getting away with that. Or he wouldn't if I was willing to admit what I wanted. That was still up for debate.

"Do what?" I added a healthy shrug of indifference to the end of the question, just in case he wasn't clear on my nonchalance.

"Let *me*, let *you*, in on a little secret." He leaned in

close, as if to impart a world secret. "I know when someone wants someone else. It's my gig."

I scowled, pretending complete ignorance as I took another sip of coffee. I wanted this accomplished but in such a way as to still give me deniability. "I really don't know what you're talking about."

He kept smiling as he leaned closer. "I wouldn't do it for him. I'm not doing it for you. I say when and how. I'm Cupid. No one tells me when to do my thing but me," he rattled on as he went to the fridge, needing more milk.

"He tried to get you to spell me?" He'd said he was going to play dirty but I was still surprised to find out he'd asked.

His eyebrows rose and he put a hand over his mouth as he made a fake gasp of surprise. "I don't know. Is what you're doing considered asking?"

"I'm not asking you to do anything but if I were to ask something, or perhaps you just gathered a certain feeling, I would think you would do whatever you could for me since you owe me. And, of course, you gave me that whole spiel about being part of the gang? Gangs help out other gang members." I rethought that sentence really quickly in my mind. *Nope, nothing outright incriminating.*

"And here you are, asking for me to wrong you again."

"If you hadn't screwed with me, I might not even be interested in…certain things."

Cupid laughed so hard, he started choking on his

last sip. I watched as he walked over and had to spit out his mouthful of coffee into the sink. When he finally got his breath back, he turned and said, "Darling, you wanted him even when you hated him. Please, don't try that bullshit on me. And what you're doing makes absolutely no sense. If you both want it, and know you want it, what do you need me for? Just go at it already." He stopped speaking as Luck sashayed into the kitchen in her sheer robe, negligee and furry heeled slippers before he continued, "This one can surely help you out with how to get things started. Unless that's not the problem?" The corner of his mouth went up with ease now.

"Help with what? What are you all talking about?" she asked with full red lips. If it were anyone else, I would think the morning appearance had more to do with having company but not with Luck. She never completely turned off the sex bomb.

"Nothing."

Cupid pulled Luck over to him with an arm around her shoulders. My coworker, who would've run screaming from him a week ago, went willingly into his embrace simply because of the prospect of gossip.

"Karma wants to bang Fate but I think he's playing hard to get. Now, she's trying to get me—"

"Pure speculation," I said, breaking his sentence.

The interruption bought me all of a micro pause while they looked at me strangely with squinted eyes and then Cupid resumed. "She wants some of my mojo."

"You people are the absolute worst." I couldn't

even muster up enough emotion to yell anymore, just turned to pour some more coffee.

"Well, this is an interesting turn of events," Luck said to Cupid, as I lifted the lid off the sugar bowl and scrapped out the last half teaspoon.

No more sugar? I couldn't drink my coffee like that and I needed it badly. One person could only take so many insults in a small period of time.

I pulled open a cabinet above me where I hoped to find some more, while Luck and Cupid continued to discuss my situation.

"So he wants her but doesn't want her. But, wants her again but now he won't do it even though he does? I'm so confused," Luck said.

"No more than them," Cupid replied.

They both broke out laughing while I searched some more cabinets for much-needed sugar.

Skateboards skidded across the hardwood floors, surely leaving marks, and the Jinxes strolled in.

"What are the hooker and the love bus laughing about?" Bobby asked.

"Goddamn heathens! Who finished the coffee and didn't put on a new pot!" Billy started shouting.

For once I was happy about their big mouths and the opportunity to change the subject.

"Make a single cup." I pointed to a Keurig machine off to the side.

"I know you're still fairly new and shit, but I only drink *that* blend." His little finger tapped on a bag of gourmet grinds with a local coffee house sticker.

"Why are there skid marks across my floor?" Fate asked from the doorway since there was no room left to actually enter the kitchen.

Three blond heads dodged out of the kitchen, presumably to avoid taking responsibility for the marks on the floor. They were followed by Luck and Cupid who appeared to want to gossip in private for a change.

Fate walked in, reached above the cabinet over the fridge and pulled out a large bag of sugar, which he plunked down next to the empty bowl, sitting lidless. He grabbed a coffee mug of his own, his side brushing mine as he made himself a single cup and then leaned a hip against the counter.

"There's more bags in there." He tilted his head toward the cabinet he'd just opened.

"Thanks," I said and then waited to see if he would bring up the subject of last night because I certainly wasn't going to.

After a couple more sips I determined that would be a *no* on both fronts.

"Where did you get all the sugar?" I asked, partly out of curiosity, since I hadn't seen any in the stores recently, and partly to fill the horrible silence that had my fingers twitching.

"I stocked up a couple weeks ago," he said.

My spoon stopped swirling mid stroke. "You did? On sugar?"

He raised his eyebrows and made a face toward my coffee.

"But how did you know I took my coffee so

sweet?"

He shrugged. "It was a guess."

"Based on what?"

"You've never seemed to be able to beat that sweet tooth."

"I never fought it so why would I have beaten it?"

"You've tried in the past."

"When?"

"Not in your last life but many times before that."

"Did you have jobs with me in the past? With my fate? Is that how you know so much stuff about me?"

All of a sudden Fate wasn't leaning. "Some."

Murphy walked into the kitchen and coughed, the word "Bullshit," was barely disguised by his ruse.

"Murphy, I heard Bernie might need some help with the cats. Hear anything about that?" Fate asked, his eyes narrowing.

Murphy's jaw dropped a bit and then he finally replied, "Not a word."

Fate nodded, patted Murphy on the back and left the kitchen.

The second he was out of earshot I rounded on Murphy. "What did you mean, Bullshit? Fate didn't have jobs with me? Spill the beans."

He rapidly shook his head. "I was just coughing."

"No you weren't."

"Karma, do you know what cats do to me? I sneeze, my eyes water and itch. They make me wish I were dead." He sighed like someone truly exhausted or desperate and his eyes silently pleaded.

"Okay," I said and took my coffee to drink on the deck while I pouted. What kind of lame immortals are we to be taken down by some cat dander?

CHAPTER TWENTY-SEVEN

Later that morning, I leaned against the doorframe of Fate's office, which he was now sharing with Cupid, the air mattress sitting deflated in the corner. He was bent over some papers, an elbow on his desk and fingers at his temple.

He looked up and I saw his face soften. I'd gotten used to that, the way he looked at me differently from anyone else, as if I were special. I'd thought perhaps it would've stopped after last night, but it was still there, at least for a bit longer anyway. I wasn't sure what I'd do the day he stopped but I pushed away the thought. I had a purpose today and meant to accomplish it.

I tucked my hands in my jeans and glanced down at the floor for a second before I spat it out. "I need a favor."

He nodded, giving me his full attention. I walked in and shut the door.

"It's about Charlie." My tongue nearly tripped over

having to mention Charlie to Fate, knowing he'd never cared for him and not sure of the reception of my request.

"Your Charlie?" His eyes lost their softness.

I nodded, not feeling comfortable with the word "your" preceding anything to do with him, especially when he was so clearly anything but that.

"I'd like to get him and his new fiancée somewhere safe. You know, like you did with my parents? Once this situation calms down, if it does that is, I'm going to talk to…" I stalled on Knox's name. "I'm going to ask for a raise so I'll be able to start repaying you."

"Forget about the cost. Tell me why you want him gone?" He leaned back and rested his head on the seat, the picture of relaxation except nothing about this line of questioning made me feel calm. I had to turn on my courtroom skills to keep from fidgeting.

"Because even if I'm not with him, I still want him to be safe. It's not as if I suddenly can turn off all emotions simply because it's over." I walked about the room and fiddled with the plantation shades so I didn't have to meet his unflinching stare.

"You still love him?"

"I'm not *in love* with him, but yes, in a way, I'll always love him."

He nodded. "I'll handle it this afternoon."

The mood in the room shifted slightly and the tension in my shoulders eased, the air coming into my lungs a little easier. I walked back to the door but paused before I left. "I'd like to be privy to the details."

"You'll have to stay in the background. Even with everything the way it is, that might still be a problem."

"Understood."

***

Fate and I pulled up to a clinic in the middle of Myrtle Beach at two p.m. that afternoon. It looked like a makeshift emergency medical center that had been thrown up quickly in a closed down storefront. I'd heard of places like this and wasn't surprised that Charlie would be running one. That was the epitome of who he was.

From where we were parked across the street, I could see her, his new fiancée, helping out with the line of patients visible through the glass front. And then there was Charlie, appearing from the back room with his white jacket. The place was busy but he was still smiling like always. It had been one of the things I'd loved about him and still did, his easy smile.

"How did you know he was here?" I asked.

"His destiny has been on my radar for a while. There's a remote island in the Pacific that he was going to do some pro bono work in a year or so. I checked it out and that area seems less affected than most places. It was a fairly easy tweak to push the trip up earlier." I felt Fate's eyes on me, not Charlie, as he spoke.

"Was it always going to be her going with him?"

"I don't know that," he said but I expected that to be a lie.

I watched as Charlie stopped to look at a file she was holding, his hand coming to rest on her back. He couldn't resist touching her in some small way when she was nearby. The only thing that surprised me about today was it didn't hurt as badly as I thought it would. I knew why I'd come.

The feelings had been fading for a while. The thoughts of him coming less and less until recently, days would go by without him popping into my mind at all. But still, I'd needed to see him one last time. I'd clung to what might have been so firmly that I'd needed this goodbye, even one sided as it was. I'd needed to see them so I could wish him well, let him go and close the book on that part of my life for good. It felt more akin to losing a dear friend than a soul mate.

I was okay.

"Do you need to go do something?" I asked as we both remained seated in the car.

"No. It's already done. They'll be packing tonight and catching a ride with a military plane early tomorrow morning. They'll be there later that evening."

"Then why did we come here?"

"Because I thought you wanted to see him."

I did. "I'm ready to leave."

CHAPTER TWENTY-EIGHT

Knox strolled into the garage as I hoisted up a box of supplies from a recent run Murphy and Luck had made. I dropped it onto the bench with a humph.

"Want some help?" he asked, coming to stand beside me.

"Sure," I replied, more from obligation than truth. The hard-found quiet of the empty garage was already dwindling and I hoped he'd be a silent worker.

Without speaking, he started lifting boxes and supplies to the upper shelves that I'd had a hard time reaching. Okay, maybe this wouldn't be too bad.

He stopped moving and turned to face me, a hand came down on the bench at his side and he looked downward, shaking his head slightly. This had the feelings of a speech of some sort coming on, and not a good one. The signs of disapproval were flowing off him like the stench of a mad skunk. I shoved a bottle of olive oil into an open nook as I waited for him to form the words to match his unhappy appearance.

"I wasn't going to say anything but I feel I have to." His shoulders rose as he asked, "Why are you with him?"

I'd known he wasn't happy about something but I hadn't expected it to be my personal life. It was made more awkward since I had no desire to answer and I didn't think he'd take the hint of silence.

"I appreciate your concern, but this isn't something I'm open to discussing." I lifted a case of oatmeal, the sides denting as I forced it into a spot it didn't really want to fit into. If I went back to work, maybe he would too.

He didn't.

"I feel as if I know you, and I don't think he deserves you. I might not have been in the office that long but I've heard the stories."

And there he went, jabbing full force, right into my soft spot. This is why animals in the wild don't sleep on their backs. There's always some asshole walking around and ready to poke them in the gut.

I shoved up the sleeves of my long shirt as his words clicked into place. They gave the sense of something more detailed than the office gossip. "What exactly is it that makes you feel you know me so well?"

"Paddy used to talk about you, the way you could do things. Sometimes I feel I know you better than myself."

The looks he'd given me in the past, as if there had been a familiarity between us I hadn't been a party to, now made more sense. "You're new here, and I do like you. But you need to butt out." And I needed to start sleeping on my stomach.

He slammed a fist down on the bench. "And watch while he uses you?"

"If by use, you mean be the only one who has stood by me, no matter what was going down and what it could cost him, then he can use me all he wants." I dropped the box in my hand and left the garage, heading for the shower and perhaps the only place left to get some peace.

Fate wasn't in the bedroom when I got in there, which was a good thing with the way I was feeling. I knew where my loyalties lay and would defend him to Knox all day long. He'd bailed me out of enough situations to more than deserve defense but it didn't quiet my own doubts.

I never reached my haven. Fate strolled into the bedroom, pulling his shirt off as he did, looking as if he'd had the same destination in mind.

"You getting in the shower?" he asked.

"Yes." I turned my back on him. Logically, I knew I shouldn't let what Knox said affect how I was feeling right now, but when did logic ever factor into feelings? If I could handle this logically, I wouldn't feel anything for Fate at all. I wouldn't be worried about ending up in a puddle of emotional muck while he walked away, finding a new shiny toy. Unfortunately, I couldn't shut off my feelings when it came to him and Knox's words were ricocheting around my brain, trying their best to do maximum damage.

Fate's arm came up and blocked the bathroom, more teasing then serious. "What's wrong?"

"Nothing's wrong." When he didn't move, I shrugged and redirected toward the dresser, pretending I needed something from within.

"Now I know it's something," he said, remaining in place.

"I just want to get in the shower." I shuffled through the drawer searching for some article of clothing that didn't exist.

"Are you mad because of last night?"

It was another poke in an already sore belly that had me finally spewing my complaints. "I work with you, I sleep in the same room with you, same bed. Sometimes it's a little hard to face the other people in this house when everybody knows you tried to get rid of me. I do have some pride. Or at least I used to."

The playfulness was gone in a blink. "Who cares what anyone thinks?"

"Maybe we need to change sleeping arrangements."

"Why? You plan on moving into Knox's room?"

I rested an elbow on the dresser and put my forehead on my palm. "No."

"That's where this is coming from though. Isn't it? What did he say to you? You were fine when you went into the garage. He goes in and now you're not."

"This has nothing to do with him."

"It shouldn't but that doesn't seem to be the case."

My back still to him, I heard his movements to the

door and I wished I'd kept my mouth shut. This was what I got for starting to talk again.

Being closer, I moved in front of it before he got there

He stopped short when I wouldn't get out of the way. "Move."

"Why?" The look on his face said it was to go punch Knox in the gut but I was hoping I was wrong.

"Because I'm going to punch Knox in his mouth so that he learns to keep it shut."

I'd almost had it right.

"You can't hit him. He's on our side."

"He's on someone's side but it's not mine." He stood there, staring me down, trying to physically intimidate me out of the doorway.

I shook my head.

His hands went to my waist and lifted me out of the way and deposited me to the side. What the hell? Why let me think I had a chance in blocking him?

He stormed down the hall, and I ran after him.

"Where's Knox?" he asked, pausing briefly in the living room to ask Murphy, who was sitting on the couch.

Murphy hooked a finger towards the garage. Fate took off in that direction, now both Murphy and I following him.

He threw the door open. "What did you say to her?"

He didn't wait for a reply, and I wondered why he even asked because he decked him a second later.

Knox was lying on his back as I ran to grab Fate's

arm to make sure he didn't continue beating on him but stopped dead. It sounded like a bomb was exploding.

The fight was forgotten as a threat from beyond loomed. The walls of the house were still shaking as we all raced outside as quickly as the garage door would open.

"Don't go beyond the twenty feet," Fate yelled, even as he himself did.

I was too stunned to move immediately. Every single house surrounding us was in flames, five in total. My hand covered the scream I wanted to release as I reminded myself we were the last occupied house on the block. The twenty feet radius was clear as the flames came close enough to lick the boundary in places but didn't touch so much as a blade of grass within that distance.

I was glad I hadn't undressed completely and my knife was still at my ankle when I spotted them. Five of Malokin's guys were about fifty feet from us. Fate spotted them at the same moment and took off.

Disregarding his warning, I sprinted off right behind him.

They ran as soon as they saw us coming and I was amazed at how much speed I was getting from my legs. I overtook Fate after the first block and launched myself on the closest target a couple minutes after.

We fell to the ground and skin shredded on pavement. He rolled on top of me but I quickly managed to get the better position. My knife going up and under his ribs seconds later.

I was back on my feet and looking for my next target as Knox was breaking the neck of one and Fate had another pinned to the ground. Murphy hadn't caught up to us yet.

I ran ahead, looking for the other two, but they were gone. Knox joined me but without any luck.

When we circled back around, Fate had one guy with his back on the ground. Murphy was beside him, having finally caught up.

"Where is he?" Fate demanded the guy as he held him by the throat.

"Fuck off," the guy said through broken teeth.

"I will kill you."

"Do it." The guy meant it. He'd rather be dead than disclose anything on Malokin. I couldn't say I was surprised.

Fate, obviously believing him as well, grabbed the guy's head and smashed it against the asphalt below him. Considering what I knew about Malokin, it was about as good an ending as he was going to get.

He stood and the four of us looked around. The rest of the house's inhabitants were standing on the lawn taking in the chaos.

And then I noticed the house in front of us, its walls still in flames except for one. Upon it, a message charred into its surface.

Almost even

We wouldn't be *almost* anything after he found out

271

we'd just killed three more of his guys.

CHAPTER TWENTY-NINE

My eyes shot to the clock on the side table. Four a.m.; I'd only been asleep for an hour but I knew I wasn't the only one having trouble sleeping after watching the houses around us burn to the ground. After Fate had lectured the Jinxes for over an hour about getting drunk on the job, we'd all sat around the living room scrambling for a new plan. No one had come up with one. It hadn't been a good night by any standard.

Now here I was with clammy skin, throbbing pain and still no plan. The pain, which had started at the tattoo and worked its way down my leg, was now climbing through my chest until I feared I was having a heart attack, except that was supposed to be impossible.

I tried to keep my body still so I wouldn't have to answer any questions from Fate, who lay beside me. I must have finally fallen asleep last night while he was showering because I didn't remember him getting into bed. Any talk of separate rooms, along with further mention of the Knox incident, was as gone as the houses that had burned down. Still, he was way over on the other side and the gap between us felt a lot larger than a few feet.

"Karma?"

I should've known he'd wake up just when I wanted him to sleep. I answered the question I knew was inevitable. "It's the tattoo."

There was pause a before he spoke again and I could imagine the pieces falling into place in his head, like they had for me. He had less information but he had more knowledge. This wasn't just the tattoo and it wasn't getting better.

"How often is this happening?"

I tried to think back to when it had first started. It was hard to pin down time and frequency on something so sporadic. Falling short of a concrete answer, I came up with the next best thing I could. "I guess you could say just enough to remind me there's something wrong whenever I start to forget."

"Show me," he said as he moved over to my side of the bed and started tugging the covers out of the way.

I pushed down the shorts I sometimes wore to sleep, knowing exactly what he'd find, and what Lars had found as well. "It looks the same. It always looks the same." I didn't need to look at it to know.

"What's it feel like?" he asked, prodding the area that now lit up the bedroom with a warm glow.

"Most of the time? Normal."

"And the *not* normal times?" he asked, leaning too

close to me with a too knowing stare.

"A stabbing pain that radiates."

"So badly that you can't walk," he said, obviously remembering the time he'd witnessed it act up.

Fate rose abruptly, startling me with the burst of action. He was on his feet throwing on pants as I still lay abed. "We're getting it out."

It wasn't a question or a suggestion.

"We don't know if it's doing anything bad," I said, rolling onto my side and watching him.

"It radiates pain that is getting progressively worse. Sounds perfectly healthy to me." He threw me a look that said *don't act stupid* before the shirt he was putting on covered his face. He moved next to open one of the drawers I'd taken over and tossed a shirt and a pair of jeans at me. "Get dressed."

I propped myself up on one arm, thinking of the merits of removing it and the main reason I didn't want to. It was the sticking point that made me hope that every time it hurt, it would end up working out. "I don't want to be cut off. I don't want to think that this is it for me. *I don't want to walk this Earth forever.*"

"Is this existence that bad?" he asked.

I sensed he was taking it as a personal insult. It was a ridiculous notion since I'd be walking this Earth alone. Not once in all the time we'd been together had he mentioned deeper emotions and it wasn't for lack of opportunity.

"Forget it," he said with an edge in his voice. "It doesn't matter. It's got to come out. Cutty will do it."

275

I gathered my hair up into a ponytail, realizing I wasn't going to be adding any hours to the sleep count tonight. He wasn't going to let this go. "Cutty does stitches. How the hell is he going to handle this? It's a little different."

"He'll know."

My stall tactic not working, I realized I was going to have to keep pursuing my true argument and probably the real reason I never wanted anyone to know it was a problem. I didn't want this to be it. "I still haven't agreed to do it."

"I'm with Fate," an old gravelly voice declared.

I snapped my head towards Paddy, who was standing in the middle of the room.

Fate turned his full attention to him, both fists clenched as if he were struggling to maintain his temper. "Popping into my bedroom is off limits."

"Fine," Paddy said, all of a sudden making use of his cane as if he were too weak to stand on his own.

"Were you spying on us?" I asked, finding the timing to be a bit more than coincidental.

"Absolutely not!" He lifted and banged his cane to the ground before quickly moving back to the subject of the tattoo, or more accurately, the piece of him that resided there. "But it has to come out. I fear it was a grave mistake and I need it back."

"Can you take it back?" Fate asked.

"And will I be cut off forever when you do?" I added.

He shrugged and looked at both of us. "I don't

know." He walked over to the opposite edge of the bed I was sitting on and looked like the old man he appeared to be for a minute. "When I gave you a piece of me, I did it in part thinking it would make you stronger, more able to help with this Malokin situation. It was never supposed to grow."

Paddy rolled up his sleeve to the place he'd pull off the chunk of himself he'd donated to me. It had been a pinch, unnoticeable after he'd done it and his skin had sealed back up. Now, a large chunk of flesh was missing, like he'd suffered some accident and lost part of the muscle from his arm.

"This is the thing of it, what I am, what I'm comprised of, likes to stay together in one unit. This I knew. It's the same with the four. We like to be close, or used to, but we wouldn't drain each other.

"What I didn't realize was how strong you would be. I figured if there were a pull, it would be exerted from me and I could control it. It wasn't supposed to be like this, you pulling from me. I didn't even believe it was happening at first. I thought it was Malokin somehow, but then..." His eyes went to mine and I knew he was thinking back to the day at Kitty's. "I realized it was you," he finished, cutting off what I believed he'd meant to say.

He slowly got to his feet again and this time I almost believed he did need the cane. "If we leave it in you, I'm not sure what will happen."

"Can you get it out?" I asked, feeling like I was quickly losing any other options.

"I don't think I should," Paddy said.

"Why? You put it there, just suck it back out somehow. Do whatever it is you can do?" If it was going to happen, I wanted it done as quickly as possible so I didn't have any time to dwell on the implications of the loss.

"If you're already draining me from a distance. It's not wise." He stood and moved across the room, putting some distance between us, as if the thought of me having such power unnerved him.

Fate stepped forward, blocking my view of Paddy. "I won't have one of your three do it," Fate said, talking about Fia, Fith and Farrah.

"Surely you'd feel comfortable with Fith?"

"Why would I possibly trust him?"

"Well, considering—"

"No. Cutty will have to do it." He turned to me again. "Get dressed."

I didn't bother arguing. I already had my clothes in hand and was already heading to the bathroom.

CHAPTER THIRTY

An hour later, we walked into Lars's closed tattoo shop, Fate's hand firmly wrapped around mine. I'd given up on my rule to keep all affection to a minimum once I realized I was not only possibly dying, I was killing Paddy along with me. It didn't matter that he'd been the catalyst. I was sucking him dry and it was a hard thing to live with. Hurting Paddy was unintended, but so were lots of other things, like giving someone the flu. It still felt like shit.

"Hey," Lars said as we walked in. I smiled even as I noticed he seemed more uptight than he had been the other night. Cutty was there as well. Paddy, who had said he'd meet us here, was flipping through tattoo books as if he were contemplating getting a piece done. I wouldn't have been surprised by anything he did.

Then I saw her—Lars's *guest*—the one they called Faith. I wouldn't have missed her. She still had patches of her human karma clinging to her new form. It was as if the brightest sunlight I'd ever seen was filtering through the leaves of a tree while she sat under it on a spring day. I'd never seen anything like it. And the smell. I breathed deep and started walking towards her, before Lars stepped in my way aggressively and pissed me off. All I wanted to do right now was get near some good karma. It was like a steak dinner complete with a chocolate cake desert when I hadn't eaten in weeks.

"You can't hurt her." He was deadly serious. I could see it in the set of his mouth, the way his eyes stared me down. He'd take me out before he'd let me touch her.

I looked over at Fate, not from fear but annoyance. I didn't fear any of his men because I trusted Fate to always have my back. Still, it would've been nice to get some help to move the hulking form out of my way.

Fate shrugged a silent response I read to mean *yeah, I know he's all out of whack but just let him get it out of his system.*

I shook my head, patience wearing thin tonight.

"I don't want to hurt her. I just want to say hello and introduce myself." And maybe stand close enough to get the stench of the bad karma I'm surrounded by constantly off of me, even if it was only for a precious few minutes. I needed this before they started digging into me.

"Just remember, I was the grim reaper and I was fucking good at it."

I looked over at Fate again, trying to not roll my eyes. *Really? How long am I supposed to do this?*

I interpreted Fate's shrug and bounce of his head to mean, *I think he's almost done.*

"Lars, I promise, I will not touch your pretty princess." I withheld *now get the hell out of my way* but with major strain.

"Are you giving me your word?"

"Yes. Now step aside. I feel like you're a dark cloud hovering over me."

Finally he stepped aside.

I couldn't breathe deep enough as I got close. I felt like I was getting almost high off just the remnants of her aura. Holy shit, when she'd still been human, she must have been glorious. And her face was perfection. Between her karma and her angelic looks, she was downright ethereal.

She looked nervous as I approached her and I could understand. Being introduced to this world by Malokin when you weren't of his ilk must have been jarring to say the least. I held out my hand, trying to reassure her I wasn't looking to kill her. "I'm Karma."

"Faith," she said, as she tentatively took my offering. Her eyes darted to the men behind us, watching. "Can they hear us?"

"Probably. But I think the office is sound proofed," I offered, seeing how she clearly didn't want to be overheard.

There was a tiny single nod to her head as her eyes darted to Lars and back to me. She headed toward the back but before we could enter the office, Lars was blocking our way.

"Where are you going?"

I looked to Faith, expecting her to take the lead but she didn't. So I stepped up.

"We want a minute to talk without all of you guys hovering."

When he didn't budge, it hit me like a sledgehammer to the back of the head. He's totally into this girl. This wasn't just a crush. This was a killing blow. Wow, how the mighty have fallen.

"We're fine. Get out of the way," I said, waving my hands and demonstrating I wanted a clear path with him out of it.

His overprotective ways might have pissed me off if I didn't understand. I could see it in his eyes, if I harmed this girl even an iota, he'd rip me apart. Why? Because Lars was utterly in love with her to the point of absurdity. Or maybe there was nothing absurd about it. Maybe it was beautiful.

Why couldn't Fate be a little more like that? I knew he had my back, but this was *I'll tear you piece by piece because the sun rises with this girl in the morning and my life would be perpetual darkness without her*.

"We're fine," I repeated, giving him some slack since he was new to the whole caring-about-someone-other-than-himself phenomenon.

Finally, he nodded back and stepped out of our way.

Faith stepped into the office and I followed, closing the door behind us.

"How are you doing?" I asked, even though I could

see the answer clearly in the drawn look about her eyes.

"Getting by. I'd heard you were human first."

I nodded but remained silent, hoping to encourage her to speak what was bothering her.

"Does it get better? I mean, it's not bad, I just feel…"

"Lost?"

"Kind of."

It was obvious she wasn't a natural complainer. I liked her already. I knew from personal experience how lousy the last few weeks must have been but she wasn't going to cry the blues. It was a good thing too. In our situation, you needed to be able to suck it up or you'd crumble under the pressure. All she was looking for was answers.

"It gets a lot easier." I nodded a head towards the door that closed us off from the rest of them. "I'm not sure if they start seeming less crazy or we get more so, but you'll adjust." And then I couldn't stop myself from digging for some dirt. Maybe I was getting more like my coworkers. "You two involved?" I asked when it was so clear something was going on with them.

"I don't know what you'd call it," she answered, somewhat evasively.

"He's very protective of you. I've never seen him act like that."

"He also thinks I might have been the scum of the Earth in my mortal life so I'm not exactly sure why." She said it somewhat jokingly but there was an edge to her voice that made it very obvious how much it hurt her, at least to someone who was listening.

I leaned against the wall and crossed my arms. "There's an easy fix to that."

She sank into his office chair, defeat written all over her as her shoulders slumped. I came around and perched my hip on it.

"I know what you do. And I know if you told him I wasn't a bad person, he'd believe you. But do you know how that feels? That he needs to hear it from someone else?"

"Why make this difficult? I can tell you care about him and that he cares about you. A handful of words from me and you two can get a—maybe not a fresh start but something better than the place you're in now."

"And be with a man that can't take my word? Can't believe I'm a decent person unless someone else tells him so?" She shook her head.

There was a knock on the door before Fate yelled, "You almost done?"

Faith stood. "I'd appreciate it if you refrained from telling him anything."

I nodded, even though I had my doubts. It would be so much easier to set this right but I respected what she said. And to hell with it, I had my own issues. If she didn't want me butting into hers, I should be happy to leave it alone.

I opened the door to Lars looming close by and Fate looking inpatient. Faith followed me out, walking right past Lars without a word, his eyes following her as she moved across the room. Yep, that relationship was seriously hitting the skids.

Lars moved in closer to me. "Well?" The one word asking for information he desperately wanted and only I could give.

A huge part of me felt for the big stupid jerk but my eyes met Faith's. I got it. If Fate had to go around asking people if I was a good person, I'd be pretty teed off too.

"I couldn't get a read on her," I lied.

The disappointment in his face made me want to smack him upside the head.

"Nothing?"

"Yes." I was short with him and walked away abruptly. I couldn't help it. If he was going to be this stupid, maybe he deserved to lose her.

Fate was back at my side, his hand wrapping around mine.

I looked to the table that had been set up in the middle of the room. A line of instruments sat next to it, a scalpel among them. Oh goodie.

I let go of Fate's hand to lie down on the spot so clearly meant for me and unzipped the jeans I wore. I glanced over to make sure the shades were drawn before I tugged them down and took off the wrapping I kept over it.

Fate pulled a chair up close and grabbed my hand again but my eyes were only on the tray and Cutty.

"Karma, I'm going to give you a shot of something to numb up the area," Cutty said as he moved into place.

I nodded. "Good idea."

"Don't look at them," Fate said by my side,

drawing my attention back to him. "Look at me."

I did. He was sitting there, a smile I know he didn't feel on his face. Both hands now wrapped around the one of mine and my breathing grew ragged.

"Don't be scared." One hand reached forward to brush the hair from my eyes and then cupped my cheek. "I won't let anything bad happen to you."

Suddenly I was scared to death, and it had nothing to do with Cutty or the fact that they were going to slice into me at any moment.

I looked at his dark hair waving back from his face, the light green flecks in his eyes, which, when he stared at me like he was right now, seemed to glow. The way his hand grasped mine with such confidence, like he wouldn't ever let go, and there was no denying it anymore.

I loved him. And it didn't seem to matter how *he* felt or what *I* wanted to feel. It just was.

"If you don't stop looking at me like you're completely freaking out, I'm going to make them stop," he said. If he hadn't been smiling, I might have believed him, but he was clearly teasing me.

"I'm okay." More accurately, I was okay with what Cutty was about to do. It was the love that scared me to pieces. How had this snuck up on me? I'd thought I'd been doing such a good job keeping my emotional distance.

"Close your eyes and I'll tell you a secret," he said as I felt the needle entering an area near my tattoo.

Listening to him speak softly to me, it was as if we

were the only ones in the room. I closed my eyes, my face still turned toward him and took the excuse to break eye contact and retreat, at least visually, into my own head, to try and come to terms with the overwhelming feelings hitting me.

"The first time I met you was approximately seven hundred years ago. The Black Plague struck a little town in France you were living in. You were fourteen at the time. Your father was dead and your mother was recently struck down by the disease. You had five younger siblings you were caring for when you got sick. But you were supposed to make it. I came to your bedside, ready to intervene if necessary. As soon as I saw you, I knew I wouldn't have to. Even then, ravaged with sickness, you were the most beautiful mortal I'd ever seen.

"I still remember you turning to one of your younger sisters who was petrified to leave your side, fearing her last caretaker would die if she so much as stepped a foot away, and telling her you weren't leaving her. And I knew you weren't going to need me. You'd make it all on your own.

"Three hundred years ago, you were a girl of twenty on a ship sailing off the Massachusetts coast during a storm. The boat smashed into the rocks. Every passenger, even the hardest sailors, all died except for you. Waves pounding your body, over and over again, taking you under until I thought you couldn't possibly make it. Just when I thought I'd need to intervene, I saw you break the surface. You never quit. As others tired and lost their strength to go on, you kept fighting. You fought for hours, longer than I thought a person could even will their body to swim in such frigid waters, but you did it.

"The fight in you, the pure essence, was like nothing I'd encountered. Not in a human, ever. Not before and not since. I was captivated."

"It's not going to work," Cutty said, interrupting the moment and I felt Fate's hand tighten on mine.

"You didn't even try yet." I hadn't felt the scalpel on my skin.

I opened my eyes and sat up partially to get a view of the area myself. I was as unmarred as I'd expected.

Cutty tossed down the scalpel onto the tray as if annoyed with the item. "I can't get through the skin."

"Try farther away from it," I said, wanting this to be over if it was what needed to be done.

I looked about the room at the other people gathered who'd been watching, and I could see the answer on their faces before Cutty said anything.

"I tried all the way up to your ribs. Whatever is going on, it isn't something I can get at."

Fate grabbed my hand. "It's going to be okay."

"Sure." I nodded.

His hand wrapped around my nape, as if trying to impart his own conviction in a belief that was looking hazier and hazier. "It's going to be okay."

"Okay," I said, more for his benefit.

I got up and started to right my clothes as Fate and his guys seemed to have been answering some silent invitation I hadn't received to gather, one by one, into the office. Faith was minding her own business on the other side of the room, looking over something by the register, clearly trying to give me my space.

I sat on the bench and Paddy sat down beside me.

"You know I care for you," Paddy said.

"I do." As much as someone like him could but there wasn't any need to get insulting. I'd already stolen a chunk out of him, might as well leave the feelings intact if possible.

So wrapped up in my own thoughts, it took me a moment for the way he'd said the words to hit home. This wasn't a let's chat about our feelings because it's looking a little ugly right now type thing but something altogether different. It was an apology. The prospect of what he was apologizing for put a golf ball sized lump in my throat.

Paddy started speaking again. "The others, they would've done something immediately at any hint."

I nodded, listening and letting him do the talking. I didn't want to jump to conclusions but the more he talked, the worse the feeling became.

"If it were just I…" Paddy shrugged. "I'm tired. I've been around long enough to have lost the thrills of being alive in the typical sense. I could let it all go tomorrow. But there's certain things that can't happen."

"But it's not so just say it."

"If this continues, it's going to be too dangerous for you to…remain."

We sat, staring at each other. I got it. I understood

on a larger level why he felt this was necessary. But it didn't stop sharp claws of hurt from shredding through me. I'd known for a while that I could only trust Paddy to a point, but having now reached that limit still felt like a betrayal.

"I didn't ask for this. And whatever it is that's happening, I can't even use it," I said, pleading my case and trying to buy time until I figured something out.

"I'm sorry, but if we can't stop this," he motioned to the chunk in his arm, concealed by clothing, "even if I didn't, they would."

"Do they know what is happening?"

"Yes. I felt I had to tell them. I know this was my idea in the first place and I'm trying to fix it."

"I understand." But I wouldn't go down meekly. I'd let him think I was fine with playing the sacrificial lamb. I wasn't but he didn't need to know that.

We fell into silence again but not the calm companionship of friends. No, this was a silence born of regrets and fear. The fear was mostly me. He'd kill me. I had no doubts about that. I'd like to think he was the one with regrets but that might've been wishful thinking.

Fate walked over and stopped in front of where we sat in silence. His eyes flitted between the two of us and I knew he was picking up on the tension. You would've had to have been deaf, dumb and blind not to, and Fate was none of those things.

"You ready?" he asked, probably sensing my desire to leave.

I nodded.

I didn't say another word until we were several miles from the tattoo shop and I knew Paddy was gone. Even then I hesitated. What if in some small way Fate felt the same? That maybe it would be better to get rid of me than jeopardize the long time establishment?

No. I wouldn't think like that. For all the faults I could lay at Fate's feet, he'd been loyal, more loyal than perhaps I'd deserved.

Finally, when I knew we'd be at his house soon, I managed to get the words out. "If we can't stop what's happening to me, they're going to kill me. I got the sense that Paddy will do it himself if needed."

His knuckles turned white where he gripped the wheel. "Why didn't you tell me back there?"

"I thought it would be better if I didn't. We aren't at that point yet."

"The point where I kill him?"

"Or he kills you."

"I wouldn't have been the one that died."

God, how I hoped that was true. "He's strong, even with me draining him."

"I don't make idle promises. I wouldn't have died." He slammed a fist against the steering wheel. "Fuck. You know he won't show his face again now. If I see him I will kill him."

We pulled up to the house, three thirteen year old looking boys walking on the roof with rifles in hand.

Fate slammed the gears into park in the garage and I thought the car door was going to fly off the hinges from the force of him closing it. I watched him walk into the house, too mad to speak.

I got the anger part. It had been growing in me since we'd left Lars's shop, and I was starting to wish I'd had it out with Paddy there.

I looked upward. I didn't know who I was talking to anymore, whether it was God, the four, or some other universal power. I wasn't sure it mattered.

"You think you've got me beat? That I'll walk softly into death? Throw my body on the top of some heap reserved for martyrs and saints?" I let out a cross between a sigh and a laugh. "Shows what you people know. You've got me pegged wrong then. Go ahead. Try and take me." I held out my hands as I stood alone in the garage. "Go ahead. I know you hear me."

One of the stockpiled guns fell off the shelf and landed pointing directly at my chest.

"What? Can't do it?" I said, not budging a hair as I stared down the barrel. "Come on. Give it your best shot!"

"What the hell you doing?" Bobby stood in the doorway.

I watched as he walked in and wondered how much he'd seen.

"And what crawled up Fate's ass? He's shooting arrows at anyone that even goes near him."

He crossed the room and walked over to the gun that was aimed right at me. He picked it up and looked at the clip. "It's fully loaded. Strange for stock not being used. Also looks like it's jammed." His sweet innocent eyes looked right at me and I saw a glimpse of the real age before his chin went up a hair. "Looks like I'm betting on the right horse." He winked as he tossed the gun back on the bench.

"I wouldn't bet too big. Not sure there's going to be a winner in the bunch."

"Not much left to hold onto then for a rainy day."

The kid had a point.

CHAPTER THIRTY-ONE

We'd been home for hours. Fate was silent the majority of the time. As tired as I was, rest didn't want to come. I'd finally decided to give up and watch another day turn to night.

The sand was moist under my feet as I walked to the water's edge, letting the breaking waves lap at my ankles. The telltale signs of the universe at work swirled in dark shadows on the horizon and I wondered at its plan—or lack thereof.

The shadows over the ocean seemed to swell as I stood there. "I don't know what to do," I mumbled to myself, not caring if any of the four heard. Not caring if Paddy appeared. Not caring about anything but figuring out how to save the only world I'd ever known from descending into utter chaos forever and not being destroyed as I did it.

A stronger breeze pushed the hair back from my face and I looked up as the black mist was building about thirty feet in, right above the surface of the water. Something was different though. It wasn't swirls forming but what looked like the shadowy outline of a person. It didn't look male or female but was something that could've been either. It didn't have features and I could see the hint of clouds behind. It slowly started walking toward me, gliding above the water and I couldn't figure out whether I should run or not.

It stopped ten feet away.

"Who are you?" I asked.

It didn't respond but dropped its head. Its shadowy body dissipated back into swirls and then was gone.

"Holy shit! What was that crap?" Buddy asked, slurring and staggering as he made his way across the beach, Billy and Bobby tailing him.

I threw my hands up in the air. "Not sure."

Billy looked like he was going to say something but it was ambushed by a belch before he could continue. "You get this type of visitor a lot?"

"No," I said, leaving them on the beach, staring at where the shadow person had stood, and headed back to the house.

Fate was in the kitchen when I walked in. We hadn't discussed last night yet, or, more accurately, the failure it had turned out to be. I wasn't sure what to say and guessed he had the same problem.

I poured myself a coffee as I watched him transfer the sugar from one bowl to another. I'd known more than a few people in my life who did housekeeping when they were stressed but I'd never pegged Fate as one of them. "Why are you doing that?"

"What? The sugar?" he asked, holding the bowl up.

"Yes."

"You didn't like the old bowl," he said.

He was right. I didn't. I'd never said anything but I'd hated the shape of it and how hard it was to get my spoon in easily after it was halfway empty. He put the new bowl in its spot and walked into the living room.

I followed him, something stuck in my craw now. "Why did you buy that new comforter on your bed? That wasn't the one you used to have before I moved in."

"It's a heavier down. You get cold when you sleep."

I froze as it truly hit me for the first time. My mind ran back over the last several weeks. The sugar, the shampoo, the throw blanket on the couch that looked just like my favorite one I'd had in the condo before it burned down. Every time I turned around, there was another little mark or sign.

Fate loved me. He never said the words but he told me over and over again. I'd been too busy listening for something to be bothered with what his actions were screaming. I fell onto the couch, stunned.

He stopped moving around to look at me. "How is it that you see everything else so clearly but not this?"

"But you never say..." I couldn't bring myself to say the word love to him.

He stood in place, the moon casting a glow around him. "I've seen countless wars, upheaval, the worst atrocities. I've known hundreds of thousands of people and watched them suffer. And yet the thought of anything happening to you brings me to my knees. Label that however you want."

He didn't sound like Fate anymore and that thing, that indescribable essence I'd felt before, was pouring off of him.

"You seem different somehow."

"Sometimes I mute myself slightly around others. I'm not doing it now but I'm still me."

"And I still don't know what that is exactly."

"Does it matter?"

"Don't you think I should know who you are?"

"You do know me."

He was right. I didn't need a name or label for him. I did know who he was, and I loved him.

I stood, needing to be near him more than I'd ever needed anything in my life. I took several steps closer before I launched myself at him. He caught me as I wrapped my legs around him.

I was kissing him before he could speak and then he was pressing against me, a wall at my back. Then we were moving again.

"Where are we going?"

"The bedroom."

"Why?"

"Because there are too many people in this house? And although I'm not overly modest, I can't help but feel that you might get shy if they were to walk in on us."

"Walk in on us making love?"

"Something along those lines."

"You don't like that word."

He laughed. "That word isn't a good fit for what we're about to do," he said and then he was kissing me again and I was oblivious to the surroundings.

I didn't realize we'd made it to the bedroom until I heard the door slam and I was falling onto the bed. My hips were lifting as he tugged my pants off; my shirt was yanked over my head next.

"What about you?" I asked, breathless but wanting to see him as well. I leaned up and grabbed his shirt, pushing it upward and he quickly tugged it the rest of the way. He made haste with his pants and his erection sprang free. I only caught the quickest glimpse before he pushed me back down on the bed, following.

His mouth covered mine, his tongue plunging as his fingers plunged below.

"And I was worried you wouldn't be ready," he said, clearly pleased by just how ready I was.

I pushed him onto his back before I straddled him, my hands pressing his shoulders to the bed and slowly lowered myself onto him.

I rose up, holding him tight to me even shallow as he was. He groaned as his hands clenched on my hips pulling me downward and driving deep inside.

His hands held me flush to him before he drove deeper. Minutes or hours, I lost all concept of time as my senses were driven down to the pure sensation of where we connected.

Then he was over me and I was arching into him,

throwing my head back as he thrust harder within me and waves of pleasure were coming so close together I didn't know if it was one massive orgasm or I was coming repeatedly.

He rolled over as we both caught our breath. I felt like a well-used rag doll that had lost its bones as I lay there beside him.

"Was I too rough?" he asked, as his palm grazed my breast before trailing down my stomach, still slick with sweat.

"Not even a little. I should probably be asking you that question."

His hand drifted lower still and then his finger was slipping into me as his thumb pressed against the hood of my clitoris.

I threw my head back, letting out a sigh of pleasure as I arched into him.

"Good, because I was afraid you were going to tell me you needed a break." He rolled on top of me and was filling me again.

"How many times can you do this?"

"Let's just say it might be a really long night."

CHAPTER THIRTY-TWO

I woke up with my cheek pressed to an ice-cold surface and could see the bottoms of massive columns and the strange light that flowed through their floors. It was definitely Paddy's home. There wasn't a marble or granite supply on Earth that carried something of this variety.

The sound of footsteps echoed around me and I didn't think they were Paddy's. Thankfully, I'd gotten up for water in the middle of the night and thrown on a t-shirt and shorts or I'd be lying there naked before my host.

Of all the possibilities I hoped for when I looked up, Fia standing above me, and alone, was my least favorite. Paddy was willing to kill me, but Fia gave the impression she'd enjoy it. So of course it was Fia.

"You could've just invited me over for tea," I said as I got to my bare feet, not feeling comfortable lying prone and helpless anywhere around her.

She narrowed her eyes as she looked me over. "Don't talk. Just listen."

She was already pacing away from me as she spoke, which was a good thing, so I did as she asked. More distance played in my favor. I might not be able to outrun her but damned if I wouldn't give it a shot.

"On September 14, 1186, according to astrologers at the time, the five known planets aligned. In actuality, every planet in the galaxy aligned. If the significance of this eludes you, due to your lack of knowledge, Genghis Khan, arguably the greatest Mongol leader ever to live, was born that day. I stress the fact that he was born, not created. To give you scope. Genghis had already lived several lives before that one and had an essence of greatness about him, but still had never amounted to much. It was being born on that day that instilled him with the final ingredient to become what he did." She finally stopped walking to nail me with a stare. "Do you have any idea what you share with Genghis Khan?"

I hated pop quizzes. As far as I was aware, no one liked them. Figured it would be her style. "Shiny dark hair?"

Disdain was probably the most accurate description of her reception to my answer. I wanted to tell her it was her own fault for quizzing me on material I wasn't prepared to be tested on but didn't. I was actually quite curious where she was going with this.

"The date, September 14, 1186, is what you have in common. Except instead of simply being born, you were created that day. No one new was supposed to be created that day. Certain dates are strictly recycles."

"Recycles?" I had a feeling I knew what she meant but I wasn't leaving this place to only think later *shit, what did she mean by that*? I was certain if I got out of here alive, I wasn't going to get a do-over.

"Old souls being reintroduced. As if that weren't enough, it happened at the location of one of Earth's most powerful chakra points, in Glastonbury, England. Some drunk slob tumbled a barmaid in a pile of hay. That was your lofty beginnings. It lasted all of two minutes and this is the mess I end up with."

She flittered her hand toward my messy self. She was the one who'd dragged me out of bed, but again I held my tongue, wanting the information she had.

"You were always meant to exist but the when and where you came into existence was an accident. It gave you a pull in this Universe that should never have happened. That's why you can bend things to your will. Why even Paddy's essence is being drained by you. There is a weight to your being that acts almost like gravity. It's why the guards react to you as they do. They think you *are* part of the Universe." She snorted after this statement, marring her refined demeanor and it made her seem oddly human, if only for a second.

"Why did Paddy never tell me any of this?" I asked. And why couldn't I beam myself out of here if I was so special? This might have been the most uncomfortable biography ever, and the orator wasn't making it any better.

"Because he doesn't know why you are the way

you are. He thinks you're some sort of miracle toy he amuses himself with. Only I know the details because you were my mistake.

"Every so often, windows of opportunity arise. We each took turns guarding against *this*," she tilted her head toward me with a lemon face, "happening. The night you were created was my responsibility. But so many other windows had come and gone with no issue, I grew complacent and bored of safeguarding, the way only time can make you."

She shook her head and I thought I saw some self-disgust there this time, which was a nice change in direction.

"I didn't even realize it had happened until you'd died and been reborn a few times. I tripped over you a century later, by accident, and then put the pieces together. It was too late to kill you at that point, since you'd already been created."

I weighed the pros and cons of interrupting again but decided the question merited it. "Why couldn't you kill me?"

"You were already made. Once created, a soul never truly disappears." She paused, as if her next words were much weightier than anything she'd previously said. "Except in one circumstance."

Holy shit. The pieces started to fall into place and the larger picture was alarming. "If I were recruited. You were the one that wanted me to be Karma because it was the only way to get rid of me." The implications made the strength disappear from my legs and I wasn't sure how I remained standing. "The train wreck. That was you?" Shock had stolen my voice and the words came out more of a whisper.

"Yes. It was the only way."

This whole thing from the beginning had been her. *She'd* stolen my life, not Malokin. If I had found out this information a couple of months ago, I would've tried to rip her apart even if it meant the end of me. But as I stood there, as much as part of me mourned my human life, I wasn't as angry as I'd thought I should be. Part of me felt compelled to attack her simply on principal but then I could lose Fate.

She moved about the massive hall like structure, oblivious to my thoughts, as she started speaking again. "When Paddy was willing to bring you here, I thought that alone might kill you but he'd given you a piece of him. That was a critical mistake but he's always had a soft spot for you. Even now that you are draining him, I doubt he'll be able to go through with killing you, not that he could if he wanted to. And my only shot was if all four us tried. I thought I might have had Paddy convinced but it didn't last. After the initial fear of dying himself sank in, he started rambling on about having an even stronger connection to humans because he was experiencing the fear of his own mortality." Her hands fluttered in the air as she got disgusted. "Or some utter nonsense he was spewing. I had a hard time listening to the whole tirade.

"As if I didn't have enough issues, Fate took a liking to you. He's Fith's child, if you didn't know, conceived when Fith was going through his Greek goddess phase. It was some minor strumpet, long gone now after Hera had found out she'd moved in on Zeus. The point is, Fate kept stepping in to protect you as well and he's no slouch himself. You shouldn't have made it past the transition. Yours was deliberately bad on purpose. But if it wasn't Paddy, it was Fate.

"You kept gathering up steam and I kept covering up what was going on. The longer I hid the secret, the harder it was to come clean. I've had to hide and cloak things about you the last twenty times you've been born. Burying your natural energy under tragedy after tragedy. Century after century of compounding the lies made it even harder. It was my final act of trying to hide you that threw off the balance. I'd been tweaking here and there, messing with things that I shouldn't have, and it finally thinned the balance enough to allow Malokin to exist."

"So you created this mess?" All this time we'd been looking outward for the problem.

"And the girl wins a prize. Took you long enough to figure it out."

"Why not just let me be? Is it so bad that I exist?"

"Like I said before, you're like gravity. You'll slowly pull energy toward you until you yourself throw off the balance just by being you. You're dead already. It's just whether you go alone or take everything down with you."

"You don't know that."

"You're right. And there's nothing I can do about it anyway."

"Then why bring me here? Why didn't you just kill me?"

"If only. I would've shot you in the garage if it were that easy. I can't. I've tried. But if I can't get rid of you, at least I can use you to get rid of Malokin."

We'd finally come to something we could agree upon.

"What do you want me to do?"

I was slammed none to gently back in bed as if the meeting with Fia had never happened, Fate staring at the place I'd just appeared.

"What just happened? You flashed in and out of sight for a second."

"A second?" Time warp, that was interesting.

"Yes."

"I know how to get rid of Malokin."

CHAPTER THIRTY-THREE

The office building stood before me. I put the key into the rusty lock and left it open as I continued on towards the office.

Fate, Angus, Lars, Cutty and Bic were in the room directly above me and had been camped out there since the previous evening, in preparation for this meeting. We had to take every measure possible to make sure Malokin thought I was alone.

Everyone else had stayed behind. If it went bad, at least there would be staff to try and carry on.

We needed to get Malokin as close to the retirement door as possible. That door was the only way to strip him of the energy he'd accumulated on this Earth and dissolve what he was back into the natural balance.

This part was mine to play, much to Fate's aggravation. The larger the entourage, the less likely we'd get him near enough. We'd thought of many different scenarios but Fate finally had to concede that we were right. It had to be me and I needed to be alone.

It was a lot easier said than done. I still had to get him in the vicinity and then hopefully, between us all, we could force him through the door. Lars had set up a trip wire of sorts that would alert them as soon as Malokin's energy entered the inner office.

I walked over and settled down at my table, waiting with ankles crossed and my heels resting on its surface. The clock struck noon just as he appeared in the doorway, alone.

He needed to cross the room to me, where I was closer to Knox's office. He strolled in a couple steps with his usual swagger but then stopped.

"Why are we meeting here?" he asked but didn't seem overly worried about being in the den of his enemy.

"Because this is the place they're most vulnerable."

He was so calm that I wondered if I was the one missing something about what was going on here. It wasn't like I'd expected him to show nerves. That wasn't Malokin. He wasn't the type to ever seem weak, but to be this calm?

"That was what you said when you called but why would I believe you want to help me?"

"If you didn't, why'd you come?" Why *had* he come? Something about this felt very wrong.

He looked down at his wristwatch. "Slow afternoon?"

And now he was joking. I'd never heard him joke, ever. Under the calm veneer, he seemed almost…happy?

"The four who run everything are starting to see me as a threat. It's coming down to them or me."

He stood barely inside the doorway, taking in my relaxed position while I tried to maintain it. I'd been so concerned about keeping him at ease and now I had to force it for myself. The guys were one floor above me. I needed to keep that in mind and proceed with the plan. It wasn't as if I were truly alone.

I dropped my feet and headed toward Knox's office, praying he'd come closer and follow me in. I heard his steps behind me and tried not to tense at having him at my back. The masquerade of calm was easier once he was beside me and in sight again.

The interior office felt even smaller with him in there and I took a step closer to the opposite side. We both looked toward the door. The light was blaring underneath, and if Fia were true to her word, when I opened it, the heart of the Universe's power would be blazing in all its glory.

I thought back to what Fia had explained to me. "That door is a mainline. If we can destroy it, it cuts the head from the beast. Upper management can add another connection but not quickly. It buys time to gain strength."

He walked closer to the door and let a few fingers trail over the surface. I knew it didn't look like much, just your average interior door—except for the light of the Universe blazing behind it. "Are there more of these?"

"Mainlines to the heart of the Universe? Not that

I'm aware of." I guessed there were but Fia had only told me the bare minimum. Not that I would've passed the information on.

He tucked his hands in his pockets. "How do we do this?"

I'd just walked him up to the key to his victory and he acted like I'd handed him a brunch menu. I had to play this hand though and see the plan out.

"I was hoping you would help me figure that out." *While I open it and kick you through it.* It had been at least several minutes since he'd come in the office. The guys should be here soon.

Malokin eyed me. "Nice try."

"You don't believe me?"

"No."

"You wanted to recruit me. You really don't think I can do this?"

"I wanted you for what you could become, not what you were."

"I've got a reason to help you."

He took a couple of steps back. "Open it."

Get him in here and open the door if possible. That was the plan, but all of a sudden I didn't want to do it. I was being silly. I needed to do this. I'd have the door wide open, the guys would come and a simple shove and this part of the nightmare would be over. As far as what Fia said about me being a problem, if we could fix this, we could fix that. As long as I made it that far.

I stepped forward and swung the door open and immediately had to turn my head. It was as if I were staring at the sun, ten feet from its surface. The room was almost blinding in its brightness and I had to squint to keep my eyes even partially open, trying to not lose track of him.

All the feelings of dread finally made sense as I heard footsteps approaching that heralded disaster. Fate and the guys wouldn't announce their approach. I wouldn't have known they were here until they'd been at the door.

"Your friends aren't coming. I'm not the one being destroyed today."

I couldn't see his face well but the gloating in his voice was more than clear. I cursed myself as all sorts of stupid. Fia had betrayed me. I wanted to curse him as well but I couldn't let my anger get the best of me. It would feed him like it had on the beach. Plus, I needed the silence to listen to how many sets of feet were approaching. It was five at minimum.

My window of opportunity was closing quickly. I had one shot to get this done myself and only if I acted quickly. There was no time to contemplate what would come next.

I zeroed in on his location, pivoted and rammed into his midsection with every ounce of strength I possessed. His feet left the ground with an umph. My momentum had us across the office and into the door before we were stopped short. His hands had grabbed the door jamb as we flew through it, halting us at this critical point. Every part of him, down to the tip of his pinky, had to be past the threshold.

"You're never going to make it out of this," he said as we struggled, his calm finally shattered.

"I promise you, I won't go down alone." I directed all my energy to pushing, digging my heels into the cheap carpet of the office trying to find more leverage.

The footsteps of his people were getting closer. I had seconds left, if that.

"You two thought you knew everything. You walked right into our trap."

His words were like venom, trying to stir my anger, but I pushed it out of my mind. I couldn't feed him anything. I had to think of good things, like a life with Fate. Then I felt something start to burn around my tattoo. It felt like a hot poker was being pressed against my skin and that feeling quickly expanded, but instead of collapsing in pain, a burst of power shot through me. The resistance disappeared as his fingers slipped off the frame.

He was gone, and I fell to my knees, almost landing through the doorway myself.

There were too many and I was drained. I willed myself to get up off my knees, thinking if I just dug deep enough I could do it but my body wouldn't obey. I could hear the people shuffling into the office as I fell forward, trying to use my hands to push myself upward, when I was jerked backward and a blade slid across my throat.

I heard a roar of anguish in the distance. Fate had arrived but it was too late. Another cry, this one from the agony of someone dying nearby. There was fighting all around as I lay there on the floor, in a pool of my own blood. Then he was there, cradling me with fingers pressed against my throat. I knew it was too late and from the look in his eyes, so did he.

I did it. I mouthed silently, using the last of my strength to raise my hand to his.

"I knew you would." He pulled me closer, hugging my body to his and rocking me. "Don't go. Please, don't go."

My eyes fluttered shut as I heard him whisper, "I love you."

I tried to say it back but couldn't as everything faded away.

CHAPTER THIRTY-FOUR

Blackness everywhere. I'd never experienced absolute darkness. No one had. It didn't exist in our Universe.

"Where am I?" I said, even though I was alone in the blackness, just to see if I had a voice. Was this the nothingness they'd talked about? But how could I have thoughts?

"No," a voice answered.

"But I was killed. I shouldn't exist at all. How can this be?"

"Because I can do anything."

"Was that you? The shadowy form I saw a night ago?"

"I am everything. The sun, the moon, the planets, the air you breathe, the molecules that created you."

"What happens now?"

"What comes next is your choice. Make it wisely."

"Can I go back?"

"Yes, but not as you were."
"Why are you doing this?"
"Because I want to. Make your choice."

The smell of flowers from the florist shop I was working at part-time filled the air of the car. Kit, one of the younger floral arrangers I'd become friends with, always gave me one of the older bouquets to take home on the days I worked. She said it was important to surround yourself with flowers, especially in winter when things seemed the bleakest before the spring.

Nothing seemed bleak this week though. I was driving a brand new Audi I'd won in a lottery some crazy lady outside the mall had talked me into entering. The only reason I'd paused by the table in the first place was everyone kept tripping as they approached the area and I couldn't quite figure out why.

I enjoyed driving it so much I'd been taking the long way home, even though I had a ton of studying to do for my finals next week. I didn't particularly care to drive past this part of town, since it still had burned down buildings from the riots that had happened before my birth.

My mother had told me all the stories. She'd said they'd stopped just as she'd gotten pregnant with me and that I'd been her miracle baby. The thought was ridiculous but I didn't argue with her. She was whimsical like that. She had all sorts of crazy tales to tell, like how a guy in white silk rested his hand on her belly before she'd even known she was pregnant and congratulated her. Or how Santa left a crib for her under the tree. She still swears that the Tooth Fairy really had been the one to put money under my pillow every time I lost a tooth.

She occasionally said some normal things too, like never to pull over to help a stranger when I was alone at night. But when I saw the old guy who looked like he was twenty years past his due date standing next to an ancient Honda, I had to. The car looked like it might have been even older than he was and he was leaning on a cane. There was no way I could drive past. What if he didn't carry a cell phone?

Strangely, I'd never had a nightmare in my life but leaving this man out here in the elements not knowing if he'd be okay might cause my first. I pulled the car up behind him and threw it into park, tucked my own phone into a back pocket and walked around to where he stood.

"Sir? Do you need some help?"

"Thanks." He held out his hand to me and grasped it in a firm shake. "Name's Paddy." His cap sat low on his brow and although he was clearly in a distressing situation, it didn't seem to dent his jovial manner.

"I'm Justine." I pointed toward where his hood was open. "I'm not very good mechanically but I think I've got jumper cables in my trunk." I pointed back behind me toward my own car.

"Nice car you have there. Very responsible of someone so young to be so prepared."

He lifted his cane toward my car and it gave me the

strangest image of him waving it violently at kids. I shook my head. Lack of sleep was making me think really weird thoughts.

"Not really. I have the strangest luck of parking next to people with car troubles. It doesn't look like you have a flat but I've got a pump as well if it's needed." I was up to a count of two flats and one dead battery just this week alone.

"I'm not sure if it's the battery but let's give it a try while we wait."

"Wait?" I looked around getting a little nervous. "Wait for what?"

He frowned for a second. "A tow truck to show up?"

I nodded, wondering if Paddy wasn't a little senile.

"Oh look! I think we might have some more help," he said, completely enthused that another car was pulling down the street.

I turned to see headlights coming from the distance but with no indication they were going to stop and help. Just as I made out the shape of a pickup truck, it started slowing down.

It passed us and parked in front of Paddy's car. The door swung open and a guy of similar age to me hopped out, but where I felt like a girl of twenty, he looked all man.

"Need some help?" he asked Paddy, and then his eyes shifted to me and stayed there. I wanted to look away but couldn't seem to do it.

"I'm Paddy, that's Justine. We'd love some!"

"I'm Pol," he said and grasped Paddy's hand.

When his hand touched mine, a zap of static zinged us both.

"Justine has some jumper cables in her trunk," Paddy suggested, then mumbled something under his breath neither of us could hear.

He stepped closer to me. "Let's go get them and I can hook them up to my truck."

"Sure," I tilted my head toward my car and we headed over together.

"Pol is an interesting name," I said, scrambling for something to say.

He smiled and then laughed a little. "It's short for Polaris. My mother said as soon as she got pregnant with me, everything else in her life seemed to flow exactly as it was supposed to, like I was her little North Star, guiding her direction."

I laughed with him then. "I get it. I've got one of those mothers, too."

"Do you know him?" he asked, motioning to where Paddy stood. "You shouldn't pull over for people you don't know."

It should've been strange to be lectured on safety from someone I just met but I felt like I knew the guy. "He looked too old to do me much harm."

"Well, I'm here, so even if he turns out to a be the oldest serial killer still alive, don't worry, I won't let you die." The corner of his lip turned up and he winked in a conspiratorial fashion.

I hesitated, afraid it would sound like a cliché, but

then asked anyway. "Do I know you?"

He stopped what he was doing and leaned his hip against the trunk of the car. Something about the way he moved seemed so familiar.

"You know, I feel like I know you too. Do you go to the University of South Carolina?"

"No. I'm at Coastal Carolina but I'm a transfer. I went to Clemson for the first year."

"Transfer..."

He said the word again, letting it roll over his tongue. Then he just stared at me and kept staring. His face changed and his posture straightened, as if he wanted to grab me.

"What?" I asked, giving him an opportunity to explain when I should've been putting more space between us.

"I remember." His arms wrapped around me and he spun me off my feet in circles as he kept repeating, "I remember." Instead of being scared, I started to laugh with exhilaration and I didn't understand why.

When he finally stopped, he stared at me in a way that made me feel like the most precious thing he'd ever discovered. I should've thought he was crazy. I kept thinking I should be trying to get away from him, but instead I asked, "What is this about?"

"You've got a birthmark on your hip."

Maybe he was crazy. I didn't want to move away from him but I forced myself to move out of arm's reach. "How do you know that?"

"Because it used to be a ying yang sign."

My hand went to the spot and I could almost envision what he was saying being there.

"'I won't let you die.' I said it to you the first time I met you. You were sick, a transfer to the agency, hired by Harold."

I watched his face as hazy memories came to me. They were like dreams I was having a hard time remembering.

"You were there. And I was really mad at you," I said, not sure if they were real or if I was under some sort of hypnosis.

"Because you wanted to be left alone and I wouldn't leave you."

"I thought you were being mean," I said, not sure where the words and thoughts were coming from.

"I was keeping you alive. Then when you got beat up doing a job for Malokin, I said it again." He stepped forward and I didn't move away. "Karma, I need you to remember. You have to remember me."

His hands were on either side of my face and there was a desperation there I felt mirrored deep inside myself, as if my not remembering would cost me something too dear to pay.

He moved his hands to my shoulders and was shaking me, as if that would make something snap loose and give him what he wanted. Then they were in my hair, his lips closing on mine in a kiss that jolted me to my core. I'd never been kissed like that, as if he were trying to touch my very soul. There was that same desperation in his kiss but also love, waves of it flooding through me from his touch.

And then the memories came. It wasn't a gentle flow but an avalanche that would have had me falling to the ground under the wave of emotions if he hadn't held me up. My lips trembled as the tears flowed.

"Fate?" I remembered dying in his arms, thinking I would never see him again.

He crushed me to him and I couldn't stop the sobs from escaping me.

"I let you die," he said, his voice uneven and broken. "Malokin knew we were there. The room we were waiting in was sealed off and by time we busted through, it was too late. I'm so sorry."

"It wasn't your fault. It was Fia. It was a trap. But I'm here and so are you." I pulled back quickly. "How did that happen?"

"After you died, I was desperate. The door was open, blasting light, and I carried you through it with me, not caring what happened next."

"But I thought that wouldn't work? Was it Paddy?" I swung around, looking for him, but he was gone, along with the Honda.

Then I saw the paper fluttering in the breeze under my wiper blade and I remembered all the messages that used to appear.

"That wasn't there before," I said, walking over and grabbing it.

"What is it?"

I looked down at the writing. "I think it's…" I looked over it again as Fate peered over my shoulder.

"A want ad?" he asked.

Feeling down or uninspired? Change your luck! We're actively recruiting new employees. Take the first step toward an exciting new career that offers travel, excitement and chance to make the world a better place. Get a chance to work with our new management and grow with the company.

If interested, stop by our office and ask for Paddy, Fith or Farrah.

"Looks like she's gone. I wonder how?"

Fate grabbed the paper and crumpled it before he pulled me into his arms. "It doesn't matter. Nothing but *this* matters."

His face broke into the most beautiful smile I'd ever seen. He kissed and held me like his life depended on it. I knew mine did.

EPILOGUE

I grabbed a ticket from the booth, ignoring the usher's warning that the film was almost over. It didn't matter. That wasn't why I'd come.

The place was empty except for him, as if the world had aligned for the convenience of my meeting today. It had taken me a while to track him down, after all this time, but I'd finally found him. He was no longer the teen I'd met in Wal-Mart. Time hadn't been kind to him, and he looked much older than the early forties I knew him to be. Maybe being the leader of an underground gang of anarchists did that to you.

I made my way down the aisle and took a seat, leaving a chair buffer in between us.

There was a loud sigh before he spoke. "Great. I'm so excited I can barely express it." His words were exaggeratedly flat. "I thought you were retired?"

"I am," I said, sounding no more enthused than him. I hadn't wanted to see him but I'd felt compelled. If Fate

323

had known I was here, he would've killed me. We'd decided we were going to live out at least one human life together in peace before we even contemplated going back to work.

We'd bought a little house a few blocks off the beach. He'd taken a job with the local police department and I was working as a therapist in the hospital. It wasn't a glamorous life but I was happier than I'd ever imagined. We were planning to get pregnant by the end of the year, and we'd even got a dog.

Still, I'd had to come.

"What do you want?" he asked.

He looked at me through antique-looking glasses and I could see the scars on his face and wondered how much I didn't know about his actions.

"Wanted to let you know I was in the neighborhood." And bringing a child into the world knowing that he existed might have been the exact reason I was there.

"Why show up at all? You're powerless. You're out of the game."

"Am I?" I asked as I met his gaze. He didn't scare me. I'd seen every side of this life and knew that certain things were worth dying for.

"You don't wield the power you used to have."

"Don't I?" I asked, really looking at him, wanting him to see the truth of who and what he was dealing with.

He leaned as far as his seat would allow him. "How can that be?"

I didn't know myself but I didn't tell him that. It had started creeping back in after I remembered. When I'd been given the choice to return, I'd thought I'd lose that part of myself, that special something that allowed me to twist things to fall into place the way I wanted. But I hadn't. Paddy's piece was gone, but I was the same me I'd always been. If I could get hold of the Universe I'd ask if that was what he'd intended but it wasn't like I could pick up the phone and call him.

Perhaps when he had told me I couldn't return as I was, he'd only meant the Paddy part. Maybe Fia had been wrong. Maybe I'd been created just the way I was supposed to be.

"It doesn't matter," he said when I didn't explain. "Go back to your little house with your fellow retiree. This isn't a fight you can win. Without evil, there is no good."

"But I'll never give up trying."

"Neither will I."

Follow Donna on social media to be notified when the next book in Karma Series, Lars's story, and other new releases become available.

www.donnaaugustine.com

https://www.facebook.com/Donnaaugustinebooks

https://twitter.com/DonnAugustine

Books by Donna Augustine

Karma Series
Karma
Jinxed
Fated

The Alchemy Series
The Keepers
Keepers and Killers
Shattered
Redemption

You can find out more about Donna
Augustine here: